THE GIFTS

A Jacody Ives Mystery

BY LINDA S. PRATHER

Echelon Press
9735 Country Meadows Lane
Laurel, MD 20723
www.echelonpress.com

First Echelon Press paperback printing: May 2006

10 9 8 7 6 5 4 3 2 1

Cover Artist: Nathalie Moore

Printed in the United States of America

Dedication

To my sons, Charles and Steven, who encouraged me to follow my dreams, work hard, and make them come true.

And Coby W. Fuson, who taught me that love didn't require a person to change, it only enhanced what they already were.

Acknowledgements

Gladys Stewart, Joyce M. Coomer and Cathy Martin, my friends, co-editors and harsh critiques. Without you, this work would not have been possible.

A very special thank you to the management and staff of Bob Evans Restaurant, Highway 27 South, Somerset, Kentucky. Thank you for allowing us to use your restaurant as a meeting place in the final stages of this book.

PROLOGUE

Corrine Larson bit her lip, stifling a scream as she turned slightly, struggling to open her eyes. She'd never heard a death rattle, but she recognized it now, deep inside her chest, with each shallow, painful breath. Her body was begging to shut down. She didn't know if he had beaten her for one hour or six. She was dying, but the son-of-a-bitch wouldn't get the satisfaction of knowing she wanted to die.

Corrine managed only a narrow slit with her left eye, just enough to stare at him, convey her hatred. He'd used her, and because of her, others would die. She fought the thoughts threatening to overwhelm her, concentrating instead on the new pain caused by the salty tears coursing down her face. Her tortured mind honed in on her one satisfaction, that one ray of light in the darkness: *She hadn't told him everything.*

He whistled softly, a haunting rendition of *I Saw the Light* as he loaded the gun. Corrine drew in one last ragged breath, closed her eye, and allowed the feel of the cool damp concrete to soothe her burning body. It was almost over.

Her thoughts turned to Sarah and her child. She'd written an article once about a psychic who believed your dying thoughts could travel across time and space, influencing the outcome of events to come. She hoped the psychic was right. Maybe she could at least undo some of the damage she'd done, warn Sarah.

Rough hands jerked at her hair, raising her from the bloody warehouse floor. She felt the cold steel pressed against the back of her head, heard the sound of the gun cocking. Funny, she had always thought her dying thoughts would be of Rob or Gavin; instead, she could think of nothing but Sarah and her child. As the bullet shattered her brain, she held the image of Sarah in her mind and silently screamed, *He's coming Sarah. He wants to destroy you.*

Murder is a sin. You'll go to hell.
It wasn't murder–it was self-defense.
He hated the voice in his head. She was always bitching at him. Always butting in. Preaching. A cruel smile twisted his handsome features. Today it didn't matter. Today was a day of celebration. Soon he'd have what was rightfully his. All the years of waiting would be over. Whistling softly, he pulled away from the dumpster and parked the car. Just a few little things to finish. He pulled the police cap down low as he entered the apartment building.

"Evening officer, can I help you?"

"Just delivering some luggage to Ms. Larson."

The security guard checked the register. "Looks like Ms. Larson is out this evening."

"Yeah, I know. She gave me a key and told me to set it inside the door. Working on some big story and needed to meet the mayor or somebody. Don't know why the city wants to waste the taxpayers' money and use me as her damn courier, but here I am."

The guard grinned. "Yeah, I know what you mean." Shrugging in sympathy, he turned his attention back to the crossword puzzle. "Go on up."

He walked slowly, taking his time. The bitch had been tougher than he'd thought. She'd cost him a whole fucking day. He wouldn't rush things now, though. Everything had to play out just right. All he had to do was make it look like she'd never left town.

What if she told someone?

The thought enraged him. He cursed softly as he slipped the key into the lock. That was the trouble with women–they talked too damn much. He frowned as the pain in his groin started again. No satisfaction. He hadn't even wanted her. Too old. He liked them young; firm, breasts just starting to bud. The throb increased as he thought about the young girl he'd glimpsed just inside the alleyway on his way into the building.

And she wouldn't scream, would she?

He clenched his fists. The bitch just wouldn't scream. Unclenching his fists, he ignored the voice. It didn't matter. He had what he wanted. After setting the luggage inside the door, he relocked it and pulled out the faded snapshot from his shirt pocket. She would scream. It was all her fault. Six long years. But time had given him a bonus. Oh, yes, a definite bonus. Maybe he'd let Sarah live and just take the child. He liked that idea.

The throbbing in his groin increased, reminding him he had a mission to complete. Checking his gun, he screwed the silencer into place. The cameras had seen only what he wanted them to see, but the guard would have to be dealt with. He chortled. Everyone knew about the corruption in the police ranks. The bitch had actually written an article on it. By the time they stopped chasing that lead, he'd be long gone.

The security guard glanced up as the elevator doors

opened. "Everything okay, buddy?"

"Everything is just fine now," he said, raising the gun. He snickered at the look of surprise that crossed the guard's face, right before the bullet pierced his heart. The world was full of stupid people.

Murder is a sin.

"I told you, it's not my fault. She's the reason I have to kill."

You like killing.

He whistled as he exited the building and glanced at the dumpster. He didn't like killing. He was just cleaning up the trash.

Clouds hung low in the sky, threatening to open up any minute. He listened to the whimpers coming from the alley. She was still there. An omen. It really was his lucky day. He approached her slowly, his voice low and gentle. "Aren't you a little young to be out this late at night?" The girl stopped her whimpering and looked at him. He saw the fear reflected in her deep blue eyes slowly dissipate as she looked at the uniform. She nodded. Smiling, he held out his hand. "Come on, I'll take you home."

Excitement coursed through his body as she placed her small hand in his. This one would be a screamer. Whistling softly, he buckled her in and brushed the blonde curls away from her face. "Did you know tomorrow is Mother's Day?"

CHAPTER ONE

Gavin McAllister groaned, fighting the pink swirls, the arms reaching through the mist. They were calling him, their tiny hands reaching through the fog, begging, pleading. *Help us, Gavin. You have to hurry.*

Terror built inside him. He could hear the laughter in the distance coming closer. Hollow, evil, maniacal laughter. Felt the eyes boring into him from the darkness just outside the mist. Black eyes. The quintessence of all that was evil.

The mist turned red, seeping into his brain, enveloping him in pain. Excruciating pain. Laughter. Pain. Black eyes. Screams.

Too late. You're too late, McAllister. Every day is Mother's Day.

"N-o-o-o!"

Like all the times before, the scream jerked Gavin from the nightmare. Throwing off the covers he sat up, trembling, and glanced at the bedside clock. Four fifty-five a.m. He groaned and ran a hand through his thick dark hair, waiting for the trembling to stop. The nightmares were getting stronger, the screams louder, closer. Different. This time there had been blood and pain. The knot in his stomach still hurt, and there was a strange ache in his chest. An eerie sadness.

"What the hell have I done?" he whispered.

His gaze strayed to the phone, mentally willing it not to

ring, but knowing in his heart it would. It was Mother's Day, and somewhere out there was the body of a young girl. The phone would ring. It always rang.

Feeling less shaky, he made his way through the dark apartment to the kitchen. Hesitating, he gritted his teeth and flipped the light switch, his gaze immediately going to his hands. He expected to find them covered in blood. The blood of the innocent. The blood of those who came to him in dreams, the ones he couldn't save.

He cursed softly as he ground the coffee beans, started the pot to brew, and headed for the shower. He might as well be ready. It would be useless to try to go back to sleep.

The hot water from the shower helped clear his head and ease the knot in his stomach. He needed to write down the dream, compare it to the others. Five years. The son-of-a-bitch had been inside his head five years, playing games with his sanity. Gavin examined the image in the mirror, searching for answers he could never seem to find, listening to the words echoing inside his head. *Too late. You're too late, McAllister.*

"Shit," he muttered at the sound of the phone ringing. Wrapping a towel around his body, Gavin walked to the bedroom. He didn't need to look at the caller I.D.; he knew who was on the other end.

"Hey, Rob."

"We'll pick you up in thirty minutes."

"I'll be ready."

Dressing quickly, Gavin picked up the overnight case sitting by the bed. Rob hadn't told him to pack a bag this time. The ache in his chest deepened, the eerie sadness spreading. This time something was different. As he sat down on the edge of the bed, he bowed his head, his thoughts in turmoil. He should have refused to work with Rob on this. All the steps he'd taken to protect his adopted brother, even changing his surname to McAllister, would be worthless if the truth came out. He was running out of time.

The ringing of the doorbell pulled him from the depths of despair. He couldn't go there now. There would be time for that later.

"You're early," Gavin stated, noting the grim faces of the two FBI agents.

"Yeah, well, traffic is kind of light this time of the morning." Rob Walker pushed past Gavin and tossed his jacket on the nearest chair.

"I hope you made it strong," Carl Jackson muttered, closing the door.

"Just the way you like it, Carl."

Gavin turned his attention to his brother pacing in the small kitchen. Something was bothering Rob. Something more than the early morning call.

"I'm getting too old for this, guys. The only reason a man should get up at five in the morning is to go fishing." Carl followed Gavin's stare and turned to watch his partner pacing back and forth.

Gavin squeezed Carl's shoulder and shook his head. He'd heard this song and dance the past ten years. Carl Jackson had been with the Bureau more than forty years. No matter how much he moaned and groaned, he would never retire.

"Catch this guy and I'll buy you a fishing boat." Rob stopped pacing and poured three cups of the strong coffee.

"The way it's going, I'll be too old to use it," Carl muttered.

"We'll catch him, Carl. No matter what it takes, we'll

get this demented bastard!" Rob gripped the coffee mug, his light blue eyes darkening into grim turbulent pools.

Gavin studied his brother over the mug of steaming coffee. "Something eating at you, Rob?"

"Yeah, the son-of-a-bitch got personal."

Gavin raised an eyebrow in silent question.

"Hollywood Cemetery. Hit us in our own backyard."

Traffic was light, and Gavin used the time to gather his thoughts. He'd never told Rob or Carl about the dreams. He'd entered the investigation unofficially on his own time, and he'd been surprised when Chief Walsh called him in, asking for his help. Well–not his help–the help of the famous private investigator, Jacody Ives. The master of uncovering secrets, unmasking killers. Gavin had long ago forgotten where the character in his books stopped and he began. Somewhere along the route, the two had become one. Or maybe they'd always been one.

The sun was just rising over the James River. Gavin watched its reflection shimmering, creating dancing diamond glints on the rippling water, as the rays penetrated the shroud of mist that surrounded Belle Island. Gavin's thoughts turned inward, pensive, as he watched the fog separate–a thousand ghosts dissipating in the early morning light. Places, like people, rarely showed the ugliness of what lay just beneath the surface. Unlike the majority of tourists who traipsed and jogged over the hiking trails, Gavin saw the ugliness of the island. It had once been a Civil War prison harboring almost 10,000 prisoners. No one was sure just how many prisoners had died and were buried here. There were no marked graves. History was forgotten. The small island had been turned into just another tourist attraction for hikers and joggers. He wondered if the tourists ever thought about the bodies they strolled over.

He turned his attention to the road as they crossed the Robert E. Lee Bridge and pulled up to the gates of the cemetery.

"Stop a minute, Carl." After exiting the vehicle, Gavin examined the gates for signs of forced entry.

Rob scowled, watching as Gavin examined the gates. "Nothing. How did he get past the gates? There's no other way in."

"Told you he's a fucking ghost," Carl answered.

"What do you think, Gavin?" Rob asked.

Rising from his crouched position, Gavin flexed his legs to ease the cramps. "Ghost or man, let's see if we can't send him to hell."

They returned to the car and resumed their trip deep into the cemetery.

Gavin's thoughts turned to the history of the cemetery. Harvie's Woods had been named after Colonel John Harvie and covered acres of ground, winding over hills and valleys. Some magazine had referred to it as America's most beautiful garden cemetery. Gavin had always thought of it as the Garden of Angels. That was what he remembered from childhood. The haunted faces and sad eyes of the angel statues that must forever stand in silent vigil.

Presidents John Tyler and James Monroe were buried here. His mother had always said its random, timeless beauty housed the eternal dreams of people's lives, their loves, laughter, sorrows, and hopes.

"Remember when Mom and Dad brought us here all the time?" Rob turned around in the seat facing Gavin. "Said they wanted us to know our history. Learn reverence for the past and hope for the future. We ran around reading the epitaphs for hours."

Gavin laughed. "Yeah, you would read the epitaphs and then rush to the history books to find out who killed them and why."

Rob grinned at him. "What about you? You couldn't wait to uncover what the epitaphs didn't say. Always looking for secrets."

"Your parents were both history teachers weren't they?" Carl asked, glancing at the two brothers.

"Yeah. Mom always said you could chart the future by knowing the past." Rob's face turned thoughtful, his eyes reflecting the sadness that thoughts of his parents still evoked even after eight years. "Ever wonder what would have happened, Gavin, if Mom and Dad had known you were a twin and adopted Cory, too?"

Gavin shook his head and laughed. "Hadn't thought much about it. Of course the Larsons could also have adopted both of us. Then I wouldn't have to spend all my time looking out for you."

Rob grumbled something unintelligible.

Gavin continued to grin. "*Esprit de l'escalier*, little brother?"

"Pontificator."

Gavin ignored the comment, continuing his teasing. "Of course if the Walkers had adopted both of us, then Cory would be your sister. Not getting cold feet are you?"

"No way. Cory is everything I ever wanted in life. Which reminds me, don't forget about tomorrow. Tux fittings for both of you." Rob grinned at Carl.

"Shit, we really got to wear them monkey outfits?" Carl grimaced.

"We'd better, unless we want Cory to take off our heads." Gavin laughed. "I have been thinking though, Rob. When you and Cory get married, that makes my brother my brother-in-law, and my sister my sister-in-law. So, when you two have kids, what does that make me?"

"The babysitter." Rob smirked.

"Not in this lifetime. I'll be the favorite uncle. Distant uncle, that is," Gavin stated.

"Hey, don't forget about Uncle Carl. I've had to watch this sorry wimp sit around moon-eyed for a year now before she finally said yes. I gotta get something out of this." Carl feigned his best pained look.

Gavin laughed. "Okay, you can be the favorite uncle...and babysitter."

The laughter stopped abruptly as they arrived at the center of the cemetery, taking in the scene before them. Carl pulled over to the side, parking the car out of the way.

"Why here?" Rob wondered out loud.

Carl shrugged, but Gavin had been wondering the same thing. Was the killer sending some message to them? Disposal sites were often picked at random. Convenience played a key role. This site had taken some serious thought and planning.

"Looks like the Blue Boys have secured the perimeter," Carl stated flatly.

"Don't let them hear you call them that," Rob cautioned as they exited the car. "Politically correct, it's Boys in Blue, or better yet, Officers in Blue."

"Shit, everybody calls them that," Carl muttered.

The medical examiner looked up and shook his head as they approached. From all appearances the young girl could be calmly sleeping, her blonde curls brushed delicately to the side, head turned, hands positioned under her cheek. A picture of innocence nestled among the angels watching over her. Her clothing had been carefully arranged to protect her from prying eyes. Gavin knew what the medical examiner had found beneath the clothing. What had been found four times before.

"Morning, Rex. Was it here?" Rob asked.

Rex Bray nodded as he handed over the plastic bag containing a small pink gift card.

"Kept it under wraps until you guys got here."

Rob nodded his thanks. Rex had worked the previous cases with them and knew to keep news about the cards quiet. They'd been lucky so far. Rex had managed to convince the other medical examiners of the importance of keeping the cards secret. All they needed was a worldwide panic every Mother's Day.

"Who found the body?" Gavin asked.

Rex nodded his head toward the young officer standing about twenty feet away. "Talk to Officer Preston. I think he was the first one on the scene."

Rob and Carl approached the young officer, flashed their badges, and introduced themselves.

"Rob Walker and Carl Jackson, FBI," Carl stated. "This is Gavin McAllister. Who found the body?"

"Groundskeeper when he came in this morning. Said he thought maybe she'd gotten lost and just fell asleep on the ground. Didn't realize she was dead until he got closer."

Gavin breathed deeply, letting it out slowly, frustration causing the knot in his stomach to catch, twist. The more people who had walked over and around the scene, the harder it would be to find anything of significance. Not that the bastard had ever left anything of significance. Even the cards were generic, found in any department or drug store across America.

Carl nodded at Rob. "We'll need to interview him."

Officer Preston shook his head, glancing, and then averting his gaze from the small lifeless body.

"Be a little hard. Poor guy suffered a heart attack right after he called it in. I found him when I got here. He died on the way to the hospital."

Gavin walked a short distance from the trio, studying the ground, searching the faces of the angels. The groundskeeper's death would be put down as natural causes, but Gavin knew it wasn't natural. It should be recorded as a homicide. The bastard had gotten two for the price of one. And they were still stuck with no clues. Literally, another dead end.

"Okay, you guys can leave. We'll take over from here," Carl stated.

Officer Preston nodded. Gavin knew the young officer was glad to turn this one over to someone else. Glad he wouldn't have to be the one who had to look into the eyes of grieving parents and tell them their child had been murdered.

"Let's go to work," Rob growled.

Gavin watched as Richmond's finest exited the scene, and wondered, work on what? The cities had changed, but nothing else. Five long years, and not one clue other than those damn cards.

"Yeah, let's go to work," Carl muttered.

Gavin glanced at Carl's slumped shoulders, realizing for the first time just how old Carl really was. He should have retired years ago. The once black springy hair was now totally white. The Bureau had tried to retire him to a desk ten years ago, but Carl had fought like hell. Chief Walsh had finally given in and paired him up with Rob. Gavin figured the chief thought Rob could take care of Carl if they got into trouble. It was the other way around. Carl had ended up taking care of both of them after their parents' death.

Rex Bray had just finished packing up his equipment and was overseeing the loading of the body.

"Same as usual. Repeated lashings with some type of belt or paddle, genitals show signs of vicious rape. Death by suffocation. Can't tell you more until the autopsy." He shrugged, knowing there wouldn't be much more to tell.

"Think anybody saw the card?" Rob fingered the package hidden in his jacket pocket.

"Don't think so. It was under the body and I put it out of sight as soon as I arrived. You need to get this guy."

"Yeah, we know," Rob stated, pulling the package from his pocket.

Gavin noted the look on Rob's face, and took the package from him. "I'll read it."

Rob simply nodded. Gavin knew that Rob and Cory wanted children. A case like this screwed with your head. Made you doubt your ability to protect your own child. He knew that Rob was thinking about that now.

Pulling on tight surgical gloves, Gavin took out the small card, grimacing as he read the message.

A gift for you.

Ah, sweet little one, the salt of your tears, the music of your screams brings such joy to my ears. Every day is Mother's Day.

T

Not quite the same. Gavin shivered as he ran his

fingers over the words on the card. *Every day is Mother's Day.*

The ringing of Rob's cell phone broke the uneasy silence.

Gavin mentally shook himself, pulling away from the darkness of his thoughts. He stopped looking at the card to listen to the one-sided conversation.

"What's up, Chief?"

Frustration and anger darkened Rob's features.

"We just started here. Wait a damn minute. This is our case!"

Rob listened another second before slamming the cell phone shut.

"The chief wants us at the office. You too, Gavin."

"What's up?" Gavin asked.

"He wouldn't say. He's sending Johnny and Brad out to the scene."

"Shit, they're just novices. Not ready for this kind of scene." Carl reached for a cigarette. "Damn," he grunted, realizing he'd left them in the car.

"Yeah, well, tell it to the chief," Rob snarled angrily as he strode toward the car.

Gavin felt as if he were wearing lead shoes, each step a slow painful process. The wind had picked up, and the rustling through the leaves whispered around him. *Too late.*

CHAPTER TWO

Sheriff Sarah Burns pulled off the road and parked near the site of Saturday night's tragic accident. Unnatural deaths were rare in Glade Springs, and she couldn't shake the feeling that she'd missed something. An image of Morgana Nelson clutching the body of her daughter, her heartbroken cry echoing through the morgue, flashed through Sarah's mind.

Maybe it was only wishful thinking. The Nelsons were good people, and Johanna had been their only child. The accident made no sense. Johanna wasn't the typical eighteen-year-old. She didn't run off to Edgewood or Richmond after graduation, looking for a larger city, more excitement. She didn't stay out late. She didn't drive fast. She didn't drink. So why had she been here, driving so fast she missed the curve? The toxicology reports weren't in yet, but the body had reeked with the smell of alcohol. The Nelsons had questions, needed answers.

Climbing out of the Explorer, Sarah walked toward the curve as she closed out the noises around her, traveling the path Johanna had driven. Emotions were strong here. She could feel the sadness–and the anger. Johanna was upset.

Sarah moved into the curve slowly, feeling the shift in the emotions surrounding her. Panic took over, quickly turning to fear. She retraced the path the car had taken as it skidded off the road into the huge oak tree.

Crouching near the point of impact, she placed her hand on the earth and closed her eyes. For a brief moment she felt physical pain and then all emotions ceased.

Sighing, Sarah stood up. She wasn't sure what she had expected to find. Let it go, Sarah, she chided herself. Some questions have no answers.

Heaving another sigh, Sarah started toward her vehicle. She was tired, looking forward to a quiet evening at home. Last night's dream had upset her. All day she'd been haunted by the image of the dark brown eyes filled with pain, the heart-wrenching cry that had jerked her from an uneasy sleep. The whispered message that had kept her lying awake, trembling as she listened to the sounds of the night.

She hated the dreams. Hated the feeling of helplessness they created inside her as the dying reached out, sending messages to loved ones, or crying out for vengeance against their attacker. Only this time the dream had been different. This time the message was for Sarah.

Sarah shook herself mentally, pushing away the memories, the fear. It was just a dream. And this was just a horrible accident. Accidents happened—especially when teenagers drank. Her foot touched the passenger tire track imprinted in the soft earth near the tree. A feeling of panic clutched at her, growing stronger, making it hard to breathe.

"Jesus," she muttered as she stepped away from the track, breathing deeply.

Kneeling, she touched the earth, holding her breath, as emotions flowed through her fingertips. Unlike the driver's side, the panic here continued to escalate. There was no physical pain, no ceasing of emotion. This was what had been bugging her. The something missing. Johanna Nelson had died almost instantly, but she hadn't died alone. Someone else had been in the car with her when she crashed into that tree.

The trip to Parham Road was a forty-five minute drive from the cemetery, but Carl seemed determined to make it in twenty. Gavin watched as Carl weaved in and out of traffic, cursing and blowing his horn. The old man's hands were gripped tightly around the steering wheel. They were all feeling it. Ninety percent of all investigative work was instinct, and instinct told them something was bad wrong.

"God, I've got a bad feeling about this," Rob stated, breaking the uneasy silence in the car.

Carl nodded. "Yeah, me too."

Gavin remained silent. The knot in his stomach had returned, a burning, gnawing pain. His heart still ached with a loneliness that spread throughout his soul. Somehow he knew what waited for them would forever change their lives. Time had run out.

Jennifer Warner looked up as the three men entered the office. "You guys must have been moving," she stated, looking at her watch. Only twenty-five minutes had passed since she'd placed the call for the chief. "The chief wants…"

Rob brushed past her, heading for Chief Walsh's office. "Yeah, we know what the chief wants."

Not bothering to knock, Rob opened the door, ready to blast out his anger and frustration. One look at the chief's face stopped him.

"Close the door and sit down, Rob. Carl. Gavin, it's good to see you again."

Gavin nodded, watching the chief fidget with paperwork on his desk as he waited for them to take their seats. Gavin remained standing. He studied Chief Walsh's face. Walsh was a hard man, but a good man. His face revealed little, but the pale gray eyes held a look of compassion and sadness. Whatever he was about to say, it wasn't good news.

Chief Walsh sighed. "There's no easy way to say this. The body of Corrine Larson was discovered in a dumpster outside her apartment this morning. She was murdered."

"No."

Gavin heard his brother's whispered word as he reached out, grabbing onto the chair to steady himself, struggling to breathe. He knew he should go to Rob, but his head felt light, as if a huge fist had slammed into his gut, knocking the breath from his body. Shock washed over him in waves.

"That's not possible. She's not even here. She's off somewhere researching a story. It's not her. We're getting married next week." Rob was rambling.

"It's her, Rob. She's already been identified by a co-worker at the paper. I'm sorry." Chief Walsh avoided meeting Rob's eyes.

Leaping up from the chair, Rob yelled at the chief, "It's not her!"

"Where is she?" Carl asked the question quietly, his voice filled with reverence.

"County morgue."

Carl nodded. He knew what had to be done. Rob had done the same thing for him five years ago when Sharon had been killed in an automobile crash. You had to see the body. It was the only way. Taking Rob's arm Carl pulled him toward the door. "We'll call you," he stated, as he opened the door and pushed Rob through it.

Gavin stood silent as Carl pulled and pushed Rob through the door, not waiting for an answer, or for Gavin to follow. Carl knew Gavin would follow. After all, Gavin was the strong one. Right now, Rob needed Carl the most. Partners were often closer than brothers. They knew each other's secrets, pains, hopes, and dreams. Gavin knew them, too. He knew that Carl was wishing for a cigarette. And he knew Carl regretted not listening to his wife, taking early retirement and buying that fishing boat.

The trip to the morgue took less than ten minutes. Carl parked the car in front, ignoring the "No Parking" sign. The morgue was dreary on a good day. Today it was dark, malevolent.

"It's not her, Carl."

"You gotta do this, kid. You gotta know." Carl placed his hand on Rob's shoulder.

Gavin felt as if his face had turned to stone. He wanted to say something, but no words would come. Instead he watched, his thoughts muddled, painful, as Carl offered Rob comfort. It should be me, he thought. I should be comforting him. A cold, steady reserve enveloped him. A numbness that seeped through his heart and mind. No, not me. This is my fault.

His legs felt stiff as he followed Carl and Rob. He retreated deeper into his mind, seeking the comfort of his alter ego, Jacody Ives. Jacody would know what to do. And he wouldn't feel anything. Couldn't afford to feel anything. Too many demons in his head. Too many losses in his life.

A sliver of pain sliced through Gavin's heart as Carl pushed open the double doors. *Too late, McAllister. You're too late.*

The attendant barely glanced up as he stated, "Viewing room is upstairs. Who do you want to see?"

Carl glared at him before flashing his badge. "No viewing room. We want to see Corrine Larson."

The attendant looked at the badge, shrugged, and glanced down at the papers before him.

"Number eighteen."

"She ain't no goddamn number, buddy," Carl growled.

The attendant started to make some flippant remark, but changed his mind as he looked into the murderous glint of Carl's dark eyes. "Hey, it's not personal."

No one bothered to answer. This time it was personal. Too personal.

Gavin followed slightly behind the others, still examining his feelings. Cory was his twin, the other half of his soul. Would he hurt worse if he'd known her longer? Fate had separated them as babies. The Larsons had adopted Cory only one day before the Walkers adopted him. For twenty-nine years he hadn't known she existed. Only that something was missing from his life. Something vital. Now, she was gone, just as if she'd never been there.

The attendant had stopped in front of drawer number 18. He reached for the handle and Carl stopped him.

"Get out."

Rob stood frozen in front of the drawer. Inside lay his hopes, his dreams, his future. With trembling hands, he grasped the handle and pulled out the shelf. His eyes focused on the white sheet over the body, his hands shaking as he reached to pull it back.

"Want me to do it?" Carl moved closer.

Rob shook his head and took a deep breath. It wasn't her. It was all a mistake. It couldn't be her. Rob touched the sheet and slowly pulled it away from the body. Pain hit Gavin, a bolt of lightning, starting in his gut, forcing the air out of his body.

"Dear God..." Reaching out, Rob touched her hair and drew back his hand, looking at the traces of dried blood on his fingers. Her blood.

"Son-of-a-bitch." Carl pulled him away from the body, holding him as Rob bent forward, retching. The smell of vomit filled the air.

Gavin forced himself to look at the body. It bore no resemblance to the pretty young woman he remembered. Gone was her laugh, her love of life. He didn't feel the same shock as Rob. Somehow he'd known. He'd known since he woke up this morning that the dream was different. Laughter filled his head. *You're too late.*

Gavin felt his jaw tighten. Everything seemed distant. He heard the sobs of his brother, smelled the vomit. Watched silently as Carl wiped the blood from Rob's hand with his handkerchief. He welcomed the numbness that spread from his mind, through his body, settling around his heart. Turning to what remained of the other half of his soul, he whispered, "As God is my witness, Cory, I'll find whoever did this. And may God have mercy on him, because I won't."

Gavin pulled the sheet up over the body. He wanted to say something. Needed to say something. For the first time in his life, words failed him. He closed the drawer.

"Let's go, kid. We can't do anything else for her. We need to get Rob out of here."

Gavin nodded, following Carl out of the building. He checked his watch. Five hours had passed since the early morning call. A lifetime. The warmth of the sun touched his face as his gaze drifted to the morning edition of the *Herald.* The headline branded its message inside his head.

"LOCAL JOURNALIST TORTURED, RAPED, EXECUTED."

CHAPTER THREE

Gavin sat nursing his third glass of brandy, as the apartment grew dark around him. In the past two days he'd grown to hate the light. Everywhere he looked he saw Cory. She was everywhere in the apartment–the drapes, the paintings on the wall, the furniture, the French cameo vase. He remembered her face the first time she'd come here, her words. *Gavin Colin McAllister, this is a disaster.* She'd immediately set about changing everything in the apartment. Her zest for beauty an inspiration, she'd turned the drab apartment into a home.

Gavin rose from the sofa, walked to the bar, and poured another glass of brandy. No matter how much he drank, he couldn't get the headline out of his head. Just words. He was a writer, made his living with words. He knew the impact of the words was in direct correlation to the emotions of the reader. Words could be twisted, knives to open up wounds long hidden. Maneuvered to evoke buried nightmares. Bare the soul, expose the wound, and you had a best seller. Make them laugh. Make them cry. But above all, make them feel something. He was an expert at manipulating words for emotion.

But he'd seen the body.

He emptied the glass of brandy, welcoming the burn in his throat. The blinking red light on the answering machine was a constant reminder of his shame, his guilt. He should have erased the message. Instead, he tormented himself by playing it again.

Gavin, it's Carl. Rob collapsed. I'm taking him to the hospital. I'll call you.

Carl would call, but he wouldn't answer. It was better this way. Better for all of them if he simply disappeared. The darkness followed him. And wherever the darkness was, death was close behind.

Gavin, you have to help them.

Cory was standing in the shadows of the living room. "Cory?" His mind registered what his heart refused to believe. Cory was dead. He closed his eyes, counted to ten, and reopened them. She was still there, her beautiful ethereal form a light in the darkness.

Gavin, please protect her.

She drifted across the room, stopping in front of the stack of mail he'd tossed on the coffee table. She smiled at him, a small wistful smile that broke the ice around his heart. Tears began to flow down his face. "Cory?" He choked on the word, reaching for her. She drifted away from him.

Protect her Gavin. If she dies, my death will have no meaning.

Swallowing the lump in his throat, he wiped his eyes. "I don't understand, Cory. Who?"

Her light shimmered, fading into the darkness.

Gavin stood motionless, his mind blurred by the brandy. He was drunk. That had to be it. Hallucinating.

How many hallucinations ask you to protect someone?

"Go away, Jacody." Gavin groaned, slumping on the sofa, head between his hands. He'd never cried before. Not even at the death of his parents. He felt strange inside, hollow.

She came here to tell you something.

"God, I need a drink."

You can run, but there's no place to hide, Gavin. We have to protect them.

"We?" Gavin laughed hollowly. "You're a character in a book. There is no we."

Now we're getting somewhere. You have to protect them, or her. A mystery. Secrets.

Gavin curled his hands into fists. Raising his head, he focused on the red blinking light of the answering machine. Jacody had always been his voice of reason. The hero. Now, it was his turn. There was no story, no book rights. Cory was dead, and Rob needed him. And if Cory was right, somewhere out there, someone else needed him.

He picked up the stack of mail. The wedding invitation on top started a new wave of pain, but he tossed it aside, digging through the envelopes until he found the small postcard. He ran his fingers over the writing, closing his eyes. He allowed himself a moment of grief, feeling her love, her warmth wash over him. Trembling, he opened his eyes to read the card.

> *Gavin, I've found a great story. I'm worried though, because it may have something to do with this case Rob is working. The Mother's Day thing. I'll call you tonight. Love, Cory.*

TORTURED, RAPED, EXECUTED

He fought the rage that threatened to consume him. Fought the tenebrosity that pulled at his soul. Cory deserved better than that. She'd died to protect someone.

He examined the card, the old building burning its image in his mind. The Lodge, Glade Springs, West Virginia.

Cory's words echoed in his mind. *The Mother's Day thing.* What was it Rob had said? *The son-of-a-bitch got personal. Hit us in our own backyard.*

It wasn't a story this time. This time it was personal. The demon of his nightmares had no name, but now he knew where to look for him. Glade Springs had secrets. And no one uncovered secrets better than Jacody Ives.

CHAPTER FOUR

Sarah swore softly as the overflowing cup sent scalding coffee over her hand. Ignoring the pain, she focused on the TV, ears straining to catch every word of the morning news. "Richmond Police say there are still no clues in the execution-style murder of Corrine Larson. Larson, whose body was discovered in a dumpster outside her apartment complex early Monday morning, was a three-time award winning journalist for the *Richmond Herald*."

The story continued, but Sarah stopped listening as the erratic beat of her heart pounded inside her head. Monday. She'd tried to put the dream out of her mind. Rationalized it. Just a dream brought on by the death of Johanna Nelson.

Rubbing her temples, Sarah brought her attention to the screen just in time to see a pretty young brunette with deep brown eyes smiling at her. "No," she whispered.

"Mommy, that's the pretty lady."

Sarah jumped. She'd been so focused on the news story she hadn't heard Nikki enter the room. She struggled to control her emotions, turned off the TV, and forced a smile as she turned to her daughter.

"What pretty lady, honey?"

"The one in my room last night. I'm hungry."

Sarah shook herself mentally. Was it possible? She knew it wasn't impossible that Nikki had inherited what her grandmother called "her gift," but dear God, she was only five years old.

And the spirits had never actually materialized to Sarah. They only came to her in dreams.

Sarah struggled to control the shaking of her hands as she pulled down a box of cereal. This was definitely one of those situations they didn't cover in Sheriff 101.

"How about a big bowl of cereal?"

"Okie, dokie."

Sarah felt a pang of fear as she watched Nikki bounce up to the table. She always seemed to bounce, her strawberry blonde curls in constant disarray. So full of energy, bursting with life. So tiny. So helpless. Too young. She was much too young for the dreams.

"Here you go...one bowl of cereal and a glass of OJ, just for good measure." Sarah forced her voice to sound natural. Taking her coffee, she sat across from Nikki, wondering where to start. She questioned people all the time. But how did you question a five year old? Especially a five year old who seemed to take the appearance of a strange woman in her bedroom in the middle of the night as a normal occurrence.

"Nikki, tell me about the pretty lady."

"I'm not supposed to tell. Can I stay with Millie today?"

Sarah controlled her impatience, taking her time, choosing her words carefully.

"Why aren't you supposed to tell, sweetheart?"

Nikki shook her head as she scooped up another mini-wheat. "It's a secret."

"Nikki, look at me." Sarah felt her patience waning as Nikki chewed slowly, making a huge display of swallowing loudly before meeting her mother's eyes. "You shouldn't have secrets from Mommy, remember? We talked about this."

"It's okay, Mommy. I know when people are bad. She's a nice lady. I think she's lost."

Sarah sighed in frustration. Nikki had always been the world's best secret keeper. Her soft blue eyes pleaded with Sarah for understanding, for trust.

"Okay, you keep your secret...for now. But, young lady, if you see her again, you have to promise to tell me."

Nikki bobbed her head, smiling.

"Get dressed. I'll call Millie and see if it's okay for you to stay with her today."

"Whoopee!"

Sarah couldn't help but laugh as she watched Nikki dance up the stairs. Nikki was her life. Without her...

"It was only a dream," she whispered. Corrine Larson had nothing to do with her life, or Nikki's. Still, a cold chill ran down her spine as she dialed Millie's number. She remembered the feeling of dread, pain, and death that had jerked her from the dream. But most of all, she remembered the heart-wrenching cry, *He's coming, Sarah. He wants to destroy you.*

"Morning, Sheriff. I was beginning to worry about you."

Sarah raised an eyebrow, looking at her favorite deputy, Joshua Cross, before glancing at the clock.

"It's only eight-thirty."

"Forget something?" Joshua raised an eyebrow, mocking her.

"Oh, shit," she muttered. The toxicology report on

Johanna Nelson. "Did they call?"

"About ten minutes ago. Doc Hawthorne says to call him when you get in. Got something on his mind."

Sarah nodded. Doc Hawthorne had delivered Johanna Nelson, watched her grow up, and he'd been the one to tell her parents about her death. She was sure he had a lot on his mind. There were still unanswered questions about Johanna's death, questions that would probably never be answered, as the case seemed no more than a tragic accident. Johanna had been drinking, lost control in the curve, and hit a tree. Death had been instantaneous. And then there was what she had felt at the scene last night. Dammit, that was always the problem. She never knew when it was real. Had there really been someone else with Johanna?

Sarah hesitated, tempted to tell Joshua about her suspicion that Johanna had not been alone in the car. "Damn," she muttered, grabbing a cup of too strong coffee as she headed for her office. And how would she explain her suspicions? *Joshua, I have this gift, and it tells me things.* She was sure that would go over great.

Grabbing the phone, she dialed Doc Hawthorne's number. The sooner she made the call, the sooner Johanna's parents would be allowed to lay their daughter to rest. Maybe Sarah could also lay her doubts to rest.

Five minutes later, Sarah grimaced as she slammed down the phone. The call to Doc had done no more than raise additional questions. Although Johanna smelled of alcohol, blood tests revealed she had not been drinking. Sarah knew there was something else. Something Doc had not told her. She couldn't put her finger on it, but it was there. She'd have to go see him in person, take a look at the autopsy report, and find out what he was hiding. The knock on her door did nothing to improve her mood.

"Come in."

"Everything okay?"

"Just fine," Sarah muttered sarcastically. "Doc says Johanna wasn't drinking."

Joshua seated himself comfortably in the old armchair Sarah had purchased at a yard sale.

"Don't surprise me none. Never knew that girl to take a drink."

"Then what the hell happened out there, Joshua? What am I supposed to tell her parents?"

Joshua shrugged, chewing a toothpick. A habit he'd taken up when he'd stopped smoking three years ago.

"You'd better put something on that burn."

Sarah glanced down at her hand. She'd almost forgotten about burning herself that morning. The skin was now a fiery red.

"It's not that bad. Did you need something?" Sarah wanted to be alone. She rubbed her temples. Everything seemed to be off kilter.

"Just worried about you. You look a little pale. Maybe you should have Doc take a look at that hand."

Sarah stopped rubbing her temples. Genius. A perfect excuse to pick the old doctor's brain. "Yeah, I'll do that. But I'm fine, really. Nikki hasn't been sleeping well lately, so, of course, neither have I."

"I'm afraid you're not gonna sleep too well in the next couple of weeks, either." Joshua tossed a mystery novel on her desk. "Know him?"

Sarah glanced at the novel. "G. C. McAllister?" She read the title, *A Jacody Ives Mystery–Pool of Tears*. "No, I've never heard of him." She glanced from the book to

Joshua.

"Got a reputation for being a pretty ruthless bastard. Fancies himself as some kind of private detective like his character. Travels around to small towns looking for secrets. Digs around until he finds a good story. Rumor has it he's destroyed a lot of lives."

Sarah frowned. "What does that have to do with us?"

"He just made a reservation at The Lodge. Be here two weeks from today."

Sarah felt the blood drain from her face. She forgot about Johanna, forgot the burn on her hand, and the need to talk to Doc Hawthorne. The dying words of a tortured soul seemed to echo in the room.

He's coming, Sarah. He wants to destroy you.

CHAPTER FIVE

Gavin hated hospitals. The smell of sickness and death permeated the air around him. The sooner he got this over with, the better off he'd be.

He'd had to fight Carl about telling the chief about the postcard, but at least he'd agreed that they shouldn't tell Rob. Somehow the two of them would have to manage the investigation without Rob's getting involved. All Gavin needed was a little time.

Stopping at the desk, he waited for the frizzy-haired receptionist to acknowledge his presence. She ignored him as she continued her animated conversation. "Well, you know and I know it was Marcus. Why, everyone knows the baby belongs to him."

Gavin cleared his throat. She glanced up, rolled her eyes, and frowned. "Hold on a minute." She placed the caller on hold. "Can I help you?"

"Rob Walker, admitted last night."

Punching a couple of keys on the computer, she glanced at the screen.

"Psychiatric ward, Room 403."

Gavin didn't bother thanking her. She probably wouldn't have heard him anyway. She'd already gone back to discussing the mysterious Marcus and whatever he'd done that had her hormones raging.

Walking slowly down the quiet hall, he checked the numbers on the closed doors until he came to 403. Taking a deep breath, he pushed open the door. Bile rose in his throat at the sickly sweet smell of fresh flowers. The room was full of baskets, all bearing cards of "Get Well Soon." Idiots. The world was full of idiots.

Guilt washed over Gavin as he noted Carl sitting next to the bed, a book across his lap. It was apparent the old man had been here all night. Gavin's head ached from too much brandy, too much pain. "I should have been the one here," he cursed himself silently.

Carl nodded his head toward the hallway, and Gavin followed him outside.

"They've got him pretty drugged up, but I think he can hear you," Carl whispered. "God, I need a cigarette."

"Get some rest. I'll stay here with him for a while."

Carl shook his head, shoulders slumped in resignation. "We're gonna lose him, Gavin, if he don't snap out of this. Keeps thinking he's seeing Cory. Talking to her."

Gavin didn't know how to respond. Twenty-four hours ago he would have thought Rob was hallucinating. Chances were, Rob really was seeing her.

"I'll be back," Carl mumbled, reaching for his cigarettes as he headed for the nearest exit.

Taking a deep breath, Gavin entered the room and took the seat Carl had vacated. Rob's face was pale, haunted. Gavin felt a strange new tenderness for his brother wash over him. The drugs had helped, but there wasn't any drug that would take away the pain completely. Rob would have to come to terms with it eventually.

Something seemed to be filling the hollowness the tears had created inside him. He took Rob's hand, emotions choking him. Rob had always looked up to him. Even though they were almost the same age, Gavin had always been the big brother. He'd already lost Cory. Seeing Rob now, lying here more dead than alive, was almost more than he could bear.

"Rob?"

Rob turned toward the voice, blue eyes empty. "Gavin? I lost her. Lost my love, my lady, my life."

Gavin swallowed hard, fighting the wetness behind his lashes.

"She's gone, Rob. But you're not. Neither am I. We have to go on. We have to find out who did this. Cory would want us to do that."

Rob closed his eyes. "Don't want to. Can't live without her. Want to die. Help me, Gavin. Help me die."

Unable to answer, Gavin sat holding the limp hand until the drugs took over and Rob slept again. He fought the emotions still churning inside him, tears flowing down his own face. Something inside had cracked. What the hell was happening to him?

Gavin, you have to hurry. Please protect her.

Cory was standing beside the bed.

"Who, Cory? Who am I supposed to protect?"

Gavin wasn't shocked at her presence this time. Somehow he'd known she would be here close to Rob. She smiled at him before looking wistfully at the sleeping figure. *You'll know,* she whispered before gradually fading away.

Carl picked that moment to open the door, poking his head inside. "Thought I heard a woman's voice in here."

Gavin let go of the hand he'd been holding, gently placed it on the bed, and stood up. "No, he's sleeping."

"I'll stay with him." Carl flopped into the seat, reaching

for his book.

Gavin nodded, hesitating as he reached the door. He had packing to do. Cory's funeral to plan. He wanted to talk to Rob. Really talk to him. Explore the strange feelings he kept having. Find out if Rob felt the same ache deep inside his heart. There just wasn't enough time.

"Sleep well, little brother," he whispered as he quietly closed the door.

Gavin shook hands with the last of the visitors. The ceremony had been small, but Cory would have liked that. He'd worried about the press at first; afraid they would play up her funeral. For once, they'd shown some small measure of sensitivity, allowing the family to grieve together without prying eyes. Perhaps it was because Cory was one of their own.

Closing the door, Gavin allowed his thoughts to turn to Rob. The last week and a half had passed so quickly he'd had little chance to think about anything except taking care of what had to be taken care of. Thanks to Chief Walsh, the autopsy had been done immediately, and Gavin had made the funeral arrangements as soon as they released the body. There was something healing about laying your loved ones to rest.

Gavin frowned. Unfortunately, it hadn't had that effect on Rob. He'd smelled the alcohol on Rob's breath at the funeral home. And Rob hadn't even bothered to show up at the apartment afterward. Gavin had been left to mumble assurances and accept condolences from Rob and Cory's friends. Rob was sinking fast, and there was nothing he could do to help him. Except maybe catch Cory's killer. Maybe then Rob would be all right.

Carl was sitting in the living room, drink in hand, cigarette burning in the ashtray. "Stay as long as you want, Carl. I've got some packing to do."

He wasn't surprised to find the older man still sitting there a half hour later.

"Christ, Gavin, you can't go out there alone. What am I supposed to tell the chief? Have you thought about that?"

Gavin set down the suitcase and turned to Carl. He knew what the old man was feeling. Rob had turned to the bottle, wanting to die, and Gavin was about to set out on a course that could lead to his own death. For the past five years, they'd been the only family Carl had.

"I'll be okay, Carl. You know Jacody Ives always lands on his feet." He grinned, making light of the situation. Carl wasn't buying it.

"You're fucking crazy. This son-of-a-bitch is like a ghost. What if Cory was right? What if there is a connection? What then?"

Gavin watched Carl light another cigarette, two already burning in the ashtray. The image of Cory's battered body filled his mind. "Ghost or man, I'll find him. And when I do, I'm going to send the evil bastard straight to hell."

"Going with you," Carl stated, taking a long drag on the cigarette before placing it in the ashtray with the other two. "Got a bad feeling about this."

Cory's death had opened up something inside of Gavin. Something strange, and yet in some small way, something wonderful. Surprised, he found himself crossing the room and placing his arms around the old man.

"I have to go, Carl. You have to stay here and take care of Rob for me. Can you do that?" He pulled away, looking into the huge brown eyes, over-bright with unshed tears, unspoken emotion.

Carl glanced away, muttering in a choked voice, "You damn kids will be the death of me." Hands shaking, he started to light another cigarette just as he noticed the three burning in the overflowing ashtray. "See, what I mean? You're killing me."

Hugging Carl again, Gavin laughed. "If you actually smoked them, those things would kill you."

"Yeah, maybe I should quit," Carl muttered as he stubbed out the three cigarettes. "Somebody's gotta take care of you two."

Gavin picked up the suitcase. He had to leave. "You'll take care of him?"

Carl nodded.

"I'll call you when I get settled in."

"You call me every day, you hear me? Don't you go getting yourself killed either."

Gavin smiled, but knew it was weak. Carl was the closest thing he and Rob had to a father. He was beginning to understand just how much the old man loved them both.

He stopped at the doorway and looked around the apartment. Somehow he knew he wouldn't be coming back here. Carl knew it, too. Gavin smiled again and raised a hand in silent good-bye.

"I'll take care of him." The old man's face was wet, his voice choked with emotion. Gavin hesitated only a second. He had to go.

"I know you will." The crack inside him widened as emotions he'd never felt before, never allowed himself to feel, washed over him. "I don't think I ever said it before, Carl, but I love you."

He wasn't quite sure, it could have been just his

imagination, but he thought he heard the whispered words as he closed the door behind him: "I love you, too, you dumb son-of-a-bitch."

CHAPTER SIX

Joshua Cross looked up as the young woman entered the sheriff's office. She didn't look like a local. Something about her demeanor struck a chord inside him. The shadows in her eyes, the way she held her arms across her body as if protecting herself from unseen blows.

"Can I help you?"

Her smile was stiff, and Joshua noted how she continued to look down, refusing to meet his eyes. "I was hoping maybe I could talk to the sheriff. Ms. Crawford told me she might need someone here to answer the phones or something."

Definitely not a local. No one around here would dare address Millie as Ms. Crawford.

"Sheriff's out right now."

"Oh." She reached for the door, disappointment etched on her face. "Thank you."

"Hey, wait a minute." Coming around the counter, Joshua grinned at her. "Can you make coffee?"

She nodded.

"You're hired."

"Just like that?"

"Biggest job around here. And the most important." He stuck out his hand. "Joshua Cross, chief deputy and sheriff's whipping post."

She shook his hand tentatively. "Ella Mae Thomas." She frowned. "Is she hard to work for?"

"Not if you make a good cup of coffee. In fact, you can start right now."

Joshua chewed on his toothpick, watching as Ella Mae went about the office, clearing away the dirty cups and washing the pot, not once, but three times. Sarah would probably be mad as hell, but he'd pay her out of his own pocket if he had to. Looking out the front window, he cursed softly as he saw Sarah parking. He'd hoped for more time.

Joshua had the decency to look slightly guilty as he made the introductions. Hiring was Sarah's job, but hell, the girl looked as if she could use some good news. And she had those huge puppy dog eyes–wary, like she was unsure if the hand reaching toward her was going to pet her or hit her.

Sarah glanced at the young woman, noting the drab dress and scuffed shoes as Joshua made introductions. Sarah also noticed the way she kept looking down, never quite meeting Sarah's eyes as she talked. She'd seen that look on women before. There was usually a mean son-of-a-bitch at home. Sarah met Joshua's pleading eyes over the young woman's head and smiled, sticking out her hand.

"Welcome aboard. How about a pot of coffee? Joshua, can I see you for a minute?"

She waited until the door closed behind him. "Want to tell me what that was all about?"

Joshua lowered his gaze, refusing to look at Sarah. He could feel the flush creeping up his neck and face. He knew he'd overstepped his boundaries. "I don't know, Sarah. Something about her reminded me of my mother. The wariness in her eyes. I just couldn't turn her away."

"Our budget is already pretty poor; maybe you can tell me how we're going to afford her?"

Joshua was saved from answering by the knock on the door.

"I brought you some fresh coffee." Ella Mae smiled as she placed the two cups on the desk. "I'm going to clean up the bathroom. It's an awful mess." Smiling again, she closed the door.

Sarah glanced at Joshua. He gave her a lopsided grin as he sniffed the coffee. "At least it smells good."

Picking up her cup, Sarah noted how clean it was before she took a drink of what had to be the best coffee she'd ever tasted. She grinned at Joshua.

"Great coffee and a clean bathroom? Screw the budget."

They both jumped as the door burst open.

"Sheriff, I want to talk to you. Alone." David Nix looked at Joshua, his meaning clear.

Ella Mae stood behind the mayor, wringing her hands in agitation. "I'm sorry, Sheriff, I couldn't stop him."

"It's okay, Ella Mae," Sarah stated, noting the tightening of Joshua's lips, the coldness of his eyes.

"I was just leaving, Mayor." Joshua glanced at Sarah before placing a hand on Ella Mae's arm to lead her from the room.

Sarah wished she could think of some reason to keep him there, but smiled and waved him off with, "I'll talk to you later."

She waited until Joshua had closed the door before turning her attention to the problem at hand. David Nix had lived in Glade Springs most of his life, married a local girl, and raised two daughters. He'd been elected mayor two years earlier. The term "pompous ass" came to mind every time Sarah crossed paths with him. Today, something was definitely wrong. Nix looked as if he hadn't slept in days. His face was unnaturally pale, clothes wrinkled, hair not quite perfect. Definitely not the man Sarah was used to seeing. He didn't waste any time letting her know exactly why he was there.

"I don't want G. C. McAllister in my town." Anger lashed out at Sarah with every word.

Sarah sighed. News certainly traveled fast.

"He hasn't even gotten here yet, David. And if he does, as long as he doesn't break any laws, he's our guest."

"I don't want him snooping around here. The Nelson girl's death is just the kind of thing he'll start poking his nose into. Her family has had enough pain."

"Johanna Nelson's death was an accident, David. He can't find what isn't there. Glade Springs doesn't have any secrets for him to uncover."

Sarah had hoped her words would have a calming effect, but they only seemed to upset him more. She shivered, her hands trembling slightly as she met the cold blue gaze. David Nix had the look of a madman.

"I had my doubts about you. A woman as sheriff! This town needs a strong sheriff, and if you're not up to it, we'll find someone who is! You tell him to leave, and you make sure he does!" Turning abruptly on his heel, he stalked to the door and slammed it on his way out.

"What next?" Sarah whispered to the closed door. A dull ache began to throb behind her eyes.

Joshua stuck his head inside the door. "Everything okay?"

Sarah shook her head in puzzlement. "I guess, but what

the hell has gotten into him?"

"Don't know. He's been that way since Johanna died."

Since Johanna died. "Joshua, do you know something I don't know?"

Joshua appeared to mull over her question. Sticking the toothpick between his teeth, he shook his head. "No, ma'am. Don't think I know a thing you don't know." With that he quietly closed the door, leaving Sarah with her thoughts.

"Good morning, Millicent. Miss Nikki." Clarence Archibald tipped his hat to the ladies.

Millie Crawford frowned as she placed the key in the door. "*Humph*," she snorted. *Old coot.* "Morning, Mr. Archibald," she answered in her most prim voice.

His laugh carried across the street. "When are you going to call me Clarence? It's been two months now, and you're still fighting it. By the way, you look as fresh as my new roses this morning."

Millie sent him a scathing look as she closed the door. Fresh as his new roses. He was the one that was fresh. Acting like a teenager.

"You run on and play, Nikki."

Millie couldn't stop herself from lifting the blinds and taking a quick peek to see if he was still there. A slight pang of disappointment filled her when she saw he had already entered the flower shop.

"Flirtatious old coot," she muttered to herself as she opened the bookstore for business. "Always calling me Millicent." She stopped her muttering as she caught sight of her reflection in the mirror behind the counter. The slight flush on her cheeks and sparkle in her eyes belied her age, as did the spring in her walk. The old fool had her feeling like a teenager. Maybe she'd just take a walk over there and see those new roses. He could probably use a good cup of coffee. Might even ask him over for dinner one night. Possibilities. The old coot had definite possibilities.

Humming softly, Millie flipped the sign to "open" and headed to the back of the store to make a fresh pot of coffee.

CHAPTER SEVEN

Gavin arrived in Glade Springs around two in the afternoon. The atmosphere was the same as all the small towns he'd visited in the past fifteen years, only quieter.

There had been no fanfare to meet him. In fact, he would have thought no one knew who he was if it hadn't been for the adoration of the young girl who checked him in. The town had that peaceful feel which often belied the turmoil churning beneath the surface. Secrets. They all had secrets.

Gavin saw immediately why Cory would have chosen The Lodge. She loved old things, beautiful things. He examined the room carefully. If Cory had been here, maybe she'd left something, some clue of her presence. He knew he was grabbing at straws. Even if Cory had been here, it didn't have to be this room. And the room had been cleaned thoroughly. No traces of anyone who had stayed before him.

Thoughts of Cory were immediately followed by thoughts of Rob. Opening the drapes, he glanced into the courtyard. He didn't have the luxury of time to think about Cory and Rob. If Cory had been right, he would need all his wits just to stay alive here. He had to concentrate on his surroundings. As promised, he placed a call to Carl, immediately regretting it. He listened respectfully to five minutes of yelling, succeeding in getting off the phone only by promising to call again tomorrow.

The Lodge was probably the oldest building in town. Gavin had studied the town history, but found little except that The Lodge had belonged to some long ago prominent family. The new mayor had preserved it and turned it into a bed and breakfast to pay for its upkeep. Gavin ran his hand over the beautiful antique oak furniture. Someone had spent a great deal of time and love restoring it to its natural beauty.

It didn't take long to unpack, and Gavin found himself pacing the floor, restless. He needed to be doing something. Past experience had taught him to wait. Wait and let them come to you. They always came.

Gavin stumbled, reaching out to catch himself as the blinding pain ripped through his head. The sound of demonic laughter seemed to fill the room. *Too late, McAllister. You're too late.*

Breathing deeply, he waited for the pain to pass. He couldn't afford to wait. Not this time. Someone in this quiet little town had a secret. One worth killing for.

Gavin ignored the curious glances as he exited The Lodge. He'd been wrong about people not knowing who he was. It was apparent from the stares that they all knew who he was and wondered why he was here. He'd gotten used to the curious glances over the years. It was that same curiosity that brought people to him.

Scanning the street, Gavin smiled as his gaze fell on the sign over the bookstore across the street. "Millie's–Great Coffee–Great Books."

There was something about coffee and books that opened people up. They dropped their defenses, telling things to complete strangers that they wouldn't tell their own mothers.

Opening the door, he breathed in deeply. He had always loved the smell of old books. The bookstore was dimly lit and appeared empty at the moment, except for the proprietor.

Gavin grinned. She wasn't hard to read at all. And what a character she'd make. Her gentle face had been wrinkled by the passage of time, but still held traces of the beauty she'd once been. Her clear gray eyes held a spark of mischief and warmed him in a way he hadn't felt in a long time. Large calloused hands that could discipline and comfort, all with the same touch, gripped his in a warm grasp. Mille Crawford was everyone's mother.

"Mr. McAllister, I hoped you'd stop by."

"Please, call me Gavin."

"And you can call me Millie. Coffee? You take yours black, I believe."

She didn't wait for an answer, but left him there at the counter as she disappeared into the back of the store, returning seconds later with two mugs of steaming black coffee and a plate of homemade oatmeal cookies.

Her touch had shocked him, and he'd instantly sensed just how wrong his first impression of her had been. Strong. Behind the gentle face was a very strong woman who was fiercely protective. He wouldn't be getting any information from Millie.

"Millie, can I play with the ballerina?"

Gavin turned at the sound of the child's voice. The bookstore had been so quiet he'd thought they were alone.

"Of course, sweetheart. I want you to meet Mr. McAllister."

Gavin felt something deep inside, something primal as

his eyes met the soft blue, trusting eyes of the child before him. She held out her hand and shook his.

"Hi. I'm Nikki."

He was amazed at how small and warm her hand was. He was even more amazed at the overwhelming urge he felt to pick her up and run as far and as fast as he could.

"Mr. McAllister writes books, Nikki."

A heartbreaking smile lit up the small face. Gavin found himself entranced, images flowing through his mind. He could see himself teaching her to play ball, pacing the floor while she was out on her first date, walking her down the aisle. He mentally shook himself, dispelling the images as he concentrated on what she was saying.

"I'm going to write books some day about a beautiful ballerina who travels all over the world and solves crimes and helps people."

Gavin swallowed the lump in his throat. "Wow, I hope I get a chance to read one of them."

"Of course you will. I'll even sign it for you."

He watched her grab a cookie and dance out of the room, feeling as though someone had suddenly dimmed the lights.

Gavin turned around to find Millie watching him, a determined, mischievous twinkle in her eyes.

"Isn't she adorable? Seems she just lights up the room when she comes in."

Perceptive. Very perceptive.

"Your granddaughter?" Gavin asked, as he bit into one of the delicious cookies.

"Oh, heavens no. Don't have any grandchildren. Nikki keeps me company sometimes while her mother is working. Her mother's the sheriff, you know. Tries to downplay it, but she's just as pretty as the daughter if you ask me."

Gavin sipped his coffee, pondering his feelings and thoughts. "What about the father?"

"Oh, there's no Mr. Burns. Never heard Sarah mention the father. It's just her and Nikki. Ask me, Nikki could use a father, and Sarah could certainly use a husband. Be good for both of them. You're not married are you, Mr. McAllister?"

He surprised himself by answering, "No. No, I'm not married."

Gavin left the bookstore an hour later and walked down Main Street. He wasn't sure who had picked whose brain in there. Millie had certainly been quite adept at gathering information about him. He was surprised he hadn't spilled his guts about his real purpose here.

The café on the corner was still open, but he wasn't hungry. He needed time to think. He hadn't been totally right. Millie was an encyclopedia of information. Glade Springs had no secrets. At least not from Millie. The town had been founded by David Nix's great-grandparents over a hundred years ago. They received outsiders with open arms, but with prudence. Their former sheriff had been murdered three years ago, and Sarah Burns had taken his place. Sarah was an outsider, but had earned her right to be here when she caught the killer. He'd learned something else, too, maybe something important. Sarah had been pregnant when she came here five and a half years ago.

A sudden gust of wind rustled the leaves overhead. *Protect her, Gavin.*

"Cory?" He turned and scanned the streets, but nobody was near enough to have whispered the words that still seemed to echo on the wind.

Gavin felt the same primal feeling he'd felt in the bookstore. He wanted to go back in, take the child and run.

He couldn't afford emotional entanglements. There was no place in his life for that kind of complication. He had to get past whatever had happened to him when Cory died. The best way for him to protect people was by staying the hell away from them. Besides, the only way to protect the child was to get close to the mother. And the mother was the sheriff. Sheriffs didn't often cotton to him. In fact, he'd be surprised if she didn't ask him to leave. And if his reaction to the mother was anything like his reaction to the child...

"Damn," he swore softly as he entered The Lodge.

"Mr. McAllister?"

Gavin started to ignore the call. He'd felt the young girl's adoration when she checked him in. He was tired and all he wanted to do was go to his room and lie down. Instead he smiled. "Hello. Marisa, isn't it?"

She grinned, pleased he'd remembered her name.

"I just wanted you to know if there's anything you need, anything at all, all you have to do is ask, you know."

Gavin stifled a laugh at the open invitation. She was every bit of thirteen going on twenty-five. He wondered for just a moment what she would do if he took her up on her offer. He would definitely have to watch himself around this one.

"Well, there is something you could check for me, Marisa."

"Anything you want, Mr. McAllister. Anything at all."

"A friend of mine was supposed to be here earlier this month. I just wondered if you could check the register and see if she checked in."

"Sure thing. What day was it?"

Gavin had no idea what day, but the postcard had been postmarked the seventh, and Cory's body had been discovered on the ninth.

"Check the sixth through the eighth."

He watched her flip through the register slowly, deliberately, one page at a time, looking up at him with a smile as she turned each page. Gavin smiled.

"Hmm, that's unusual. Someone tore out a page. Mr. Jones is going to be really pissed about that."

Gavin leaned over the counter, getting a better look at the book. A page had definitely been torn out. "What day was it?"

"It looks like the seventh. Yeah. That's strange. That's the night Johanna…"

"Johanna?" She wanted to talk. They always wanted to talk, and he encouraged her with a gentle pat on her hand. Secrets. There were always secrets, and always someone eager to tell.

Marisa leaned over the counter and whispered, "Yeah, they said it was an accident, but I don't think so."

"Who said it was an accident?" Gavin whispered.

"Sheriff Burns. She investigated the accident and said Johanna had been drinking and that she lost control of the car. Everyone knows Johanna didn't drink." Marisa lowered her voice again and leaned closer. "I think someone killed her."

"Why would someone do that?" Gavin continued to whisper, giving Marisa his full attention.

"Why would someone tear a page out of the register?"

Why indeed? Maybe not a mystery, but definitely a place to start.

* * *

Gavin followed the directions Marisa had given him as he drove north away from town. He sorted through the information he'd received so far. There was definitely something wrong here. Even if Johanna's wreck had been an accident, that didn't explain the missing page. Had Cory been here on the seventh? And if she had, who or what had she been looking for?

The accident site was only a few miles out of town, and he had no trouble finding it. Skid marks trailed for about ten feet prior to the point the car had left the road. The skinned bark on the large oak tree at the edge of the fence line told the rest of the story.

Small towns all had one thing in common–news traveled fast. Gavin wasn't surprised to see headlights approaching. Nor was he surprised to see the sheriff pull up behind his car. He was surprised when she stepped into view. Millie had said she was pretty, but that was an understatement. Even with her flaming red hair pulled back severely from her face, and without a trace of makeup, she was breathtaking. He had an overwhelming urge to free the long red hair, bury his face in it, and smell its softness.

"You won't find a story here, McAllister." Her voice was cold, her green eyes scornful.

"What makes you think I'm looking for a story?"

"Your reputation precedes you."

Gavin laughed, but there was no mirth in the sound. "Oh, yes, the ruthless bastard." He scanned her face, trying to find what it was about her that made it hard for him to think of anything but holding her.

"The only thing you'll find here is a sad young woman who lost control of her car and died." Sarah's voice was

54

filled with anger, pain, and something he couldn't quite decipher.

"I thought she was drinking." Gavin stated, watching the green eyes for a reaction.

Sarah didn't answer, but turned away and started toward the Explorer.

"You're not sure it was an accident, are you?" He baited her.

Sarah turned, hesitation and doubt written on her face, as she met his challenging gaze.

"If it wasn't, that's still no business of yours. Watch your step while you're in my town, McAllister. One wrong move, one citizen's complaint, and you'll find yourself with an overnight stay and a one-way ticket out of here."

Gavin looked at the marks on the tree, ignoring the challenge. "And what about Johanna? What about her pain? The dead don't rest, Sarah, until the guilty are punished."

Their eyes met and Gavin felt something pass between them. For a moment he thought she had touched him. Just a gentle brush of her fingertips across his face. A feather-light kiss. A flicker of pain darkened her eyes.

"Johanna Nelson's death was an accident. There aren't any secrets in Glade Springs, Mr. McAllister."

He watched her turn her back on him again, walking stiffly to her vehicle. He issued his own challenge. "Someone in Glade Springs has a secret, Sheriff. One worth killing for, and I'm going to find it."

CHAPTER EIGHT

Ella Mae Thomas placed the Nelson file in the drawer. She liked her job at the sheriff's office. She liked the deputies, and she even liked the sheriff on most days. She frowned. What she didn't like was going home. What if he was home? She hated him. Hated this place.

"I'm headed home, Ella Mae. Leave Tommy a note to call me if he needs anything."

"Okay, Deputy Cross."

Joshua hesitated. Ella Mae had been here almost a week and he still didn't know anything about her except that her husband traveled. She looked lonely, lost.

"You know, you can call me Joshua." He grinned at her.

Ella Mae smiled shyly, blushing.

Joshua's grin broadened. She certainly was a shy little bird. "Hey, Mary and I are thinking about taking in a movie and dinner out tonight. Care to join us?"

Ella Mae smiled again. "No, I have to go home."

"Well, if you change your mind, you're welcome to tag along."

"Thanks, Deputy…Joshua."

She stared longingly at the closed door. Joshua was nice, a good man. Dinner and a movie would be nice. But she had to go home. What if Philip was there? She never knew when he would be home. He'd be angry if he found out. She rubbed the bruises hidden by the long-sleeved blouse. Dinner and a movie wasn't worth it.

Ella Mae wrote a quick note to Tommy, her heart heavy. How had she gotten herself into this? She knew the answer to that question. What had made her think a man as handsome as Philip Thomas could love a woman as ugly as her? She knew her features were plain, homely at best. She didn't even have a good figure. She'd been so flattered with his attention, so blindly in love with him, she'd never questioned his motives for marrying her. Her eyes brimmed with unshed tears. There was no way out, no place where he wouldn't find her. And if he found her...Ella Mae shivered in the warm evening air as she placed the note for Tommy on the counter, locked the door and headed home.

Carl Jackson scanned the daily report, but found nothing new. He hadn't expected anything. His head ached and he absently rubbed the back of his neck. He'd tried to talk to Rob last night, but the alcohol did all Rob's talking. Damn foolishness is all it was. What was Rob thinking blaming Gavin for Cory's death? Pain sliced through his belly at Rob's parting words: "What if it was me, Carl? What if Cory was killed because of me?"

A light knock jerked him from his thoughts. Chief Walsh opened the door, came in, and closed it behind him. Oh, shit, here it comes, Carl thought.

"How's Rob doing, Carl?"

Carl avoided meeting the chief's eyes. "He's doing okay, sir. Expect he'll be ready to come in any day now."

"That's good news. Have you heard from Gavin?"

Carl felt the chief's piercing look, knew he was

watching him, waiting for a response.

"Talked to him last night." At least that was true.

Chief Walsh placed a sheet of paper on Carl's desk. "My door's open, Carl, when you want to talk."

Finally meeting the Chief's eyes, Carl nodded.

After Chief Walsh left, Carl sat looking at the closed door for a long time. He should have told the chief about Gavin. Should have told him the truth about Rob. He'd been with the Bureau the majority of his life. He didn't like breaking the rules. Chief Walsh was not only his boss; he was also his friend. Carl glanced at the sheet of paper the chief had placed on his desk. Forgetting his guilt, he felt a surge of excitement. Rob had damn well better be ready to go to work.

Rob opened the door on the third ring.

Taking one look at the bloodshot eyes, Carl cursed. "Jesus Christ, Rob, you gotta pull yourself together."

"Why?" Rob turned away, stumbling through the litter on the floor.

"Because you're my fucking partner, and I need you, that's why." Kicking a pile of dirty clothes out of his path, Carl slammed the door behind him.

Something must have penetrated the fogged brain cells, because Rob turned and really looked at him.

"What's up?"

"Just maybe the best thing that's happened in a long time. A lead on the Mother's Day killer. Or maybe Cory's killer." Carl lowered his voice, trying to soften the blow of his words.

Sitting down, Rob placed his head between his hands. "Get Gavin. He'll help you. I can't."

Cursing again, Carl pushed his way through the cluttered room to the kitchen. Coffee was what was needed now. Rob was still sitting where he'd left him when Carl returned ten minutes later with two steaming mugs of strong coffee.

"Get off your ass, boy. Gavin is out there somewhere risking his life. The least you can do is try to help." He placed the cup of coffee in Rob's shaking hands and tossed the trash from the nearest chair.

Rob grimaced at the taste of the bitter coffee. "What do you mean, Gavin is out there risking his life?"

Carl hesitated. He'd promised Gavin he wouldn't tell Rob, and he hadn't meant to let that slip. "Don't worry about that yet, we got work to do here."

Rob raised his head, meeting the stony glare of his partner. "Don't tell me he's hit again?" The words scribbled on the small pink card had haunted him. *Every day is Mother's Day.*

"No, but he just might have been seen this time. I'm driving. You look like shit, Rob. The drinking has got to stop."

Rob nodded. Carl had been his partner for ten years. They were family. "Let me get a shower."

"Make it cold," Carl yelled after him.

The cold water helped clear Rob's head, but the coffee was making him nauseous. Rob held his hand over the cup. "No more. Fill me in. Tell me what we've got."

"Our last victim was twelve-year-old Katlin Kramer. Disappeared on the evening of the eighth."

Rob nodded. He already knew all this. He felt a knife slice through his heart. The day Cory had died.

Carl glanced at his partner, feeling his pain and

frustration. "Give me a chance, okay? I'm too old to hurry. Anyway, a kid came up to the parents this morning. Says he met Katlin in an alley on Center Street that night. He got mad when she wouldn't put out. Left her there. Kid's pretty messed up right now. Blames himself."

Rob frowned, searching his memory. "Hell, it's been almost three weeks. Why didn't he speak up sooner?"

"Parents divorced. He'd been out of the country with his mom. Didn't know about the girl until he got back this morning. Anyway, you missed the point. He left her on Center Street."

The knife twisted, going deeper.

"That's near Cory's apartment." Rob's voice was soft, hesitant. "Carl, you don't think…"

"Method's different, but we can't discount it either. The paper didn't know what Cory was working on. She could have found something. And something the kid saw that night makes me believe she did. Says he saw a police officer driving away from the trash bin where Cory was found. Kid found it a little strange because he wasn't driving a police cruiser. According to the kid, the police officer parked the car and then went toward the apartment complex carrying luggage."

Rob tried to digest what Carl was saying, but the words kept getting jumbled. Cory would have told him. They'd studied the surveillance video on Cory's apartment in connection with her death, and the death of the security guard. They had seen the cop entering and exiting. No face. Nothing to identify him with.

"She didn't tell me what she was working on either. But I know she would have, Carl, if it had anything to do with this case. Cory would have told me."

Carl heard the anguish in Rob's voice. Cory knew they'd been working this case for five years. Five years of chasing a nameless, faceless, sick bastard. The only saving grace they had was that the news had never leaked about the cards and poetry. It was hard enough to look into the eyes of grieving parents without their knowing their child's killer had left a card. The son-of-a-bitch was leaving bodies as gifts.

"You know, when Chief Dooley checked the roster for that night, he said none of his boys were supposed to be in that area at that time. Figured the guy was a fake," Carl continued, sounding out the evidence as he related it to Rob.

"Or a dirty cop," Rob responded. He remembered the article Cory had written two years ago involving the Richmond Police Department. She'd received a lot of threats then, but nothing had come of it.

Carl cleared his throat. "It would have been easy for him to pick up the kid as he was leaving." He hesitated, knowing that what he was about to say would impact the future of both of them forever. "Rob, you know if we find a connection, they're going to remove us from this case."

"Then I guess we aren't going to find one, are we?" Rob looked at him then, the pale blue eyes determined, clear for the first time in weeks.

Carl nodded. "Guess we're not."

"Mommy!"

Sarah smiled, reaching down to pick up her daughter. Tears threatened at the corners of her eyes as she held her tight, feeling her warmth, hearing her tiny heartbeat. There had to be a way. She had to stop him. The loneliness inside threatened to overwhelm her, and she squeezed her daughter tighter.

"Mommy, you're hugging too tight." Nikki squirmed in her arms.

"Sorry, precious. I'm just so glad to see you." Sarah sat her daughter down, capturing one tiny hand in her own as she entered the house. This was her home. The only home Nikki had ever known.

"Something smells good." Sarah glanced fondly at her housekeeper and friend, Juanita Sanchez.

"You're late."

"I know. Thank José for picking up Nikki for me. I don't know what I'd do without you two."

Sarah listened to her daughter's chatter throughout dinner, hardly touching her food, as Juanita fussed around, scolding her for not sleeping enough, not eating enough, and spending too much time at the office.

"What you need is to find a good man. A woman needs a good man."

Sarah grinned mischievously and winked at Nikki. They both knew this game.

"So, are you thinking of giving up José, Juanita? I mean, I might consider it, you know, if José were available."

Not for the first time, Sarah was glad she didn't speak Spanish, as Juanita flounced out of the room. She giggled with Nikki as they retired to the porch swing. Thank God for José and Juanita. They took care of her house and her daughter when she had to put in long hours at the office.

The squeaking of the old swing was a pleasant sound as Sarah's thoughts drifted over the past five and a half years. She breathed in the cool night air, the wonderful smell of the honeysuckle vines. She loved it here. It was a perfect place to live, to raise her daughter. Or it had been.

A scowl crossed her face as her thoughts turned to her meeting with McAllister. She had been more shaken by the meeting than she wanted to admit. The sadness in his eyes had touched her, making her want to reach out and hold him, comfort him like she would Nikki. Her face warmed. No, not like she would Nikki.

Sarah knew she should leave now. It had to happen eventually. She'd always known they weren't truly safe. She glanced at the sleeping child in her arms. They would never be safe.

Pulling Nikki closer, Sarah watched the dark clouds gathering overhead. McAllister was right about one thing—there were secrets worth killing for.

CHAPTER NINE

Gavin tossed and turned, his thoughts in chaos as images of Cory, Sarah, and Nikki drifted through his mind. He didn't want to sleep. Sleep brought the dreams, the demons that had chased him all his life. He could no longer pretend the demons belonged to Jacody Ives.

Tossing off the covers, he opened the laptop and pulled up a blank page. Placing his fingers on the keyboard he began to type.

The demons were back inside his head. Laughing at him. Mocking his inability to stop them. Jacody knew that this time it wasn't a story. This time it was personal. Somewhere in the midst of this small farm town a killer lurked. Going about his daily life. Laughing, loving, following his dreams. He didn't care about the dreams he'd destroyed.

Jacody had arrived in town amidst no fanfare. He'd only been here one day, and yet already the secrets had started to unravel. What had really happened to Johanna Nelson? Was she also a victim? Marisa thought so. And then there was the missing page from the register. Secrets. The whole town was full of secrets.

And what about the sheriff? Why would a beautiful young woman hide behind a badge? And what was she hiding?

Desire coursed through him as he remembered the flashing green eyes, heart-shaped face, and flaming red hair.

And then there was Nikki. His gut instincts told him the child was in danger. He could feel the darkness closing in around her. Was the secret surrounding Nikki? Was Nikki the one Cory wanted him to protect?

He was here to find a killer. Someone had killed to hide a secret.

He didn't want to believe that Sarah was involved. It couldn't be Sarah.

Gavin closed the laptop, a sinking feeling starting in the pit of his stomach as he faced the truth. He didn't have to write it. This wasn't a story. This time he couldn't pick and choose the bad guy. His fingers shook as he dialed the number. It was only five a.m., but Carl would be up. Carl was always up.

"Hello."

"Carl, it's Gavin. I need a favor."

"Shit, Gavin, it's five in the morning."

"Were you asleep?" Gavin grinned as he heard the muttered cursing at the other end of the line, the sound of the cigarette lighter clicking.

"Don't make no difference whether I was sleeping or not. The chief is already suspicious. You're asking me to put my job on the line here, Gavin. Is it worth it? And dammit, you could get killed."

Gavin ignored the last and answered the first question. "I think so. Just a few more days, Carl. That's all I need. For Cory." He listened as Carl took a deep drag off the cigarette he'd just lit.

"All right. What do you need?"

"A background check on Sheriff Sarah Burns. Anything you can find."

"I'll do it on one condition. You meet me at O'Patrick's Friday night at six o'clock."

Almost as an afterthought, Carl added, "Be careful. We think the guy doing this is impersonating a police officer. Or he really is a police officer. Thought we had a lead, but nothing panned out."

"How's Rob doing?" Gavin changed the subject. The silence told him more than he wanted to know.

"I told you I'd take care of Rob, and I will. Don't you worry about him, you just be careful."

"I'll be careful." Gavin hung up the phone. He knew Carl was worried, and it wasn't about his job. He also knew that if Sarah Burns had a secret, Carl Jackson would find it.

The growling of his stomach reminded Gavin he hadn't eaten since yesterday afternoon. The Lodge offered its occupants breakfast, but Gavin wanted to mix with the locals. One good thing about small towns, the people got up early. If he was lucky, the café would be open. He needed to let people see him, get them talking. Someone here had to have seen Cory arrive. And someone here knew what happened after she arrived.

Morning traffic had just reached its peak as Gavin stepped onto Main Street. Motorists slowed, honked, and waved as he walked toward Leslie's Café. He waved and smiled. Every small town had secrets, but it also had good people. He needed to remember that. It was sometimes hard to expose the guilty without hurting the innocent.

The sign in the window said, "Mom's Home Cooking."

"Mr. McAllister!"

Gavin turned to watch the elderly man quickly

approaching.

"Clarence Archibald, sir. I was hoping to get a chance to meet you. Just finished your last novel, *Pool of Tears*. Would you let an old man buy your breakfast?"

Gavin waited for him to catch up.

"After you, Mr. Archibald." He held the door open.

"Oh, please call me Clarence."

"All right, but only if you agree to call me Gavin."

"It's a deal."

Leslie's Café could have been any small town café in America. Gavin smiled at the red-checkered tablecloths. It seemed that nothing much changed from town to town. The café was filling up with the breakfast crowd as he followed Clarence to a small booth near the windows.

"I hope you don't mind my barging in, but I've been a fan of yours for years."

"Well, I have to say Mr.–Clarence, you seem to be the only fan I've met since I arrived here."

"Oh, they're a good bunch. Little standoffish at first, but they'll come around. I can heartily recommend the biscuits and gravy."

Gavin felt his mouth watering from the delicious smells wafting in from the kitchen. Biscuits and gravy sounded good, along with bacon, sausage, eggs, and lots of coffee.

Clarence laughed heartily as Gavin gave his order to the waitress. "Been a while since you ate, son?"

Gavin grinned, "Been a while since I wanted to. Everything here smells delicious."

Gavin studied the man in front of him. Late sixties, possibly early seventies. He'd felt the strength in his grip and wasn't fooled by the gleam in the vivid blue eyes. This man had been places, seen things. A keen intelligence lay behind the twinkle, and Gavin wondered who would be picking whose brain over breakfast.

"So, Clarence, how long have you been here?"

"Oh, I've only been here about three months. Bought the flower shop down on Main. Decided there was enough ugliness in the world and wanted to spend my remaining days creating something beautiful. You'll have to drop by, see my butterfly garden."

Gavin nodded, lost in his own thoughts. He knew all about ugliness in the world. That's why he was here.

"How about you, son? What brings you to Glade Springs?"

Clarence hadn't wasted any time getting right down to the real issues.

"Sheriff put you up to asking me that question?" Gavin's voice turned cold.

Clarence looked offended. "I wouldn't have asked it if she had. Don't take kindly to people asking me to nose into other people's business. Just making small talk. Forget I asked."

"In that case, I apologize."

"Accepted." Clarence returned to his biscuits and gravy, and the two sat in silence as they enjoyed their meals.

"You said you'd just finished *Pool of Tears*. What did you think?"

"Not your best work, but still a good novel. *Sacred Secrets* was my favorite."

Gavin smiled. *Sacred Secrets* had also been his favorite.

"Tell me, do you really dig up people's secrets the way they say you do?"

This time Gavin laughed out loud. "Are you hiding

something, Clarence?"

"Me? I'm an open book." The dancing lights glimmering in the blue eyes told a different story.

Gavin laughed again. He was beginning to like the old man. He felt good for the first time in days. There was always something refreshing about honesty.

"Do you promise not to tell? I mean, if the truth got out, it could ruin my reputation."

"Scout's honor." Clarence grinned at him conspiratorially, eyes twinkling.

Gavin was about to reply when he felt a hand on his shoulder. He looked up to see a middle aged woman standing by his chair. Her face was haggard, dark circles rimmed the violet eyes. Eyes that held a sadness he'd seen too recently reflected in his own mirror. A sadness he still saw each time he looked at Rob. This woman had recently lost someone she loved.

"Mr. McAllister?"

"Yes, I'm Gavin McAllister."

"My name is Morgana Nelson. My daughter was recently killed."

"I heard about Johanna's accident, Mrs. Nelson. I'm sorry." Gavin knew the words would bring her no comfort.

"Then you'll help me?"

Gavin frowned. "I'm sorry, Mrs. Nelson, I don't know what I could do."

"I want you to find out who killed my daughter." The words were spoken softly, but the grip of the hand on his shoulder became increasingly painful.

Gavin searched the face of the woman beside him. This was the second time in less than a day that someone had suggested that Johanna Nelson's death was not an accident.

"Let's go, honey, you can't be bothering Mr. McAllister." Gavin met the tortured gaze of the man who'd approached them, as he gently removed the clutching hand from Gavin's shoulder and pulled the distraught woman safely into his embrace. "I'm sorry, Mr. McAllister. Johanna was our only child. It's been really tough."

Gavin nodded, unable to find words. He watched as the husband led the sobbing woman from the café. Tough was an understatement. He met Clarence's eyes across the small table, seeing the understanding and compassion there.

"Get a lot of that when you visit a new town?"

"Yeah."

They finished their meal in silence, both lost in their own thoughts.

"You look like crap, Sarah."

"Thanks, Joshua, just what every woman wants to hear when she walks into the office. Where's Ella Mae?"

"Called in sick. Said she fell last night and woke up stiff and sore this morning. I may run out there later on, see how she's doing."

"They bought the old Sampson place, didn't they?" Sarah grimaced as she sniffed the coffee. Too strong.

Joshua nodded, his thoughts elsewhere.

"I think checking on her is a good idea. Tell her to get well quick. We need her here. I don't want to have to get used to your coffee again." Sarah grinned at him. She knew he was worried about Ella Mae. Maybe she needed to have a talk with Philip Thomas.

Closing the door to her office, Sarah sighed heavily. It was only nine o'clock, and yet it seemed the day had gone on forever. She rubbed her aching eyes. She hadn't slept well, and this time it wasn't the dreams. She'd brought Nikki back to Millie's. For some reason she couldn't explain, and didn't want to look at too closely, she wanted her near. Taking a drink of the strong coffee she grimaced again. Ella Mae had spoiled her.

Joshua stuck his head in the door and grinned. "I'm making a fresh pot. You look as if you could use it."

Sarah nodded and motioned him to sit down. "You must be psychic. You told me I wasn't going to sleep well after McAllister got here."

Joshua laughed, "It doesn't take a psychic to know that no law official sleeps well when G. C. McAllister is in town. Have you met him yet?"

Sarah nodded.

"So, what'd you think?"

Sarah knew Joshua was watching her intently, looking for a reaction. She shrugged.

"Hey, Sarah, it's me, okay? I've worked for you the past three years. Surely you don't think I bought all that woman's intuition crap you throw around. You feel things or know things. I don't know, and as long as it helps us, I don't give a damn. So, what's G. C. McAllister doing in Glade Springs?"

Sarah weighed what he'd said. She'd been treading water for a long time. Sarah felt like a drowning victim, going down for the third time. She needed a lifeline.

"I don't know. He's looking into Johanna's death, but I don't think he's looking for a story. At least not one he intends to write about. There's a lot of rage inside Gavin McAllister. And something else, something very sad."

"Any clue about what he's looking for?" Joshua didn't for one minute doubt Sarah's assessment. If she didn't think

71

McAllister was here for a story, then he wasn't here for a story.

"He's looking for something, or someone." Sarah hesitated. "Joshua, I don't think Johanna was alone the night she crashed."

Joshua nodded. He'd suspected as much himself. "Makes more sense."

Sarah hesitated again. After all it was only a hunch. She didn't have any proof at all, except her dreams. "There's something else that bothers me, Joshua. I think Corrine Larson may have been here, in Glade Springs."

Joshua frowned, searching his memory. "The journalist killed in Richmond?"

Sarah nodded.

"Wouldn't somebody have seen her? I mean, somebody had to see her if she was here."

"What if she came in late and Johanna checked her in? What if Johanna was the only one who knew she was here?"

Joshua jumped to his feet, startled. "Good Lord, Sarah, do you know what you're saying?"

Sarah nodded, rubbing her aching temples. "I'm saying we may have a killer in Glade Springs."

CHAPTER TEN

"Good Lord, Mary, she said she fell. She doesn't have the flu." Joshua watched impatiently as his wife continued to pack items of food for Ella Mae. The conversation with Sarah earlier had left him on edge. He wanted to get out to Ella Mae's and back to town as quickly as possible. He didn't want to leave Mary alone after dark.

"Oh, that's right. Wait just a minute." Mary disappeared into the bedroom returning with a small jar of odd-looking gel.

"Grandpa's liniment. Works wonders for sore muscles."

"Yeah, and smells like a polecat."

"Joshua Cross, you keep a respectful tongue in your head about my grandpa."

Joshua ginned, catching her as she huffed by him. "I love your grandpa. After all, if it wasn't for him, I wouldn't have you," he whispered as he ran his hand gently over the swell of her stomach. "Sure you don't want to go with me?"

Mary smiled up at her husband, locking both arms around his neck. "I wish I could. Doc says not to take any chances, and the road to the old Sampson place is pretty rocky."

Joshua nodded, holding her close. She'd had two miscarriages in the past three years. This time they weren't going to take any chances.

"I'll be back as soon as I can. How about dinner at the café?"

Mary smiled. "I'll be waiting."

It was getting dark, but Joshua continued driving, hands clenched tightly around the steering wheel. Mary would worry, but dammit, he couldn't go home yet. Not this way. Why? Why the hell did women feel they had to protect the cowardly bastards?

The memory of Ella Mae's bruised and swollen face still burned inside him. She'd fallen all right. The same way his mother had fallen time and time again. Emotions washed over him. Rage, hate, love, and guilt. He'd felt no remorse when his father died. He hadn't killed him, though God knows he'd wanted to many times. But then he hadn't tried to save him either. It had taken every ounce of his eight-year-old strength to drag his mother's body from the burning car.

Pulling the Jeep to the side of the road, he cut the engine and rested his head on his hands. He hadn't been able to save her, either. She'd died in his arms as he sat there watching the car go up in flames.

Heavy sadness descended upon him. He wouldn't be able to save Ella Mae either–not unless she wanted to be saved.

Joshua relaxed his hands on the steering wheel, turning his thoughts to Mary and the child growing inside her. His child would never know the pain he'd had to grow up with. Never know the fear. Love flowed through him, chasing away the last of his rage. It was too late for dinner at the café, but he'd make it up to Mary. It was time he went home.

Gavin threw off the covers and stumbled to the bathroom to splash cold water over his face. What the hell had he just seen?

He examined his hands, expecting to see them covered in blood as they had been in the dream. His heart beat erratically, still caught up in the need to run as fast as he could. Nikki was out there, somewhere in the night. The killer was stalking her, getting closer with each ragged breath Gavin took. He didn't know whose body he had stumbled over. He hadn't recognized the man, but the face had changed and he was holding Rob, trying to stem the blood flowing from his chest.

He stared at his hands again, just as he'd done in the dream. There were bodies everywhere. Small bodies of children. Rob, Carl, people he'd never seen before. There was blood everywhere. He'd seen Cory then, just outside the circle of bodies. *Hurry, Gavin. You have to hurry. Please protect her.*

Drying his face, he avoided meeting his eyes in the mirror, afraid of what he would see there. Returning to the bedroom, he sat down heavily on the bed. At least now he knew who she had sent him here to protect. Nikki. Placing his head in his hands, he saw an image of the bodies strewn about. "Cory, what the hell did you stumble into?" he groaned.

CHAPTER ELEVEN

The soft gray light of dawn filtered through the kitchen window as Sarah sat, gripping the mug of coffee as if it could somehow ward off the darkness surrounding her. She couldn't remember how long she'd sat there, but knew she'd slept only a few minutes before the dreams woke her. Someone was going to die.

A glimmer of light glowed softly near the door, and Sarah felt the hair rise on the back of her neck as the shape slowly took form. She recognized Corrine Larson from the pictures. The young woman held out her hands.

You have to stop him, Sarah, before he kills again.

Sarah gripped the mug tighter, her voice trembling. "Stop who? Who am I looking for?"

The figure shimmered, a sad wistful smile tugging at the corners of her mouth. *You know.*

Sarah watched as the light dimmed and the figure slowly faded. The words echoing in the room. *You know. You know. You know.*

No, it couldn't be him. They would have told her if he was out.

She had to know. Fingers shaking, she flipped through the address book until she found the number. It was only four a.m., but he would understand. She prayed silently as the phone rang for the third time, "Please be there."

"Jones."

"Captain, it's Sarah."

"Sarah, it's four in the morning. What's wrong?"

"Just tell me if he's still in jail. Please." She knew her voice sounded desperate, but she felt desperate. She heard the deep sigh on the other end of the phone.

"He's still in jail, Sarah. I'm to be notified immediately if he's released. I told you, Sarah, you're safe there, honey. Don't worry about Williams. If he gets out, I'll take care of him."

Sarah felt the air rush from her lungs, realizing she'd been holding her breath. "Thank you, Captain. I'm sorry if I woke you."

"Any time, Sarah. You call me any time."

Replacing the receiver, she noticed the trembling in her hands, the wetness on her face. Fear. She was actually trembling in fear. "Damn you, Todd Williams."

Refilling her coffee mug, Sarah sat down at the kitchen table. Her eyes focused blindly on the soft gray light. The words continued to echo in her mind as tears streamed down her face. *You know.*

Gavin entered the sheriff's office with some trepidation. It went against his grain to ask for or offer help to local officials. He'd been breaking his rules ever since he arrived. Getting involved. He wasn't here to get involved in the death of Johanna Nelson, unless it had something to do with Cory. Still, the dreams last night had left him shaken, and the pained face of the father and sobs of the mother had haunted him. Those poor people needed answers. No, they needed closure. Johanna needed closure.

"Can I help you?"

Gavin studied the face of the young woman behind the counter. Heavy makeup did little to conceal the bruises around her eyes, the cut and swollen lip. Not his business. He didn't have the time, and it just wasn't any of his business. Not this time.

"Yes, I'm Gavin McAllister. I'd like to talk to Sheriff Burns, please."

"She's in her office." Ella Mae nodded toward the hall.

"Thank you." Gavin followed the nod to the closed door down the hall, but found himself hesitating at the door. Taking a deep breath, he knocked.

"Come in."

Once again he was awed by her quiet beauty. She looked as tired as he felt, but more than anything she looked soft and womanly, her eyes gentle, arms wrapped around the child on her lap. Shock registered, making her eyes darken as she met his gaze across the desk.

"Mr. McAllister."

Nikki glanced up and smiled. "I'm drawing a ballerina."

Something ached deep inside Gavin as he watched the two of them. Something he didn't have the time or energy to analyze.

"I was wondering if I could talk to you."

"Nikki, why don't you go show Ella Mae your ballerina. I'll be ready in just a minute."

"Okie, dokie." Nikki smiled up at Gavin as she left. "We're going to the park. Do you want to come?"

Gavin knelt to answer her, surprised when the tiny arms reached out and wrapped around his neck.

"Nikki…"

He heard the panic in Sarah's voice.

"Maybe next time," he whispered as he disengaged himself and watched as she bounced happily down the hall.

"She doesn't normally do that with strangers."

"We met at the bookstore. I guess she doesn't consider me quite a stranger."

"Still, she knows she isn't supposed to–" Sarah stopped. She didn't want to discuss her daughter with Gavin McAllister. "Please, sit down. What can I do for you?"

Gavin sat, taking her cue. All business now.

"The day I got here, the young girl at The Lodge told me she didn't think Johanna Nelson's death was an accident."

Sarah frowned. "Marisa Hutchins?"

"I guess. I know her name is Marisa."

Sarah nodded and waited for him to continue.

"Yesterday morning at the café, Mrs. Nelson approached me and asked me to help her find out who killed her daughter."

Sarah sat up straighter. She hadn't been aware that the Nelsons thought their daughter had been killed.

"I don't want to get involved in this. Maybe you could talk to them."

"I'll do that. And I'll talk to Marisa, too." Sarah hesitated. "I'm sorry I was so rude to you the other day. Things have been stressful around here the past few weeks."

Gavin smiled. "I didn't take it personally. As you said, my reputation preceded me."

Sarah smiled, extending her hand. "Well, if there's nothing else, Mr. McAllister, I have a date with a very vivacious five-year-old."

The touch of her hand shocked Gavin, and once again he found himself saying things he'd never meant to say. "I have to go to Richmond today. I'll be back tomorrow. Maybe we could talk about why I'm really here."

Sarah nodded, "Good."

"Well, thank you, Sheriff. I don't want to take up too much of your time. I've met that vivacious five-year-old, and I don't want her mad at me."

Sarah laughed, the ache inside Gavin magnifying. Did she know how beautiful she was when she laughed?

"Nor do I. She's going to start getting impatient if I don't hurry. Come on, I'll walk you out."

Dark eyes followed the progress of the Explorer. They grew darker with anger and hatred as he stared at the black-haired man standing waving after them. The fucking whore. He touched his groin. Pain. The ache was becoming a constant pain now. He needed to hear her scream.

It isn't Mother's Day.

Fuck off, bitch.

It didn't matter. It never had really. Every day was Mother's Day. He followed the man as he walked to The Lodge and came out a few minutes later carrying a small bag and briefcase.

"We'll see you tomorrow, Mr. McAllister."

"Take care, Marisa."

The car pulled out of the parking lot. Pain. He had to ease the pain. Fucking whore. He'd show her who was boss. He watched the young girl, his hunger growing. So young, so sweet. His mouth filled with saliva as he stared at her lips. He could almost hear her screams.

The warm sunshine felt good as Sarah watched Nikki build sand castles. She wished her thoughts were as pleasant. Why had Nikki hugged Gavin McAllister? She'd never hugged Joshua, and she'd known him for years. And why hadn't she pushed him for an answer when McAllister had said he'd tell her why he was really here?

Her face flamed red as she remembered. *Because the touch of his hand had your hormones roaring, that's why. Time to stop thinking.*

"Nikki, we have to leave soon. Juanita will have dinner ready, and you know how grouchy she gets when we're late."

"Okay, Mommy."

Nikki rose from the sand pile, dusted off her jeans, and reached for her mother's hand.

"That was easy," Sarah laughed, as they walked toward the Explorer.

"I'm hungry."

Sarah laughed again and buckled her in the seat. "Why didn't you tell me? I've been starving for the last hour."

"You were having fun, so I didn't want to make you leave."

Buckling her own seat belt, Sarah reached over and brushed back the tousled curls.

"Oh, so it was me having fun?"

"Mommy, why don't you like Mr. McAllister?"

The question caught Sarah off guard. Nikki was watching her closely, her expression too serious for a five year old. Sarah chose her words carefully.

"Sometimes adults have problems dealing with each other. I don't dislike Mr. McAllister, sweetheart."

"Oh."

"And that brings up a question I have for you. Why did you hug Mr. McAllister?"

Nikki smiled, "I like him. He looks like the pretty lady. I think he's lost, too."

Sarah felt the familiar chill go down her spine. "Nikki, have you seen the pretty lady again? You promised me you'd tell me if she came back."

Nikki screwed up her face as if giving the question great thought. "I'm sorry, Mommy, I forgot."

"When did you see her, sweetheart?"

"This morning. She said when the bad man came she'd help me hide."

Sarah drove in silence. She knew Nikki didn't understand what she was seeing at night, or what was being said to her. But Sarah did, and the thought terrified her. Nikki was in danger. There could be no other reason for Corrine Larson to keep appearing to her, talking to her. She was trying to protect Nikki from something, or someone. *You have to stop him, Sarah, before he kills again.*

"Nikki?"

"Yes, Mommy."

"I want you to listen to the pretty lady, okay? If she says it's time to hide, then you go with her. Mommy will find you."

"Okie, dokie."

Sarah shuddered as the sun went down. She'd always loved the night, but now it seemed darker than usual. She found herself watching the road, the bushes, the trees, looking for places someone could hide. She tried to remember exactly what Nikki had said. *When the bad man comes.* That was it.

"Mommy?"

"Yes, angel?"

"Mr. McAllister isn't the bad man. He's one of the good

82

guys."

Sarah nodded. The thought both pleased and terrified her. If it wasn't Gavin McAllister who was here to destroy her, then who was it? She trembled as the words once again echoed in her mind. *You know.*

CHAPTER TWELVE

A gentle flush crept up Millie's face as Clarence asked for a second helping of meatloaf. Old fool. Probably die of heartburn tonight, and it'd be all her fault. His comment about needing to put a little spice in her life had angered her. She'd show him spice. Her tongue felt on fire, and she gulped her second glass of water. Had he complained? No, just laughed and kept right on eating as if nothing was wrong.

"You don't have to eat it to be polite. I know it's too hot. Here, I'll fix you something else." Millie reached for his plate, only to have it pulled away, his dark eyes twinkling with laughter.

"My own fault. I'm the one who said I needed a little spice in my life."

"Humph. That wasn't what you said," Millie grumbled.

Clarence covered her hand with his. It was a good hand, warm, strong, calloused from long hours of working in the earth.

"How about we compromise? Is that jam cake I smell? Sure would go good with a cup of your coffee."

The gentle squeeze on her hand had the effect of sending her running to the kitchen, eager for a moment to pull herself together. Sadness enveloped her. Why not just enjoy what he was offering? A relationship without trust just couldn't work, that's why. And he didn't know. Didn't know the truth about her. Millie swiped away the single tear that had escaped. And she couldn't tell him.

The town had grown quiet as Millie and Clarence sat in comfortable silence in the old porch swing sipping coffee. Clarence had noticed her withdrawal when she came back from the kitchen, but took it in stride. Time. She'd come around in time. After all, they were both too old to go anywhere else.

"I brought you a present. Actually, two presents."

Millie set her cup on the porch and took the small package.

"What is it?"

"I always thought half the fun of presents was opening them." Clarence hesitated. "Just don't take offense, okay?"

Millie opened the package, taking out the small .38 caliber pistol and the article on Millicent Garrett Fawcett.

"But..." she stuttered, finding herself suddenly speechless.

"Well, you always seem to get mad at me when I call you Millicent. Thought you might like to know why."

Millie scanned the article on Dame Millicent Fawcett.

"She was a great woman. Maneuvered and wooed political friends for fifty years. Set the stage for women's suffrage in England. She reminds me a lot of you." Clarence placed his arm along the back of the porch swing and continued. "When she started her campaign, married women didn't even own their own clothes and certainly didn't own or have access to their money, whether it was inherited or earned by their own labors. Why, if it hadn't been for her long-standing, assiduously won political friendships and achievements, the suffrage movement would have been lost."

"I never heard of her." Millie stared at Clarence, leaning back into the arm placed behind her and continuing to read the article.

"Sort of like what happened here. Historians preferred to write about the violence than the hard, day-by-decades of political strategies that actually got the job done. Fawcett is almost a footnote to suffrage history."

Clarence waited until Millie finished reading the article before continuing. "Always admired strong women. And you remind me of her. I see how you go about every day, not nosing in other people's business, but still always there to lend a hand. Lady Bounty. Sort of in the background. You make things happen in this town. And I know you don't need a gun. But, well something's been bothering me lately. There's some suspicion that young Nelson girl's death wasn't an accident. Feel safer knowing you had it. A woman ought to know how to shoot a gun."

Millie felt her eyes grow wet. She wouldn't cry. She was touched by the gifts. Practical, yes, but the old coot cared about her. He just didn't know her.

"Thank you, Clarence." Millie's voice was husky, and she trembled slightly as the arm resting lightly behind her tightened, pulling her close.

"Gotta keep my best girl safe, don't I?" The words were light, but the gleam in his eyes told her he knew how she was feeling and wasn't going to push it tonight. He'd give her all the time she needed. Time wouldn't change the truth. She hadn't touched a gun in twenty years, but he wouldn't have to teach her to shoot. She'd grown up with a gun in her hand.

"Well, guess I better get home. Much as I hate to admit it, the old body does need more sleep than it used to. Why don't you bring Nikki by tomorrow? Show you ladies my new butterfly garden."

Millie nodded, still too upset to trust herself to speak.

"Good night, Millie." Clarence placed a light kiss on her cheek.

Millie watched him until he was out of sight. He'd called her Millie. Warmth spread through her until her gaze fell on the small pistol and article. Lies. Everything about her was a lie. Clarence was a good man. She couldn't do that to him. A tear coursed down the weathered old face. With trembling hands, she placed the gun in the closet and pulled down the old shoebox. She'd already lost so much. Tears flowed freely as she pulled out the faded photograph, her eyes lovingly memorizing every feature of the face smiling at her.

Gavin stood in the doorway of the dimly lit bar, waiting for his eyes to adjust to the light. It didn't take him long to spot Carl, seated against the wall, facing the door. Typical.

He started toward the table, stopping short when he saw Carl's face. He looked as if he'd aged ten years in the past week. Cory was right about one thing–he needed to hurry. Not just to protect Nikki, but also for Carl's sake. If anything happened to that old man, he'd never forgive himself.

Carl chose that moment to glance up and meet Gavin's eyes across the room. Gavin smiled and nodded toward the door. He'd never liked bars and liked them even less since Rob had started drinking. Carl nodded, indicating he'd join him as soon as he paid for his drink.

The air was cool and Gavin breathed in deeply, ridding himself of the smell of stale cigarette smoke and whiskey.

"Where you staying?" Carl looked him over, noting the black circles under the eyes, fatigue etched on the handsome face.

"Thought I'd stay with you." Gavin smiled, hoping to lighten the older man's load, let him know he was okay.

"'Bout time you said something that made sense. I'll meet you at the apartment."

Gavin wondered briefly if he should let him drive, but shrugged it off as he started his own car and followed Carl. In Carl's present mood, it would have led to a fight. Gavin had a feeling that was coming anyway, and the longer he could delay it, the better off he'd be.

In less than thirty minutes, Carl had him settled into the guest bedroom with the smell of Columbian coffee drifting through the apartment. He'd missed his coffee. Millie's was great, but there was nothing that compared to the taste of freshly ground Columbian coffee. Carl was waiting for him, mug in hand, and he didn't waste any time getting down to business.

"What's up with you and Sarah Burns?"

The question caught Gavin unprepared. "What do you mean?"

"Come on, Gavin, don't lie to me. I know you too well. I heard it in your voice. There's something there, and before I tell you anything, you gotta give a little." Carl's words were slurred, the whiskey beginning to take hold.

"All right. I'll admit I feel something for her and her daughter. But if she's part of what happened to Cory, then what I feel won't matter."

"You sure?"

Gavin grimaced, as pain sliced through his chest. "Yeah, I'm sure."

"Then I need something with her fingerprints on it."

The pain in Gavin's chest expanded, filling his abdomen. "You don't think she's who she says she is?"

"Not unless I believe the dead wake up. The real Sarah Burns died six years ago."

Gavin stared into the black coffee, looking for an answer he couldn't find. There could be a thousand reasons a person would take over the identity of a dead person. None of them good. Some of them worth killing to protect.

Marisa flipped through the pages of the new teen magazine she'd purchased at Millie's. She studied the fashions feverishly, her dreamy eyes recreating her own staid wardrobe into the sexy outfits the girls were wearing. Her father would kill her. She laughed. She'd probably get thrown out of school.

A frown marred her pretty face. Her mother had told her she'd named her Marisa because it was different. She'd never be different here. Nothing ever happened in Glade Springs. Her life sucked. Here she was, on a Friday night, sitting at a desk waiting for one of their two esteemed guests to need something. Or maybe on the off chance someone else would check in.

Marisa thought about Gavin McAllister, her lips curving into what she hoped was a sexy smile. Now, there was different. She liked the way he looked at her when she'd told him about Johanna. At least he hadn't treated her like a child. There was something wrong with Johanna's accident. She knew it. And she hoped he uncovered it. Then he'd tell everyone that she had been his informant.

Maybe then Robby would take her seriously.

A sound from the hallway broke her fantasy, and she glanced around nervously. No one should be here but her. Mr. Green had left about an hour ago, and Mr. McAllister wasn't due to return until tomorrow.

She glanced around again. She wasn't supposed to leave her station, but what if he'd returned and she'd missed him? She checked her image in the mirror behind the desk. The clerk had told her the blue blouse made her look older, more mature. She grinned, fluffing her auburn curls and applied the pink lip-gloss she kept hidden in her pocket. Her mother would kill her if she found out that she wasn't wearing a bra today. She frowned as she preened in front of the mirror. It wasn't all that noticeable. He hadn't noticed earlier. This time he would notice. She'd make sure of that. Wetting her lips, just a little, the way the magazine had said, Marisa left the counter. Her heart started to beat a little faster. Excitement. This is what it felt like to be alive. The hallway was dimly lit, but she noticed Gavin's door was ajar. Perfect, she didn't even have to knock. She was just checking to see if he needed anything, right?

"Mr. McAllister–" Marisa stopped just inside the door, her eyes wide, taking in the disarray of the room. "What are you doing?"

She wanted to say something else, scream, but the cloth pressed over her mouth and nose was making her feel funny. The smell was familiar. She tried to remember what it was. A hand slipped under her blouse, cupping the small breast. Marisa tried to pull away, but her arms were too tired. She felt herself being lifted, placed on the bed. The smell pulled her deeper. No, she had to fight to stay awake. She had to tell him she wouldn't tell anyone. Had to make him stop.

Everything seemed to be happening from a distance. Marisa fought her way through the fog, hearing his curse as the zipper on her pants stuck. Hearing the fabric rip, feeling the cool draft as her body was exposed. He lifted the cloth from her mouth, shaking her awake. "You're going to scream for me, aren't you, sweetheart?" He placed a pillow over her mouth and nose, just as a sharp pain between her legs brought her to full consciousness. Her eyes filled with tears as she stared into the black eyes above her and screamed. *Scream for me, sweetheart. Scream for Daddy.* Marisa screamed with every painful thrust until lack of oxygen made her body go limp, her mind numb. He continued to grunt and thrust long after her body became limp and lifeless. His climax was exhilarating. He was renewed. Humming his favorite tune, he jotted the words on the small pink card. *A gift from me. You're next.*

It's stupid to leave the card. They'll know it was you. Then they'll come here.

He grinned. *Shut up, bitch.*

The voice in his head no longer bothered him. He glanced around the room. No time for his usual clean up. Dumb sons-of-bitches. He knew all about DNA. He chuckled, as he placed the card on the nightstand and doused the body and bed with gasoline. A hot fire could destroy just about anything. Striking the match he tossed it on the bed and exited the room, leaving the door open. The smoke would be noticeable in minutes. Slipping out the rear entrance, he walked quickly up the street. Let them come. He was invincible.

CHAPTER THIRTEEN

After hours of relating to Carl everything that he'd found in Glade Springs, Gavin fell into bed exhausted. His body ached, and his mind felt numb as the sleepless nights caught up with him. In seconds, he drifted into an uneasy sleep and found himself once again in the swirling pink mist. He couldn't breathe. Struggling, he tried to reach up and push the pillow away from his face. His arms were heavy, too tired to move. Gavin could hear the grunts, the whispered words, *Scream, sweetheart. Scream for Daddy.* Bile rose in his throat, choking him. Reaching deep inside, he pulled on every ounce of willpower and screamed.

"Dammit, Gavin, wake up!"

Gavin's eyes jerked open, dazed and confused. "What happened?"

"You scared the fucking bejesus out of me, that's what happened," Carl said, his hands quivering as he struggled to light a cigarette. "Screaming in the middle of the night like some kind of goddamn banshee. What the hell's wrong with you? Probably woke up the whole fucking neighborhood."

Gavin glanced around the room trying to get his bearings. He could still taste the bile, still hear the whispered words. Placing his head between his hands he groaned. "Oh God, Carl, he's killed again."

Finally managing to get his trembling fingers and the

lighter together long enough to light the cigarette, Carl took a deep drag as he pondered what he'd just heard. He'd wondered about Gavin for a long time. A lot of things made sense now. The withdrawals. The long treks through the wilderness. Constant searching for something he couldn't find. Jacody Ives made perfect sense now.

"How long you been having the dreams, son?"

Drawing a ragged breath, Gavin met Carl's steady gaze. "All my life."

Carl nodded. He'd suspected as much. Yep, made perfect sense now. "I'll make the coffee, you get dressed. We got us some serious talking to do."

Gavin focused his attention on the steaming mug of black coffee. The only sound in the room was the slight click of Carl's lighter as he lit another cigarette.

"I'm waiting."

"I don't even know where to start, Carl." Gavin looked up to meet the serious brown gaze. He'd never told anyone but the psychiatrist about the dreams.

Carl shrugged. "I'll start for you then. Read every book you ever wrote. Always wondered about Jacody Ives. Good investigator, but he never let himself get involved with anyone, did he? Had those damn demons in his head all the time. Always afraid to let people get too close. Always running away to the next town, or disappearing into the wilderness for weeks. Boy seemed awful lonely to me."

Gavin continued to focus on the coffee mug, as if somehow the black liquid held the answers to questions he'd always been afraid to ask.

Carl continued, "Then I read *Sacred Secrets*. That was your best work, son. Want to know why?"

Gavin raised his head, his eyes haunted.

"Because Jacody finally got a friend. I think the only friend he ever had was that dog."

Gavin smiled wistfully remembering Myriah. She'd been his favorite character, and Carl was right, she'd been his only friend.

"That was right after you found out about Cory. You changed then. Maybe that was what you writers call your epiphany. Don't know what it was, but you came back to us. Gavin came back, not Jacody Ives."

"Penetralia of the soul," Gavin whispered.

"Exactly." Carl took another long drag on the cigarette before stubbing it out. "You ain't alone, son. You ain't never been alone."

Gavin swallowed the lump in his throat. He knew where to start now. At the beginning.

"The first time I remember the dreams I was about five. I woke up screaming. Couldn't explain to the Walkers what I'd seen, but I knew something bad had happened. The next day I heard them talking about how the old woman at the end of the street had been killed by a hit and run driver. It scared the hell out of me. I knew the dream and the death were connected, but I didn't know how. I was afraid to sleep after that. Thought I had caused the death."

Gavin stopped, lost in the guilt he'd felt as a child. The guilt he felt now. He could never stop the killings. He was always too late. Then there was the question he'd never been able to answer: *What was inside him? What part of him was so evil that it sought out the darkness while he slept?*

Carl's lighter clicked again, a signal for Gavin to continue.

"The Walkers were great people. They tried to understand. Took me to counselors, psychiatrists. Nothing helped. Then on my eighteenth birthday, I went camping with Rob and a bunch of the guys. That was the first time in my life I slept totally dreamless. Out there beneath the stars, away from the crowds, the towns, the people. I realized then that it was better for me, and better for everyone around me if I was alone. There had to be something inside of me that the darkness sought out. I've lived my entire life afraid the dark side would break loose, hurt the people I loved.

"The psychiatrist agreed with me. Said it was my own dark nature manifesting itself in my dreams. Thought it was healthier for me to write out my feelings. So I went away, created Jacody Ives and put the demons inside his head. Five years ago they returned. Worse this time. He's playing games with me. Laughing at me." Gavin tightened his hold on the coffee mug, allowing himself to feel the rage and despair warring inside him.

The silence in the room built until it was almost unbearable.

"Of all the fucking horseshit I ever heard." Carl threw his cup against the wall, shoved back his chair, and paced the small room. "Goddamn, psycho-social babbling fools. Ain't got nothing better to do than fuck up young kids."

"Carl…" Gavin started to speak, but held his tongue, the brown eyes turning deep charcoal as they fixed on him.

"You forget that shit. You hear me?" The old man's jaw bunched up in anger. "Ain't nothing wrong with you that a little love and understanding wouldn't a'cured. Fucking psychiatrists. Goddamn idiots, all of them. Anything they can't explain with their fucking mental babble, they medicate."

Gavin sat in shocked silence as Carl glared at him before slamming out the door. The ticking of the counter clock grated on his nerves, but he knew Carl would be back– he'd forgotten his cigarettes.

"And another thing," Carl continued his tirade as he stormed in, picking up the forgotten cigarettes, "maybe it ain't the killer you're connecting with. Maybe it's the victim. Just because you can't stop the killing you see happening in your dream, don't mean you can't stop the killer. Maybe it's the next victim you're supposed to save. You ever think of that?"

Gavin sat dumbstruck. Was Carl right? It wasn't the killer, but the victim reaching out to him? Gavin felt as if a weight had suddenly been lifted from his shoulders. The victims. That's why Cory had been able to get through. That's what she'd been trying to tell him.

"Well, what the hell are you waiting for?" Carl growled.

"I…"

"Gotta do everything for myself," Carl muttered as he crossed to the coffee pot, poured another cup, and disappeared into the guest bedroom. Gavin could hear the sound of drawers opening and closing, Carl muttering about stupid assholes. Shaking his head, Gavin followed.

"Want to share what you're doing?" Gavin asked from the doorway.

"I'm packing your things. You gotta get back to Glade Springs. Protect that little girl. Ain't that what this was all about? You ain't gonna be late this time, Gavin." Carl stopped shoving clothes into the overnight bag and sat down on the bed. Maybe he could save Gavin. Rob was already dead. The bottle had killed him; he just didn't know it yet.

Gavin joined him on the bed, afraid to break the silence

as rings of cigarette smoke drifted between them.

"I listened to you talk about that little girl and her mother, Gavin. Something happened out there in Glade Springs. Something good. Don't you let it mean nothing. Don't you lose her the way Rob lost Cory. Get the dog if you want it, but you got a chance, son, for more than that. A whole lot more."

Gavin placed his arm around Carl. He was right. Something had happened to him the minute Nikki had placed her small hand in his. Something strange and wonderful. Gavin had never prayed in his life, but he prayed now. "God, please don't let me be too late this time."

"Fire's out, Sheriff. We opened the windows, but the smell is still pretty bad."

Sarah nodded, her eyes misting. "Thanks, Billy." Swallowing hard, she tried to stop the gagging reflex that hit her the second she entered The Lodge. There was nothing in the world worse than the smell of burned flesh. Tommy and three of the volunteer fire fighters were still outside vomiting, and Joshua looked slightly green, although he was holding up better than most. Dammit! They weren't prepared for this. She wasn't prepared for this.

"Are you okay, Doc?" Sarah noted the grayness of the doctor's face, the blueness around his mouth as he slipped on his mask and nodded.

Sarah allowed her gaze to drift around the room, looking for something, anything to look at besides the badly charred body of what she knew must be Marisa Hutchins. They had caught the fire in time to save most of the room, but the body was burned beyond recognition. She swallowed hard again, concentrating on breathing through her mouth. She had to focus on her job, not her feelings. Her gaze fell on the small pink card on the dresser. Picking it up, she shivered as emotions ran up her arm, making her skin crawl, chilling her to the bone. Evil had its own special feel, and this was evil. *A gift from me. You're next.*

"Anything on McAllister's whereabouts?"

Sarah could feel Joshua's searching look. She knew her face revealed the turmoil of her emotions. Struggling to control the overwhelming fear that threatened to pull her into the darkness, she placed the card inside a plastic package and handed it to Joshua, resisting the urge to wipe her hands on her uniform. God she wanted a bath.

"He told me he was going to Richmond, but I didn't ask where. Said he'd be back tomorrow."

"I'm finished." Doc Hawthorne rose, his shoulders drooping more than usual. It wasn't supposed to happen this way. He'd delivered these children, watched them grow up. He shouldn't have to sign their death certificates. "Not much more I can do here. I'd say it's Marisa Hutchins. You can wait for the autopsy to make it official."

Sarah grimaced. She didn't need an autopsy.

"The Edgewood forensic team is on their way. Said they'd be here within the hour," Joshua stated.

"Thanks, Joshua." Sarah had hated calling in outsiders, but they just didn't have the equipment, or the expertise, to handle this type of situation. Nothing like this had ever happened in Glade Springs. Gavin McAllister had a lot to answer for.

"What do you make of the card?"

Joshua was turning the package over in his hands. Sarah glanced at it, a cold chill running down her spine...*never send to know for whom the bell tolls; It tolls for thee.*

"You're next." Joshua read the card out loud and glanced at Sarah. "Who do you think he means?"

"Not a clue," Sarah lied. "We'll run it through the system, see if anything like this has happened anywhere else."

"Good idea." Joshua hesitated, "Sarah, I think this card is for you."

Sarah didn't bother answering. She'd known the second she touched the card it was for her. *You know,* echoed in her mind.

"Joshua, stay here, lock it down, and wait for Edgewood. Go ahead and do the photographs and sketches of the scene. I have to go tell the Hutchins." Sarah knew her voice was quivering. She cursed silently at life's cruel joke of giving her the ability to feel what others felt. She was having enough trouble controlling the pain and fear she'd picked up in this room. She didn't know how she was going to handle the parents' emotions.

"Sarah, why don't you stay? I'll go."

Sarah met the concerned green eyes, not trying to disguise the pain in her own. "It comes with the territory, Joshua. It's my job."

"What do I do if McAllister shows up?"

Sarah considered her answer carefully. She knew Gavin McAllister hadn't killed Marisa. The evil she'd felt in that room wasn't attached to him. He could, of course, sue the city, but at the moment she didn't give a damn. It wouldn't hurt him to cool his heels for a couple of hours. And, dammit, he was partially responsible. If he hadn't come here none of this would have happened. At least in jail he'd be safe and one less thing for her to worry about.

"Book him."

Joshua nodded. Sarah was in charge. "The Hutchins are pretty religious people. Why don't you call the new minister, have him meet you out there?"

"Bless you, Joshua. You always seem to know the right thing to do."

"Comes with the territory, remember? It's my job."

Sarah exited The Lodge, her thoughts serious. Joshua would make a good sheriff. At least she wouldn't have to worry about that when she left. She turned her thoughts to the new minister. She hadn't had an opportunity to meet him or his wife. What was his name? Cooper. Picking up the cell phone, she automatically dialed the number and hoped it hadn't been changed. How was she supposed to address him? Was it Reverend, Father, Pastor?

"Hello."

"Mrs. Cooper?"

"Yes."

"This is Sheriff Burns. I'm sorry I haven't had the time to call on you and welcome you to Glade Springs, but I wonder if I could speak with your husband, please?"

"He's asleep, Ms. Burns."

Sarah frowned. No Sheriff Burns, and the Ms. had been spoken with disapproval. It was apparent Mrs. Cooper didn't believe in women sheriffs. She probably didn't believe women should work at all.

"Could you wake him, please? It's an emergency."

"Oh, no, I could never do that. Never." The voice had changed, a slight tremor just beneath the words.

Good Lord, she's afraid of him, Sarah thought. What kind of minister instilled fear in his wife?

"Mrs. Cooper, I'm sorry, I'm a little upset, and I'm

afraid I haven't made myself clear. I know it's late, but we've had a," Sarah paused. "We've had a death in the community. The family is going to need him. Please put your husband on the phone."

"I'll have him call you in the morning."

"Mrs. Cooper..."

The phone went dead. And people wondered why Sarah didn't go to church. It wasn't that she didn't believe in God; she just didn't believe in organized religion. As usual, she was on her own.

A half hour later Sarah stood outside, breathing deeply in an attempt to control the tears streaming down her face as she waited for Doc Hawthorne. Thank God he'd been here. She should have known he would feel an obligation to do just that. He'd been there for thirteen years through every broken bone, every cough or late night fever. He wouldn't desert them now.

Sarah watched his approach, realizing for the first time just how old he was getting. She'd ignored the Mayor's ravings at the council meetings that they needed to start looking for a younger doctor, someone more up to date. How much longer could he last? And getting a doctor to come to a small town like Glade Springs wouldn't be easy. Of course, there was always Edgewood. It was only a two-hour drive, but what about emergencies? The next time the mayor brought up the subject, Sarah would be more open-minded. Not a replacement, because no one could ever replace Doc Hawthorne. Maybe a partner.

"I gave Irene a sedative. She'll sleep until morning." His eyes never left Sarah's face, the question left unspoken between them.

"Dammit, Jim, I can't stop him if he wants to see her."

Doc nodded. Edsel Hutchins wanted to see his daughter. "Call me when he comes in. I'll be there."

Sarah nodded, not trusting herself to speak. He would be there, sedative in hand. They both knew sedatives weren't going to help Edsel Hutchins when he saw his daughter's body. It was almost two a.m. and Sarah felt a desperate need to hold Nikki. To know she was safe. That, like sleep, was a luxury she didn't have. It was going to be a long night.

CHAPTER FOURTEEN

The closer he came to Glade Springs, the more on edge Gavin became. He felt, more than knew, something was wrong. He also knew from past experience that a lot could happen in twenty-four hours. His eyes burned from lack of sleep, his eyelids gritty, sandpapery. He needed to deal with Rob, but now he needed to be here. He couldn't be in both places. Somehow, whatever was going on here was tied together with Cory's death.

Gavin's shoulders and arms ached from the four-hour drive as his thoughts ran rampant. He and Carl had talked for hours, going over the dreams, analyzing every clue. He could still feel the chills that had raced down his spine at what they suspected. The five young girls were some sort of gift. The killer was making a statement to someone. Who, or what, they didn't know. What was worse, they suspected that wasn't the only time he killed. It was simply the only time he left a message.

They were guessing, but Nikki's life depended on those guesses. It all had something to do with Sarah Burns. Somehow they were all connected. Cory was the catalyst, bringing them all together.

"Shit." He felt the tension increase. Cars lined Main Street. Too many cars, even for a Saturday.

Gavin drove straight to The Lodge. Yellow tape sealed

both the entrance and exit and a deputy waved him to parking across the street. He parked the car, sitting still for as long as he could. He had to go in there. Fear clutched his stomach as tightly as his hands clutched the wheel. If something had happened to Sarah or Nikki...

"Get out of the car, McAllister!"

The deputy stood, feet planted about two feet from the car, pistol drawn. Gavin opened the door and exited, hands in the air. He knew the drill, he'd written it a thousand times.

Gavin remained silent while the deputy searched and cuffed him before placing him in the rear seat of the cruiser. As the deputy started the car, curiosity finally made him ask the question he wasn't sure he wanted the answer to.

"Would you mind telling me what I'm being arrested for?"

The deputy met his stony glare in the rear view mirror for just a moment before turning his attention back to the road. "Suspicion of rape and murder."

The fear dug deeper into his stomach, the headline glaring in his memory. TORTURED, RAPED, EXECUTED.

"Who?" Gavin's voice was barely a whisper, and he wasn't sure the deputy even heard him.

"Marisa Hutchins."

Gavin felt the blood drain from his face. Guilt washed over him at the gut-wrenching relief he felt that it wasn't Sarah or Nikki. Marisa? God, she was only a child. He wanted to close his eyes, but knew if he did, he'd see her face, hear her voice as she whispered, *I don't think it was an accident.* He remembered his conversation with Sarah the day before and shuddered. He'd told Sarah that Marisa thought Johanna had been murdered. What if he'd been wrong? Carl's words replayed in his mind. *The real Sarah Burns died six years ago.* His guilt became a heavy weight that caused his shoulders to slump. He heard the hollow, maniacal laugh inside his head. It was his fault. He'd killed her.

Sarah replaced the receiver softly. She'd wanted to slam it down a dozen times in the last fifteen minutes.

"That bad, huh?" Joshua asked gently.

Sarah nodded, meeting Joshua's eyes across the desk. "He's asking for my resignation."

"He's an idiot. This town needs you. Especially now."

Sarah nodded again. Glade Springs was falling apart. Murder did that to a small town.

"What about McAllister?"

Sarah knew they couldn't hold Gavin much longer without charging him. Dammit, he hadn't even requested an attorney. In fact, according to Joshua, he hadn't said a word since he'd been brought in. The ringing of the phone kept her from having to answer immediately. She answered it automatically, moments later wishing she'd ignored the ring.

"Edsel Hutchins is coming in. He wants to see his daughter."

"Damn."

"Exactly." Sarah lay her head down on the desk. The sleepless night and emotions from the day had drained her. Now she had to deal with Edsel Hutchins.

"Sarah…"

Raising her head, Sarah placed her hands on the desk and pushed herself to her feet. She had to take charge of the situation.

"Joshua, call Doc Hawthorne and meet him at the funeral home. Edgewood took her there temporarily until they arranged for transport. Have Tommy keep an eye on Edsel the next day or so. He's going to be angry and he's hurting. That makes a dangerous combination."

Joshua nodded, glad to see the old Sarah.

Sarah rubbed her eyes. She'd forgotten to tell the Hutchins about the autopsy. She'd have to deal with that. First, she had to deal with Gavin McAllister. She fished around in her desk looking for the keys to the jail cell. It had been so long since they'd actually locked someone up that she'd forgotten where the keys were. It would be so much simpler if she could leave him locked up. But she couldn't. And she no longer had the option of asking or making him leave town. Even if he wanted to go, he couldn't now. Until she found Marisa's killer, Gavin McAllister was the town's number one suspect.

Gavin didn't look up as she unlocked the cell.

"I wish you'd never come here," she whispered.

He raised his head, haunted eyes meeting her own. "Believe it or not, Sheriff, so do I."

"I don't suppose you'd agree to stay in jail for your own protection?" Or mine, Sarah thought.

He shook his head.

"I didn't think so, but I had to try. There are a lot of scared and angry people out there, Gavin. I can't ask you to leave, and I may not be able to protect you."

Gavin shrugged, not even noticing she'd used his first name.

Sarah felt her jaw muscles tighten. She was getting angry. There was nothing emanating from him. He had totally walled himself off. No anger, no fear, no sadness—no emotions. Why the hell didn't he defend himself, say he didn't do it?

"Where were you last night?"

Gavin shrugged again, eyes downcast.

"I know you didn't kill Marisa Hutchins. So, why the hell don't you…"

He looked at her then, his eyes fierce, and for a moment she wavered. Guilt was written all over his face. Could she have been wrong?

"And how do you know that, Sarah?" Gavin stood up and approached her, hands clenching and unclenching, nostrils flaring with each angry step.

Sarah swallowed. She hadn't really meant to say that.

"I just know you didn't do it. You're not that evil."

"Maybe I am. Maybe I…" Gavin hesitated. He didn't even know how Marisa had been killed. "You don't have to actually pull the trigger to be responsible."

Their eyes met, a struggle of wills. Something flickered in his. Passion burned with a muted intensity, warring for control with the anger building inside him. Sarah wanted to back away. Her legs refused to move. She knew he was going to touch her. Knew she was powerless to stop him. All the pain and loneliness inside her screamed out for that touch. His fingertips gently stroked her cheek, his eyes on her lips. Sarah closed her eyes as desire flowed through every muscle in her body, making her legs weak, filling her with butterflies. She accepted the inevitable. She'd known this was going to happen from the moment she'd met him. She'd fought it, but now as desire coursed through her, she waited for the moment when his lips would claim hers.

A moment that never came. Even with her eyes closed, Sarah felt his withdrawal. Felt him move away from her.

"You were the only person I told that Marisa didn't believe the Nelson girl's death was an accident. Now she's dead."

Sarah's heart clenched in pain, an anguished sound escaping her lips. He couldn't believe she...

Gavin continued, his voice cold, emotionless. "I was with Carl Jackson from six last night until ten this morning. You can verify that by calling the FBI office in Richmond. Here's his card."

Sarah's eyes jerked open at the harshness of his voice. The room had suddenly gone cold. She took the card he held out before he once again put as much distance between them as the small room would allow. She looked at the card without really seeing it. She had to look at something, anything but him. Her cheeks flamed red with embarrassment. She had thought...but he thought she...

Sarah continued to look at the card, as she struggled for control. She had to get out of here. Throwing the card on the floor she slammed the door and locked it, not trusting herself to speak. She could hold the son-of-a-bitch until she checked out his alibi. And she wasn't going to be in any hurry to do that.

Gavin picked up the card from the floor, careful not to touch where she had held it, and placed it in the holder Carl had given him. The deputy hadn't taken his billfold, which surprised Gavin. So much for writer's knowledge.

The more Gavin tried not to think of Sarah, the more she entered his thoughts. He knew he'd hurt her. Dammit, he didn't believe she'd killed Marisa Hutchins. So why had he said it? He needed to get close to her, not alienate her. Groaning, he sat down on the cot. It wouldn't be easy for him to get close to her again. He wondered if she knew what it had cost him not to take what she had offered. Closing his eyes he felt the softness of her skin against his fingertips, saw her full lips ready, waiting. The ache of desire filled him so strongly he groaned out loud. She'd left here thinking he didn't want her. His need for her was so strong he knew if she had stayed, he'd have taken her whether she wanted him or not.

The sheer force of his desire terrified him. No woman had ever had that effect on him before. Opening his eyes, he shifted on the cot for a comfortable position. He finally gave up and started pacing the small room. He needed to get out, get the card to Carl. They were running out of time, and every moment was precious. He should have told Sarah about Nikki.

After an hour Gavin realized Sarah wasn't coming back. She hadn't bothered to check his alibi. His body was tired, his mind exhausted. He didn't want to sleep. Sleep brought dreams, and the dreams brought death. He paced until it was virtually impossible for him to take another step. His legs trembled, his vision blurred. Lying down on the small cot he closed his eyes and prayed.

CHAPTER FIFTEEN

"Be a good girl." Sarah hugged Nikki before pulling Juanita to the side with a whispered, "I don't care if it is church, don't let her out of your sight."

Juanita clucked something in Spanish that Sarah didn't understand, but the tone of her voice spoke volumes. Sarah knew that Juanita would tackle the devil himself to protect Nikki. Still, a wordless uneasiness settled over Sarah. Something intangible she couldn't touch, feel, smell or see, yet it hung in the still gray light of dawn each morning, hovering just out of reach, watching.

Sarah hugged Nikki again against the child's protests. She missed her time with Nikki. Guilt washed over her. She should be the one taking Nikki to church. She wanted her daughter to grow up informed so she could make her own decisions. They couldn't hide forever. Nor could they run forever. The thoughts filled Sarah with an overwhelming sadness as she waved and headed toward town.

The Edgewood van was parked in front of the funeral home. Sarah breathed a small sigh of relief. The sooner the autopsy was performed, the sooner the body could be released. At least then the Hutchins would be allowed to bury their daughter. The healing could begin. Sarah frowned, her thoughts once again turning to Gavin McAllister. What was it he had said? *The dead don't rest until the guilty are punished.* She'd tossed and turned all night. The mayor had been right. Since Gavin McAllister had arrived, she'd thought and acted more like a woman than a sheriff. Her face flamed red as she pulled into the parking slot marked "Sheriff." That wasn't the worst part of it. The worst part was that she wanted him to see her as a woman.

"Shit." Sarah slammed the door to the Explorer. Well, she was the sheriff, and Gavin McAllister was going to start talking. Pride raised her head, straightened her spine, and her stride brooked no interference.

"Morning, Ella Mae."

"Morning, Sheriff. We didn't think you'd be in today."

Sarah didn't bother to answer, but strode determinedly toward her office. She didn't feel up to small talk today. In fact, she didn't feel like talking to anyone at the moment. The sound of male laughter brought her up short. She'd never heard him laugh before, but something inside her recognized it. For just a moment she felt jealous, before the anger set in. What the hell was Joshua doing with Gavin McAllister in her office?

Not bothering to knock, Sarah opened the door and strode in. She watched the deep red flush that started at the base of Joshua's neck. Damn him; he should feel guilty. Ignoring McAllister, Sarah focused on Joshua.

"Sarah, what are you doing here?" Joshua stuttered slightly, a child caught with his hand in the cookie jar.

"Correct me if I'm wrong, Deputy Cross, but I believe I'm the sheriff, and the last time I looked, this was my office."

The brusqueness of her tone had the opposite of the

effect she had hoped for. Joshua simply smiled, a gleam of amusement lurking in the cool green eyes.

"I was just finalizing the paperwork on Mr. McAllister. I checked his alibi."

Sarah felt her color heighten at the unspoken accusation. Joshua knew she hadn't tried to verify the alibi last night. Knew she'd deliberately left Gavin in jail overnight.

Gavin cleared his throat. "Sarah, I think it's time we talked about some things."

Sarah finally looked at him, her gaze chilling, impersonal. "I don't remember giving you permission to use my Christian name, Mr. McAllister. Even with your alibi, you're still a suspect in a murder investigation. And you're right, we are going to talk about some things. I'll let you know when I want to see you. For now, if you're finished with the paperwork, I'd suggest you start looking for a place to stay. And if Deputy Cross didn't warn you, I will. Don't leave town."

"It's your call." Gavin reached across the desk and shook Joshua's hand. With a curt nod and "Sheriff," he left the room.

Sarah stood still, her back to the door. Her anger was dissipating quickly, leaving her feeling weak, vulnerable. Tears stung behind her eyelashes. Too little sleep, too much caffeine. Flopping into the chair Gavin had vacated, she forced herself not to jump up as his warmth wrapped around her.

Joshua cleared his throat.

"Go ahead and say it, Joshua."

"I just wondered if there was something you wanted to tell me?"

"He couldn't have found a place to stay last night, and he was safer in the jail cell." Her words sounded lame, even to her own ears. "Tell me about Edsel Hutchins."

A shadow of pain crossed Joshua's face. He and Mary wanted children, had one on the way. They'd wanted to raise them in Glade Springs where they would be safe. The murder of Marisa Hutchins and the pain of the parents had almost changed his mind. No place was safe.

"He took it hard. Doc was late, something about Mrs. Cooper burning her hand. He could be dangerous, Sarah, when the sedatives wear off."

"I was afraid of that. Anyone keeping an eye on him?"

"I sent Thomas out there last night. Told him I'd relieve him this morning. We'll take turns for a couple of days. The man's hurting. It'd be easier if he could go ahead and bury her, but with the autopsy it'll probably be a couple of weeks."

Sarah nodded. A hurting man was a dangerous man. "Keep me informed. I'll talk to him if I need to."

Joshua rose to leave. "Since you didn't ask, Millie gave McAllister the rooms over the store."

Sarah wanted to throw something at the retreating figure. He was right. She hadn't asked and she should have. It was definitely something she needed to know.

Placing the card inside the overnight envelope, Gavin jotted Carl's address on the paperwork. He didn't know how long it would take to run the prints, but he couldn't shake the feeling he was running out of time.

Gavin spent the rest of the afternoon getting settled in the small apartment above the bookstore. At least here he'd be close to Nikki. If Sarah allowed her to visit Millie.

Millie had told him she only used the apartment in the winter and he could stay as long as he liked. For everyone's sake, he hoped his stay would be short. He placed a call to Carl, not surprised when he got the answering machine. He left a brief message that the package was on its way and where he was staying. There was no need to go into the rest of it. Joshua had talked to Carl to verify his alibi. Carl knew all hell was breaking loose down here. He just hoped Carl stayed put a few more days. Gavin's muscles ached from the small uncomfortable cot. He'd finally managed to sleep, but what he really needed now was a hot shower and a real bed.

The hot water washed away the dirt and some of the soreness from his muscles. He wandered into the kitchen, expecting to find it bare. To his surprise, Millie had evidently stocked it earlier in the day. Bless her. He was going to have to send her something special when this was all over.

CHAPTER SIXTEEN

Carl played Gavin's message again, listening to the tone of voice more than the words. Boy was in way over his head. Didn't have a clue. Love could blind you that way, make you vulnerable. It only took a second for life to change, mistakes to be made. Carl went over the phone conversation with Deputy Cross in his mind. The young deputy was sharp. He'd accepted Carl's explanation about the pink card, but he still might run it through the system. And if he did...

Shit, it didn't matter any more. He was going to lose his job when this was all over. That didn't matter either. What mattered was catching this bastard. Stubbing out the cigarette, he picked up his keys. It was time to kick some ass.

The drive to Rob's apartment was short, but the closer Carl came, the madder he got. Ignoring the doorbell, he pounded on the door and waited.

"What the fuck..."

Carl grinned as he took in the bloodshot eyes and wrinkled clothes Rob was wearing. He was going to enjoy this. Grabbing a fist full of the wrinkled shirt, he shoved Rob into the room and kicked the door shut.

Rob stumbled over the mess in the floor and landed on his butt, his eyes reflecting drunken confusion as he looked up at his partner. "What the hell's wrong with you?" he slurred. "Leave me alone."

Carl didn't wait for him to get up, but reached down and grabbed him again by the shirtfront. Picking him up, he threw Rob across the room. "Want to die? Is that it, Rob? Want to sit on your ass and drown in your fucking whiskey?"

"Hey, Carl, wait. I…"

Rob didn't get the chance to say anything more as Carl slammed a right fist into his stomach. Chuckling, he followed with a left to the chin. Rob fell to his knees, gagging. He knew the old man was pulling his punches, but still it hurt like hell. And it was pissing him off. Anger ate away at the whiskey-fogged cells of his brain. He shook his head trying to clear the fog. Carl was coming at him again. Raising both hands Rob pleaded with him. "Wait a minute, dammit. At least tell me what the hell you're mad about."

Carl chuckled again. "Mad? Hell, I ain't even started getting mad yet. Cory was lucky. Look what she could have wound up with. A sniveling, pant pissing wimp!"

Carl's grin widened as Rob roared out in anger and pain, coming off his knees and rushing him. He'd finally gotten through the whiskey fog.

Carl allowed Rob to land one punch before he shoved him away, laughing. "That all you got, boy? What a fucking wimp."

Landing a solid left to the stomach, Carl followed through with a right upper cut and watched as Rob smashed through the coffee table and lay still. "Lights out, partner."

Carl lit a cigarette and took a long, deep drag before bending over Rob's prone figure and gently brushing the silvery blond hair out of his eyes. "Shit, you stink," Carl whispered. Picking Rob up, he headed toward the bathroom.

Rob jumped, sputtering and cursing as the cold water revived him. A huge black hand pressed him into the bathtub. "Sit down and shut up. You smell like a fucking brewery."

Rob stopped struggling. His head ached, and it wasn't from the whiskey. The old man hadn't pulled those last two punches.

"Now, you ready to listen, or do you want to fight some more?" Carl snickered, the cigarette hanging from the corner of his mouth. He almost hoped Rob would take option two. He hadn't felt this good since Sharon died.

Rob stayed seated, the cold water pouring over him.

"Good choice, son. Good choice." Carl stood up and tossed him a towel. "Get cleaned up. I need some coffee."

Carl had cleaned the kitchen and made a pot of coffee by the time Rob appeared. Rob's left eye was swelling, and the cut on his lip was still bleeding. "You didn't have to hit me so damn hard."

Carl laughed, a deep booming rumble that set off a pounding cadence inside Rob's head. "Shit, that was just a little love pat. If I'd really wanted to hurt you, you'd still be out."

Rob knew Carl was telling the truth. Carl Jackson had been the boxing champ at the Bureau for twenty years.

Carl's voice lowered, turning serious. "Sit down, Rob. I got problems, and I need to know where you stand. If you ain't got my back, then I need to get a new partner."

The words cleared the remaining fog from Rob's brain. Taking the mug of steaming coffee from Carl's hand, he sat down at the table. His head still pounded, but his eyes were sharp and clear, his voice strong, "I've got your back, Carl."

Insistent knocking on the door jarred Gavin from the edge of sleep. A quick glance at his watch told him it was only seven p.m. He considered ignoring the knock, but the pounding was becoming more insistent. Raking a hand through his hair, he cursed as he stalked to the door and jerked it open.

"Mr. McAllister?"

Gavin didn't recognize the woman, but he knew the type. Royalty among commoners. The gleaming amber hair was perfectly coiffed. Makeup a little too perfect, lips a little too red. She didn't wait for an answer, but pushed her way past him into the apartment.

"I'm Claire Nix."

Gavin knew the name was supposed to mean something to him, but he had no idea why.

"It's imperative that I speak with you."

Gavin raised an eyebrow quizzically. Imperative. Nice word. She probably spent hours looking through the dictionary finding words that made her feel a little superior to the rest of the townspeople.

"Ms. Nix…"

"It's Mrs.," she huffed. "My husband is the mayor of Glade Springs."

That explained it. Putting him politely in his place. Gavin could ask her why she was here, but it would be useless. She would tell him, in her own time and her own flamboyant way. Closing the door, he took a seat in the comfortable old armchair, waving a hand to the couch. "Please, Mrs. Nix, have a seat."

He wasn't surprised when she glanced at the furniture

with disdain. Fifth Avenue silk couldn't sit on anything so cheap.

"I want you to leave Glade Springs, Mr. McAllister. We don't need your kind here."

"My kind, Ms. Nix?" Gavin spoke the Ms. with just the right inflection of insolence. Rage began to build inside him.

"Yes. You're a troublemaker. Look at what's already happened since you've been here. If you leave now, things will go back to normal."

Gavin sighed. If only it were that simple. Leaving now wouldn't change anything. Something was wrong with this picture. Mayor's wife, late call. He needed to think, but his mind was tired, as well as his body.

"Ms. Nix, even if I wanted to leave, I can't. Sheriff's orders."

She snorted contemptuously. "The sheriff will be handled. You just leave."

Gavin watched as she flounced from the room, slamming the door behind her. Bitch. Cold, callous, calculating bitch. His hands clenched into fists as the rage that had simmered just below the surface since Cory's death threatened to boil over. He wanted to hit somebody, and Claire Nix was at the top of the list.

CHAPTER SEVENTEEN

"Morning, Sheriff."

"Good morning, Joshua. What's going on?"

"Not much. Everything's quiet. Ran into Edsel last night. Wanted to know about McAllister. I told him McAllister wasn't really a suspect. He grumbled and left."

"What do you think?"

Joshua shrugged. Whatever he was thinking, he wasn't ready to share it. Sarah winced, knowing the distance between them was her fault.

"I sent Thomas out to his place. Told him to keep an eye on things for a while."

"Thanks," Sarah whispered. Joshua might not share what he was thinking, but he was on top of what was expected. He could be frustrating, aggravating and damned irritating at times, but Sarah was still glad to have him as her chief deputy. Reaching out, she clasped his shoulder in silent apology. "You're going to make a good sheriff someday, Joshua."

"Apology accepted."

Joshua grinned, that damn know-it-all grin that Sarah had come to anticipate and dread.

"Since things are quiet here, why don't you run over to Millie's, have a cup of coffee, spend some time with Nikki?"

Was there anything he didn't know?

"I think I'll do just that." Sarah left, his laughter causing her face to flush.

"Mommy!"

Sarah hugged her daughter. Although Nikki had only been gone one night, it seemed much longer. She smiled up at Millie, a silent thank you. Her mind and body had been so tired last night that the thought of taking care of Nikki had overwhelmed her. When Millie had offered to keep her overnight, Sarah had jumped at the chance to get some rest.

"How's my girl this morning?"

"Millie let me play with the ballerina, and Reverend Cooper brought me a little doll. Want to see?"

Nikki held up a tiny doll with long red hair and soft blue eyes. "It looks like you, Mommy."

Sarah frowned. The doll did indeed bear a slight resemblance. "Sweetie, why don't you go play and let Mommy talk to Aunt Millie."

"Okie, dokie."

They watched until she was safely out of hearing distance.

"Don't know, Sarah. He came by early this morning, had a cup of coffee, and talked to Nikki for a while. Said he had a present for her, and a few minutes later came in with the doll. Said he'd bought it for his own little girl, but she'd gone away before he had a chance to give it to her."

Sarah stood open mouthed at Millie's rambling. She hadn't asked any questions. Was everyone in Glade Springs psychic?

"Don't know if I like that man," Millie continued. "You need a good cup of coffee."

Sarah nodded. That seemed to be all she could do

lately, as words failed her. The doll had upset her more than she wanted to let on. She'd never met the minister or his wife. As far as she knew, he'd never seen her. So how did he come up with a doll with red hair and blue eyes?

Millie returned, interrupting her thoughts.

"Man of God shouldn't look quite so handsome if you ask me. And he's got black eyes." Millie picked up the conversation where she'd left off.

"Black eyes? An accident, someone hit him?" Sarah had been trying to follow the conversation but felt lost.

Millie rolled her eyes toward the heavens. "No, not black eyes. Black eyes."

"Oh."

"Humph, can't get through to anybody anymore. Whole world has lost its common sense. You've got green eyes; I've got gray eyes. His eyes are black."

"Oh!" This time Sarah understood. Maybe it was time she paid a visit to the new, handsome, black-eyed minister.

"You be careful, Sarah. Something about that man I don't like." A delitescent evil, Millie thought.

The door opened, and they both turned as Gavin McAllister stopped just inside the doorway. His eyes darkened and Sarah noted the clench of his jaw muscles. It was apparent he wasn't any happier to see her than she was to see him. Sarah broke the eye contact first, and with a quick wave to Millie, acknowledging the warning, brushed past Gavin without a word.

Sarah rammed the Explorer into gear, her foot heavy on the gas pedal, her thoughts jumbled and confused. She hadn't even said goodbye to Nikki. The darkening of the whiskey brown eyes had sparked the passion that lurked just beneath the surface of her calm exterior. Lust. That's all it was. Pure and simple lust. She ached to reach out and touch the tanned arms, feel the muscles that had rippled underneath the cream shirt when he'd stepped aside and opened the door for her. "Slut," Sarah muttered.

The church came into view, and Sarah breathed deeply, calming her tattered emotions. She hadn't been to church in years. She'd missed it at first, but then slowly came to accept it. It would be hard to sit in a pew and pray, knowing her life was a lie. God knew the truth, but still she felt sinful. One day, maybe soon, she could stop lying and start living a normal life.

Parking near the church, Sarah admired the flowers growing along the walkway to the parsonage. Evidently, Mrs. Cooper had a green thumb. Sarah remembered her last conversation with the woman. This time would be different. Exiting the vehicle, Sarah walked the short distance to the parsonage, her stride purposeful, determined. Ignoring the doorbell, she rapped on the door.

"Yes?"

The woman was definitely not what Sarah had expected for a minister's wife. Bleached, frizzy hair surrounded a timeworn face that echoed long nights, rough living, and alcohol. Her veiled blue eyes revealed nothing, but Sarah noticed the slight tremble of her hand on the door.

"Mrs. Cooper, I'm Sheriff Burns."

"I know who you are."

"Could I come in? I'd like to speak with Reverend Cooper for a moment."

The veil over her eyes lifted slightly, replaced by grim shadows. A glimmer of fear.

"He's in prayer."

The door started to close. "I just wanted to thank him."

Mrs. Cooper hesitated a brief second, the slight tremor of her hand escalating, causing the door to visibly shake. "I'll tell him," she hissed, and slammed the door in Sarah's face.

"Of all the rude–" Sarah sputtered, tempted to kick the door down. The woman was impossible. Sarah raised her hand to knock again, but stopped herself. It was clear Mrs. Cooper was afraid of her husband. And her fear of him was stronger than her fear of the sheriff. Sarah made a mental note to run a background check on the couple as she stalked to the Explorer. It was apparent she wasn't going to be meeting the handsome, black-eyed minister today. Millie had said she wasn't sure she liked the man. Sarah didn't know about the Reverend, but she was developing a strong dislike for Mrs. Cooper. Buckling her seat belt, Sarah sat for a moment, pulling her thoughts together. The radio crackled.

"Sheriff."

"Sarah, we've got another body." Joshua's voice was ragged, unspoken emotion crackled across the wires, opening the door Sarah had fought so hard to close. Sarah forgot the Coopers as she sped to town, Joshua's words echoing in her mind in perfect rhythm with the rapid beating of her heart. *We've got another body.*

Rob looked up as the door opened, irritated by the interruption. The chief had saddled him with an inordinate amount of paperwork. Penance.

Carl smirked, aware of his partner's irritation. He was glad to have things back to normal.

"Good news and bad news."

Rob groaned. "Give me the good news first."

"I got that fingerprint check Gavin asked for."

"Who is she?" Rob perked up.

"Sarah McKnight. Used to be a D.C. police officer. Disappeared from the system about six years ago after turning her partner in for rape."

"Yeah, that could make you want to disappear." Rob had started out with the police force. The code was you didn't turn on your own, no matter what.

"There's more, but I think you better hear the bad news first." Carl glanced at the no smoking sign on the wall before lighting a cigarette.

"Cory ran those same prints four days before she was killed."

Rob paled slightly, his jaw tightening. "You ready for a vacation?"

Carl nodded. "Yep, think it's time we went fishing."

CHAPTER EIGHTEEN

"He's been dead a while. Couple of months maybe. Won't know for sure until we get an autopsy on what's left of him." Doc Hawthorne dusted the dirt off his hand and stood up.

"Any idea how he died, Doc?" Sarah stood over the shallow grave, her thoughts in chaos. She felt a similar darkness here, similar to what she'd felt at The Lodge. Not quite as strong, not quite as evil. A darkness born of confusion.

"Don't need an autopsy for that." Bending down he turned the skull to the left, revealing the fracture. "Gonna be hard to identify him, though. Whoever did it pulled all his teeth and cut off his hands."

"Damn." Sarah wanted to scream. It could take months, maybe years for them to identify the body. By then, the killer would be long gone. Or worse yet, have killed again.

"Sheriff?"

"What, Thomas?" Sarah snapped out the words.

"We got company."

Sarah turned to watch Gavin McAllister make his way up the hill.

"Want me to stop him?"

"No, I'll take all the help I can get right now."

Thomas stood quietly, waiting for further orders.

"It's okay, Thomas. Find Joshua and see if he's found anything yet."

"Sheriff." Gavin stopped a few feet from her.

"If you've got any suggestions, McAllister, I could sure use them right about now."

Gavin examined the open grave. Too shallow. Whoever had dug the grave was in a hurry, but not stupid. The choice of location was good. Time and nature would take care of any trails he might have left, and the odds of someone discovering the body were poor.

"We need to talk." Gavin turned his attention to Sarah, noting the deep furrows of her frown.

"Let me finish up here. I'll meet you at the office."

Gavin hesitated. He knew how local sheriffs reacted to the FBI. Time was running out. "Sarah, my brother is with the FBI in Richmond. I could call him, see if I can get you some help down here. There're reasons he may be interested."

Sarah nodded. Her pride was no longer important. People were dying, and she didn't have a clue which way to look. And if she could trust her emotions, they had more than one killer running loose in Glade Springs. "Come on, you can use my cell phone."

They walked down the hill together and yet Sarah felt they were a thousand miles apart.

Minutes later Gavin frowned as he closed the phone.

"No luck, huh?"

"Strange. He's on vacation. They said he left this morning for a fishing trip."

Sarah laughed hollowly. "Must be nice. But I don't see anything strange about that."

Gavin shook his head, frowning. "As far as I know, Rob has never been fishing in his life."

The crackle of the radio stopped any response Sarah might have given.

"Sheriff."

"We got another one. Up the hill to the left. Better get Doc up here."

Sarah turned, but Doc Hawthorne had already started moving slowly toward the hill.

Sarah felt Gavin's hand on her shoulder, offering the comfort she so desperately needed. She longed to sink against him, be held, protected. Protected? The thought infuriated her. "You coming?"

"Right behind you."

The second grave was a duplicate of the first. Doc Hawthorne looked up and shook his head. "Female, same wounds. Teeth and hands missing."

Turning to Gavin, Sarah shook her head. "Looks like we're going to have to put off that conversation a little longer. Tomorrow?"

Gavin nodded, fear clutching at his stomach. He hoped tomorrow wasn't too late.

Sarah turned back to the scene unfolding before her.

"Sketches and photographs are finished, Sarah," Joshua stated, his voice flat, emotionless.

Sarah nodded. She knew she should probably wait to move them. Call in forensics. Dammit, they didn't belong here. They should be laughing, loving, living their life. Sarah turned to Joshua, her voice filled with anger seething just below the surface, and barked out orders. "Get the bags. Let's get them out of here."

CHAPTER NINETEEN

Captain Jones swore softly as he watched the two men approach his office. Trouble with a capital T. Their casual dress did little to disguise them. He knew Bureau when he saw it. And Bureau was always trouble.

He stood up to greet them at the door. The best way to deal with trouble was to meet it head-on. No greeting was necessary. They'd been around long enough to know he knew who they were. He waved them to seats and remained standing, setting the boundaries. They were in his territory now.

"Gentlemen, what can I do for you?"

The voice was polite, a thread of steel running just beneath the words. Rob ignored it as he took in the office in one glance. The stack of files on the right, mass of loose paperwork on the left. Understaffed. The captain probably found himself constantly amidst the tower of paperwork required to satisfy the higher-ups and keep them off his back. Tattered and worn furniture that the city should have replaced years ago. Rob turned his attention back to the captain. A tough cop, but from everything they'd learned, a good cop. He had to be tough to make it in Washington, D.C. Everyone wanted to blame the cops for everything. Even the Justice Department had made them sign an agreement that limited the use of force by officers. No respect. And crime was now on the rise again, especially murders. Even Richmond was better than this. Carl was senior partner, and Rob waited patiently for him to start the ball rolling.

Carl too had measured the captain, liking what he saw. "Tell us about Sarah McKnight."

The words were spoken softly, but to Captain Jones it felt as if the old man had screamed them. He hesitated, returned to his desk, and fidgeted with the paperwork there. *Sarah McKnight. Dear God, would that never go away?*

"Not much to tell."

Carl chuckled. Meaning, not much he was going to tell.

"She in trouble?" Captain Jones was patting down his pockets, a sign of distress Carl knew well.

Glancing around the room, Carl saw no signs to prohibit it, and pulled the well-worn pack from his coat pocket, extending it to the captain. "Smoke?"

Jones took the proffered cigarette and light, dragging in deeply, blowing out a billowing cloud of smoke. "Thanks. Been trying to quit."

"Hard job," Carl stated flatly, as he lit his own cigarette.

Rob watched in fascination as charcoal eyes clashed with smoldering blue. Two old veterans who knew the rules, the boundaries, the game.

"You first."

Carl weighed the information he had so far. Bureau policy was not to share information. He glanced at Rob and received a knowing nod. Hell, he wasn't Bureau now, he was on vacation.

"Trouble, no. We think she may be in danger. Something from her past, maybe, coming back to haunt her?"

Captain Jones sat back and digested the information he'd received, as well as what had not been said. He'd always been afraid of that. He liked Sarah. His ass could be on the line, too. He'd helped her disappear.

"Sarah left here almost six years ago. I haven't heard from her since."

Carl knew he was lying. Protecting her. They knew most of the story, but needed to hear it from him. He tried a different approach.

"All right, tell us about Todd Williams."

Jones felt the rage rising, blood rushing to his face. Shoving the paperwork on his desk to one side, he faced the agents. "I'll tell you anything you want to know about that son-of-a-bitch."

Two hours later Carl and Rob stepped into the D.C. sunshine. Neither of them wanted to break the silence. The captain had been true to his word, telling a story that sickened and angered them. No wonder Sarah McKnight had taken on a new identity.

"He sure sounded like our man," Carl stated, breaking the uneasy silence.

"I think he is."

Carl stopped walking. "Jones said he was still in prison. Checked himself last week."

"Yeah, well I think maybe we'll check him out ourselves. Jones didn't say why he checked last week. In fact, there's a lot Jones didn't say. Ever been to Ohio, Carl?"

"Fuck," Carl muttered. Ohio? Why couldn't the motherfucker have been some place where the fishing was good? "Nope, but I guess I'm going."

Rob walked away, his thoughts on Cory and Gavin.

Cory must have somehow stumbled across the Sarah McKnight story. If Williams was the Mother's Day killer, then it all made sense. Cory would never have exposed Sarah McKnight. She would have died before doing that. He glanced at the photograph Jones had given him. Odious, soulless, black eyes. Rob didn't care what anyone said, he knew in his heart he was looking at Cory's killer. Hate filled him with a burning fury.

Sarah, wake up. He's here, Sarah. Wake up!

Sarah struggled to obey the voice in her head, but her arms and legs felt disconnected. A strange smell drifted in the room, filling her senses, pulling her into the blackness. *Sarah, wake up!*

The scream inside her head had the desired effect. Sarah fought her way to consciousness with the realization that something was wrong, terribly wrong. Blackness was all around her. Someone was here. Someone dark, evil. Emotions filtered through her semi-conscious mind. Rage. Hate. So much hate. She concentrated. Nikki. She had to get to Nikki.

The sound of the door closing downstairs cleared her mind and spurred her on as she threw off the covers and stood on shaky legs. Fear was a great motivator. Nikki. She had to get to her. She stumbled, her legs still not obeying the commands her brain issued. The hallway stretched out before her. Tears filled her eyes. She felt weak, helpless. She hadn't felt this way since–no, she wouldn't think about that. That was another life, another lifetime. She was almost there. The same fear that had given her strength now seemed to paralyze her. She forced her trembling fingers to open the door and flip on the light.

Relief robbed her legs of the last vestige of strength. Sinking to the floor, she rested her head against the door jam, tears flowing down her face. Nikki lay, one hand tucked under her angelic face, sleeping peacefully, unaware of the darkness that surrounded them. Safe. It was just a dream.

Sarah pulled herself up and reached for the light just as her gaze fell on the stars floating above the bed. It hadn't been a dream. Reaching out she touched a star, recoiling from the evil she felt there. He'd been here. In her house. In her daughter's room.

CHAPTER TWENTY

Rob flinched as the gates clanged shut behind him. Glancing at Carl, he realized his partner was feeling the same thing. They hated prisons. They'd been lucky, catching an early flight to Ohio. Still, it was a little after midnight. The odds were the warden wouldn't see them, and if he did, he probably wasn't going to be too happy about it.

"Warden will see you now."

They followed the officer down the dimly lit hallway to the warden's office. Rob couldn't help comparing the opulence of the warden's office to the ragged office of Captain Jones. He allowed his glance to travel around the room, noting the cream colored carpet covering the floor, polished cherry furniture, and expensive prints lining the walls, before he looked at the man behind the desk. The warden smiled. A polished, fake smile.

"What can I do for you boys?" The warden's eyes never left Carl's face, as he emphasized the word "boys."

"We're here to see Todd Williams." Rob took over, noting the darkening threat in Carl's eyes, the jutting of the chin.

The warden's grin widened, revealing perfect white teeth. "Let me see. Williams." He leafed through the file on his desk. "Serving twenty years for armed robbery. Been a model prisoner." He glanced at his watch. "Little late, or early, for visiting. Something you boys want to tell me?"

Rob felt Carl tense at the use of the word "boys" again. "Just want to ask him a few questions about an old case we're working. Shouldn't take long. We can wait, if you want. Call Captain Walsh in the morning."

The mention of Captain Walsh's name had the effect Rob wanted. The smile faltered. "Take them down to Room 1. Have Williams brought in."

They followed the deputy down the long corridor, flinching as the doors opened and clanged shut behind them.

"Wait in here."

Rob had avoided looking at Carl since they'd left the warden's office. Knew Carl was a volcano about to erupt.

"Get it out before he gets here."

"Son-of-a-*bitch*." Carl slammed his fist against the old wooden table. "Did you see the way he looked at me? And that suit. He's wearing a fucking Armani suit. Looked at me as if I was some kind of trash. Boys. I'd like to smash that goddamn phony nose of his." Carl slammed his fist on the table again for emphasis.

Rob felt at a loss for words. If Gavin were here, he probably could have come up with something appropriate. Racism had always existed, and always would.

"Let it go, Carl. Let's talk to Williams and get the hell out of here. This place gives me the creeps."

Carl muttered something unintelligible, but sat down at the table. The door clanged open.

"Warden says you got twenty minutes."

Rob smiled. "Thank you. We'll let you know when we're done."

The deputy hesitated, but finally shrugged and closed

the door behind him.

Rob had memorized the face of Todd Williams. He glanced at Carl and received a knowing nod. Instinct. Instinct told Rob the man standing in front of him was not Todd Williams, and Carl agreed.

"Have a seat." Rob waited as the prisoner sized them up, sneered, and took a seat.

"Got any cigarettes?"

"Sorry, don't smoke," Rob answered, ignoring the sneer.

"How about the nigger? He smoke?"

Tension filled the room, thick, plausible.

Rob coughed. "Yeah, the nigger smokes. Carl, give our friend here a cigarette." He waited while Carl took out his cigarettes and passed one to the prisoner, lighting it for him.

"Let me see your hands." Rob said the words quietly, his eyes watching every move.

"Go to hell."

Carl reached across the table, grabbed the hands, and slammed them down in front of Rob. "We've already been there, you piece of shit."

It took only moments of study to see what they had already expected to find. What someone else should have found. Rob remembered the lushness of the Warden's office. The warden was scum, and when this was over, Rob was coming back and permanently wiping that smug sneer off his face.

"Good work. Who done it?" Rob asked.

"Don't know what you're talking about."

Rob sat back. It was Carl's turn to run the show. Sometimes the good cop/bad cop act had its benefits. This was going to be one of those times.

"Yeah, bet you don't. Think Williams is coming back for you? What'd he tell you? You take the heat and we'll split the money when you get out?"

Carl laughed, a mirthless sound. Knew by the look in the man's eyes that he'd hit the nail on the head. Slamming his hand down on the table, he bent over and got close to the convict. "Did he tell you Virginia still has the death penalty?"

The head came up, eyes panicky. "I didn't kill nobody."

"Yeah, well Todd Williams did. And you're Williams, right? Got the fingerprints to prove it. We're gonna fry your ass. Let's go, Rob, get this piece of shit transferred."

Rob rose, ready to follow Carl's lead.

"No, wait. I didn't kill nobody. He didn't say nothing about no murder. I ain't frying for that son-of-a-bitch."

Sitting down, Rob grinned. It had almost been too easy. "Who did your hands? And who the hell are you?"

Loyalty didn't cover murder, and two cigarettes later, Sid Williams had told them everything he knew.

Rob slammed his hand against the wall, ignoring the pain that immediately spread through his fingers. "Dammit, Carl, we don't have time to run down every plastic surgeon in Washington, D. C."

"Got no choice," Carl answered, lighting a cigarette and taking a deep drag. "Otherwise, we go in there blind." Shaking his head in amazement, Carl continued, "Used his own brother. The mother-fucker used his own brother to cover for him."

"Yeah, the profilers will have a field day with this one. And we don't have a damn clue what Williams looks like now. We better head to Glade Springs. Warn Gavin what he's up against out there."

Carl shivered, knowing he might live to regret what he was about to say.

"Have you thought about that?"

Rob frowned. "What are you getting at?"

"If Williams is the Mother's Day killer, this may be the only chance we'll get to find him, take him down."

Rob rubbed his fist, the pain subsiding to a dull ache. He knew he'd said before that catching the killer was worth any cost, but could he really do that? Could he take a chance on sacrificing Gavin? It wasn't a choice he should have to make. He hit the wall again, welcoming the pain. He didn't have a choice.

"What are you going to tell him about the fingerprints?"

Carl slapped him on the back. If anything happened to Gavin, Rob would never forgive him. Hell, he'd never forgive himself. "We'll think of something."

"Yeah, it better be good." Rob frowned as they walked down the prison corridor. Something was eating at him. They banged on the gate and waited to be let out.

"Find what you needed?" The deputy opened the gate.

"Maybe." Rob shrugged. "Has Williams had any other visitors lately?"

"Wait a minute and I'll check." The deputy left them standing in the hallway while he went inside the cubicle and checked his roster. "Yeah, says here he had a visitor about three months ago. A Jeremiah Campbell."

Rob exchanged glances with Carl, but kept his thoughts to himself. What the hell was Jeremiah Campbell doing visiting Todd Williams?

CHAPTER TWENTY-ONE

Millie opened the door on the second knock. "Why, Sarah, honey, come in. What's the matter? Is Nikki sick?"

"Millie, I need you to watch Nikki for me while I pack. I have to get out of here."

Taking the sleeping child, Millie placed her on the couch and pulled Sarah into the kitchen. She'd seen the kind of panic she saw reflected in Sarah's eyes before. Shock. "Now, you just sit down for a minute. I'll fix us some fresh coffee, and we'll talk about this."

Sarah twisted her hands as she paced the small room and shook her head. "I don't have time to talk. I've got to get her out of here."

"Running away never solved nothing, Sarah. You trust me, I know. Whatever you're running from always catches up to you sooner or later. Besides, if you're gonna lose either way, you might as well stay and face the music. Now you sit down there like I told you. Ain't nobody going nowhere until you've had some of Millie's special brew." Millie watched as Sarah numbly obeyed. Young whippersnapper. Full of spunk and fight one minute, running like a scared goose the next. Something had gotten under the girl's skin. Pulling the brandy from beneath the sink, Millie poured a healthy dose into the cup before filling it to the brim with strong black coffee.

"Here, you drink this." Millie sat down across from Sarah and watched as she took a long gulp, coughing and sputtering as the brandy burned its way into her system.

"Millie, what the hell did you put in this? Poison?"

Millie laughed. "Good brandy. Put some color in your cheeks, too, so it must be working. Drink up."

Sarah sipped the coffee slowly this time. Millie was right, she did feel better. Millie was the one person in Glade Springs who had penetrated the shell she'd wrapped around herself. She loved and trusted the old woman. The tension of the past week, the sleepless nights, and the fear of the past few hours caught up with her. Laying her head on the table, Sarah sobbed.

Millie came around the table and gathered the young woman in her arms, patting her gently on the back. "There, there, honey. It's all right. Millie's here. You just cry it out."

Millie held Sarah until she stopped crying. Then she poured another cup of coffee, putting a healthy dose of brandy in it for herself, as she listened to Sarah pour out the whole sordid story of Todd Williams. No wonder the poor girl had kept to herself, afraid to let anyone close to her or Nikki. The gray eyes twinkled as she thought of Gavin McAllister and his reaction to Nikki and Sarah. Smart as a tack, dumb as a coal bucket. Couldn't see the forest for the trees in front of him. She'd have to do something about that.

Finished, Sarah sat emotionless, drained of all feeling. Confession really was good for the soul. Millie squeezed her hand gently.

"I have to stay, don't I?" Sarah whispered.

"Yeah, honey, you do," Millie answered. Most people already knew the answers, just needed somebody to sound the questions off of.

Sarah drew in a ragged breath and glanced at the child sleeping peacefully on Millie's sofa. "Can I leave her here for a while?"

"You know that child is welcome here for as long as you need. You, too, if you want to stay."

Sarah smiled sadly, pushing back her chair and standing up. "No, it's me he wants. As long as Nikki is safe, I'll be okay. She's been wanting to go see Mr. Archibald's new butterfly garden. Would you take her for me?"

Millie hesitated, a slow flush creeping up the wrinkled old face. She'd been avoiding Clarence since the night he'd come to dinner. *Running away never solved nothing. If you're going to lose either way, why not stay and face the music?* I'm a darned old fool, Millie chided herself before answering Sarah. "I'll take her."

The knock on the door woke Gavin from an uneasy sleep. The dreams were closing in. Glancing at the bedside clock he saw that it was only six a.m. Didn't anyone in this godforsaken place sleep? Probably the mayor this time, he muttered to himself. "I'm coming," he yelled.

Gavin jerked open the door, his patience at an end.

"Millie, what are you doing here?" Something in her eyes warned him to be careful. Nikki poked her head around from behind Millie, a mischievous grin lighting up the small heart-shaped face.

"Well, are you going to ask us in or not?" Millie grumbled, unaccustomed to being left standing on the doorstep, especially her own doorstep.

"My home is your home." Gavin grinned and waved her in.

"Nikki, sweetie, you go get Aunt Millie's music box. We'll take it to the shop with us today."

The child's face lit up with sheer joy at the prospect of being allowed to play with her favorite treasure, a tiny ballerina that danced whenever she opened the lid.

"We don't have much time, so you listen to me, Gavin McAllister. Don't know why you're here, and don't care. Sarah needs you. Nikki does, too. Now you go talk to that girl, and you help her." Millie moved quickly to the bedroom and stood at his closet, tossing a shirt and pants on the bed before moving on to the chest of drawers for socks and underwear.

"Well, what are you waiting for? Start getting dressed," Millie growled, irritated by his lack of understanding and movement.

"Millie, whoa, slow down a second. What's wrong with Sarah? And I can't get dressed with you standing there watching me."

"As if at my age I've never seen a man before. Somebody's trying to kill her, that's what. And fool she is, she's decided to use herself as bait. Get dressed, you ain't got much time."

Gavin raised an eyebrow, waiting for her to turn around. Realizing she'd met her match for stubbornness, Millie relented, turning her back to him. "All right, already. You dress, I'll talk."

Gavin moved quickly, aware that Nikki might return at any second. He found his hands shaking as he buttoned his shirt, listening to Millie tell how Sarah knew who the killer was. Some old partner she'd had in D.C. She was home now, packing Nikki's clothes. Meant to send the child away while she used herself as bait to catch him.

"He'll kill her, and then he'll find little Nikki anyway. That's the way it always works. The past always catches up with you eventually."

Something in her voice told Gavin that Millie, too, had run from something, or someone. Her eyes had darkened, fixated on some distant memory of things lost forever. A single tear escaped.

"You go stop her. Tell her the truth." Millie sniffled, brushing away the tear.

"What truth?" Gavin shook his head, but found he was still frantically pulling on socks and shoes. Preparing to do whatever it was Millie wanted him to do.

"Tell her you love her, you darned idiot! Don't you let her get herself killed." With that Millie pushed him toward the door.

Gavin grabbed his keys and slammed the door behind him. He stood at the top of the steps wondering if he were crazy or if Millie was. Tell her he loved her? It hit him suddenly that Millie was right. He'd never believed in love at first sight. Written about it, but never personally believed it happened. Something had happened when Nikki placed her hand in his. And he'd known the first time he looked into Sarah's eyes what he wanted. The loneliness of the past thirty years crashed down on him. Carl had seen it. Millie had seen it. He was an idiot. He wanted her, wanted Nikki, wanted a home. He wanted a life outside of Jacody Ives. The thought of losing her now spurred him into action as he took the steps two at a time.

Gavin heard the slight whoosh, felt the bullet strike. His legs buckled. Hot burning pain flowed over him as he fought to stay conscious. He heard Millie's screams in the background, her voice carrying through the fog pulling him into the darkness. *Too late, McAllister. Too late.* Gavin fought the pain, fought the blackness, gritting his teeth. "Not this time, you son-of-a-bitch."

Millie had reached his side, her hands fluttering over his body, lifting his head. "I called Doc. You just lay still."

"Nikki?" Gavin gasped between gritted teeth.

"Nikki's fine. Just a little scared. Don't you die on me, Gavin McAllister. She'll never forgive me."

Gavin forced a pained grin, the darkness beckoning. "Tell Sarah–" A fresh bolt of pain cut off his words.

"You shush, now. Whatever needs to be said to Sarah you can say it yourself."

Gavin took a deep breath, willing himself to stay conscious. "Have...to protect...Nikki."

His eyes closed and Millie sat with Gavin's head in her lap, blood soaking her brand new dress. It didn't matter, though. Clarence wouldn't care about a little blood. Millie stroked the thick black hair, her thoughts a thousand miles away–another life. She was tired of being alone. Tired of living a lie. Tired of seeing the people she loved hurt. "Don't you worry none about Nikki. Anybody wants to hurt that child, they'll have to come through me first."

"Well, partner, that was the last one. What do we do now?" Carl tossed his cigarette in the ditch, reaching in his pocket for another one.

"I don't know." Rob rubbed the short-cropped blonde hair, wishing he had a drink. "Let's go get a drink."

"Nope. Told you, no more alcohol."

"Dammit, Carl, I need a drink."

"Nope. Just have to beat the shit out of you again. Getting too old for that."

"All right, then you come up with something," Rob yelled in frustration and anger.

"We knew it was a long shot, Rob. It's been five years. Hell, the guy could be anywhere now."

"Carl, you're a genius." Rob took off at a brisk walk.

Carl started after his partner, a slow grin spreading over his face. "Hell, I could have told you that."

It took only minutes of searching the license records to find the plastic surgeon list from five years ago. Only two had moved out of Washington.

"We're running out of time. You take Matheson, I'll take Weaver." Rob handed Carl the address.

Carl nodded, with a happy smirk. Matheson was in Florida. It might take an extra day to find him. Hell, he might be out on a fishing boat. You could always get a good conversation going on a fishing trip. Whistling, he packed his bags, hailed a taxi, and caught the first flight out. If he found Matheson tonight, he could spend tomorrow morning fishing and still catch an early flight to Richmond. A guilty flush crept up his neck. They were running out of time. All right then, one hour. That's all he needed. One hour of slinging out a line and watching his cork bob. Was that too much to ask?

CHAPTER TWENTY-TWO

Millie watched as Nikki played quietly, her face solemn. Poor little thing had been scared to death when she saw the blood on Millie's dress. Took over an hour to calm her down, convince her Mr. McAllister was going to be all right. She'd promised Sarah she'd take Nikki to see the butterfly garden. The child sure needed something to take her mind off blood and death.

Screwing up her courage, Millie peeked through the blinds. There was no sign of Clarence this morning. She knew her abrupt coldness had hurt him. Seen it in his eyes. The twinkle had disappeared, and he suddenly looked old. He'd lost his bluster, unsure of himself. Her fault. All her fault. All he'd wanted to do was care about her, and she'd rejected him.

In a flash, Millie made up her mind. Seize the day and the hell with the consequences. What good was a long life, if you didn't really live it? "Nikki, honey, help Aunt Millie close up. I'm gonna take you to see a butterfly garden."

Clarence looked up from the vase of roses he'd just put the finishing touches on as the door opened.

"Millicent?"

"Don't look so surprised, you old coot. Got me a little girl here that wants to see a butterfly garden."

Clarence grinned, the twinkle back in his eyes. He

didn't know why Millie had pulled away from him, but he knew her well enough to know the gruffness of her voice and softness in her eyes were her way of apologizing. Coming around the counter, he gave them his best exaggerated bow. "Right this way, ladies."

Taking Nikki's hand, Clarence led the way through the back doors.

Millie felt as if she'd stepped into another world. The half-acre of ground behind the flower shop had been totally transformed. Huge stones had been placed as a walkway around small trees, flowering bushes, and multi-colored wild flowers that grew randomly throughout the plot. A small pond with picnic benches along both sides filled the center of the garden.

"Why, Clarence, it's lovely." Millie stood awe-struck, breathing in the wonderful fresh smell of blossoming flowers.

Clarence flushed, pleased and embarrassed by her approval.

"How about I give you ladies a tour and a history lesson?"

Clarence noted Nikki's quietness, but figured Millie would fill him in at the appropriate time.

"This here is Monarch territory. See the milkweed?"

Nikki nodded, still clutching Clarence's hand tightly.

"What's a Monarch?" she whispered.

"See that big butterfly over there by the pond?"

Nikki nodded again.

"Well, that's a Monarch. The *Danaus plexippus*. You can tell it's a female by the color of the body. Males are bright orange with black borders and black veins. The females are orange-brown with black borders and blurred black veins."

Nikki smiled as the butterfly took off, flying over her head to land on the milkweed. A chubby worm crawled up the stalk.

"What's that?" Nikki removed her hand from Clarence's and reached out to grab the worm.

"Can't touch, sweetie." Clarence caught her hand. "That's a caterpillar. Pretty soon it'll enter the pupal stage, and then in about two weeks it becomes a butterfly."

"What's a pupal stage?" Nikki asked as she watched the pretty caterpillar crawl to the underside of a small leaf.

Clarence struggled for words that Nikki could understand. "Well, it's sort of the way a baby develops in a mother's womb. It's the final stage as the caterpillar is developing into a butterfly."

"Can we see some more?" Nikki was finally becoming excited, the color coming back into her cheeks.

Clarence grinned at Millie, who followed behind the two. "See that group over there next to the water?"

Nikki nodded, her blue eyes huge as she watched the group of butterflies.

"Those are swallowtails, fritillaries and skippers. They're doing what we call puddling. They gather around a wet place and sip up the nutrients they need for their diet."

Clarence was warming to his subject. "See that one over there?" He pointed at a tiger swallowtail. "Well, that one's doing what we call basking. See how he's got his wings outstretched there? He's soaking up the sun. Needs to let his wings warm up before he flies."

"Do they ever sleep?" Nikki asked, watching as the group around the pool took off, drifting from flower to flower.

"They roost at night. Kind of the way chickens do. They pick out the underside of a leaf or plant and usually spend about fourteen hours each day roosting from sunset until morning."

"What kind of butterfly is that?" Nikki pointed to the Rose of Sharon bush.

Clarence cackled. "That's not a butterfly, honey, that's a hummingbird. His little wings beat about seventy-five times per second. That's what makes the humming sound when he flies."

"Can I go sit by the pond and watch the butterflies?" Nikki looked to Millie for approval.

"Sure you can, honey. Aunt Millie will join you in just a minute."

Millie waited until Nikki was comfortably seated on the picnic bench before she signaled Clarence to follow her back to the flower shop. She knew curiosity was about to kill the old coot.

"Clarence, I…"

He shushed her. "No need to say anything, Millie. I shouldn't have rushed you."

"Clarence, Gavin McAllister was shot this morning. Right in front of me and little Nikki." Millie gushed the words out, afraid Nikki would come back.

"I hope I'm not interrupting anything."

They both turned, startled by the sound of the voice so near.

"Why, Reverend Cooper, I didn't hear you come in. Got your roses all ready for you." Clarence recovered quickly and headed for the front counter.

Millie glanced out the door, checking on Nikki.

"Is that Nikki out there? I'll just go say hello."

Millie stepped in front of the door, barring his way. "Not a good time, Reverend. The child's had a shock. In case you haven't heard, Mr. McAllister was shot this morning."

Millie shivered, watching his black eyes darken as he watched the child play near the pond.

"Perhaps another time, then."

Millie watched him until he picked up the roses and left the flower shop, waiting anxiously until Clarence rejoined her.

"Something about that man I don't like," she muttered.

Clarence looked over his shoulder, following the direction of her stare. He didn't normally prejudge people, but for once he totally agreed.

CHAPTER TWENTY-THREE

Carl cast the reel, settled in his seat, and breathed in the clear ocean air. A half hour. That's all he wanted. Nothing wrong with that. He deserved this. Besides, he'd be a much better person after casting his rod and meditating on the beauty of the ocean. Then he'd find Matheson, beat the hell out of the guy, and fly home.

The ringing of his cell phone cut off his happy thoughts. *No, dammit. No way.*

"Yeah," he muttered into the phone, realizing he should have left the damn thing in the car.

"Get back here."

"Shit, Rob, I just got here. Besides, what about Matheson?"

"Forget Matheson. Reynolds was our guy."

Carl forgot his disappointment for a moment. "What'd he tell you?"

"Nothing. Got his brains blown out five years ago, right after moving to Tennessee."

"So we're still going in blind."

"Not totally. Witnesses gave a good description of Reynold's murderer. Striking resemblance to Williams. Little nose change, hair color. Said he had strange eyes. Black, empty."

"Sounds like our man."

"Yeah. Meet me in Richmond. The sooner we get started, the sooner you can get back to your fishing."

Carl cursed softly at Rob's low laugh as he closed the cell phone. He looked longingly at the bobbing cork. Now the damn fish decided to bite. A half hour. That's all he'd asked for. When he caught that son-of-a-bitch, he was going to punch Williams right in the nose. Right in the goddamn nose.

The cell phone rang again, just as he reeled in his line. Asshole. "I'm on my fucking way."

"Jackson!"

"Chief, I thought you was somebody else." Carl cursed himself silently for not looking at the caller I.D.

"That's apparent. Where the hell are you and Walker?"

"Florida, sir. Just catching a few fish." Carl fidgeted for his cigarettes.

"Get back here. Gavin McAllister's been shot."

"He'll be all right. Constitution of a mule. Bullet went straight through. Not a lot of damage. Going to hurt like hell for a couple of days, though. Be best if you could keep him quiet." Doc Hawthorne patted Sarah on the shoulder as he left the room.

Sarah contemplated her choices. Gavin McAllister could destroy her life. She was sworn to protect and serve. His handsome face was pale against the white sheets, his wavy hair midnight black. Sarah felt strange inside, tender and vulnerable. She reached out to brush a stray curl back from his forehead. The feeling grew, and she knew he was awake, felt his eyes searching her face. Taking a deep breath, she let it out slowly as she turned away.

"Sarah, I'm sorry."

"Are you?" Sarah turned just in time to see the flicker of pain in the deep brown eyes. It wasn't his fault. She knew her past had finally caught up with her. She didn't know where he was, but she'd felt him. Knew he was close. Closing off her thoughts, Sarah concentrated on the job at hand. She had no choice but to see it as that, just a job.

"Did you see anything? Have any idea who might have done this?"

"No." Gavin grimaced as he struggled to sit up.

"Anything strange happen, anyone say anything to you in the past few days that maybe made you suspicious?"

Gavin frowned, trying to think back over the past few days. So much had happened since he'd arrived.

"The mayor's wife called on me. Nice lady. Told me to get out of town. She didn't say 'Or else,' but I had a feeling the or else was there."

"Did she say why?" Sarah chewed thoughtfully on her bottom lip.

"Yeah, she said this town didn't need my kind." The memory rekindled his anger, but it quickly died as a bolt of pain moved through his shoulder.

Sarah decided to end the interview. She could question him later. "Can you get dressed? Doc says you have to rest for a few days."

Gavin nodded, and Sarah left him to fend for himself. She checked in with the office and let Millie know that Gavin was okay. What she was about to do might have repercussions. The attraction between them was too strong. Needs too primal. Could she actually have him that close and not let him break her heart?

"Okay, boss, Doc says I'm ready to go."

Sarah winced at his grimace of pain as he climbed into

the Explorer. She buckled his seat belt and gave him a wan smile, realizing from the moment she'd met him she'd never really had a choice.

"So, where are we heading? You locking me up to keep me safe?"

"No. I'm taking you to my house."

The words shocked Gavin into silence. Within minutes Sarah realized he'd fallen asleep, his breathing soft and steady. She smiled, that strange feeling of tenderness washing over her. Maybe this wasn't going to be so hard after all. Sarah regretted her thoughts seconds later as he turned in his sleep, one hand falling to rest comfortably on her thigh. Desire coursed through her. She gritted her teeth against the sensation as he smiled in his sleep, almost as if he knew her discomfort. Cursing softly, Sarah stepped on the gas. The sooner she got him in bed, the better off she'd be. The total absurdity of her thoughts struck her just as she swung into the driveway.

Millie pulled the .38 from the closet. People getting murdered, shot in broad daylight. Dammit, she had to do something. This was her home. Her hands trembled as she loaded the gun. What to do? She was just an old woman. She stared off into the distance, memories of another life, before Cardona. Before she'd had to disappear. To the eyes of the world she was dead. At first, shut away from her family and friends, she'd wondered if perhaps that wouldn't have been a blessing. Then she'd come here. Dammit, this was her home now and no faceless monstrosity was going to take it away from her. She'd find him, or them, or whatever. Sarah needed help. This was out of her league.

The light tapping on her door pulled Millie from her

memories. Placing the gun in the closet, she raked a hand through the curly gray hair and brushed the tears from her face before going to the door. Clarence stood on the doorstep, hands full of roses. Life had passed her by the past twenty years.

Throwing the door open wide she squealed, crushing the roses between them as she seized him in a tight embrace. "Oh, Clarence, come in, come in. I've got coffee and jam cake." Letting go she stepped back and lowered her voice. "Have I ever got a story to tell you."

Slightly flustered, Clarence stared at the crushed roses. Jam cake, coffee, story…he looked at her flushed face, gray eyes alight with mystery and life. Taking off his hat, he grinned foolishly at her, like a teenager on his first date. "I'm your man."

Clarence sat quietly, listening to her. He never interrupted, and asked no questions. Occasionally he would cover her hand with his, squeezing gently, to let her know he understood.

Drained from all the talking Millie waited, breathless. It was a lot to take in all at once. She waited for him to speak, but he just sat there quietly, holding her hand.

"Humph, you could say something, you old coot. Can you live with that?" Her voice was brusque, but Clarence saw the fear reflected in her eyes. Afraid what she had told him would send him packing.

Clarence smiled, quickly closing the distance between them. Without saying a word, he kissed her soundly before pulling away, the twinkle in his eyes now a determined gleam. "You just let someone try and stop me."

For the next two hours they put their heads together, coming up with strategic plans, tossing them aside as too complicated or unfeasible. The seriousness of their plans never entered their minds as they laughed like teenagers, holding hands. Millie kissed him good-bye, telling him she'd be sure to lock the doors and keep the gun loaded. For the first time in years, she felt in control of her own destiny. She felt alive.

CHAPTER TWENTY-FOUR

"Damn," Sarah cursed, struggling to bring the Explorer under control. Letting her foot off the gas pedal, she breathed deeply and pulled over to the side of the road. What the hell was she thinking? Her hands trembled as she pried them loose from the steering wheel, realizing she'd almost met the same fate as Johanna Nelson. And for the same reasons. Everything was moving too fast. Her emotions had run the gamut, and now she was left with nothing but fear. Fear of losing control. She had three dead bodies, and no suspects. Gavin lay wounded in her bed, and Nikki was scared and upset. Continuing to breathe deeply, Sarah forced herself to calm down. She needed to think rationally. Allow her mind to sort through the evidence, look for the catalyst. It all started with Corrine Larson, and the death of Johanna Nelson. Sarah tightened her hands around the wheel. It was her job to protect the people of Glade Springs. If that meant stepping on toes, then she'd step on toes. Someone knew something, and it was time she asked the right questions and got the right answers. She headed to Doc Hawthorne's.

Sarah wasn't surprised to find Doc's light still burning in his office, nor did he appear surprised to see her.

"Come in, Sarah. Been expecting you."

"Why's that, Doc?"

His eyes narrowed, a scowl accentuating the deep furrows of his face. "Shouldn't of done it. Thought I was doing the right thing."

"What did you do?" Sarah was beginning to feel as if she'd fallen into the twilight zone of riddles and parables as she watched Doc Hawthorne fidget with the manila folder.

Doc came towards her, his smile sad, eyes showing the burden of too many years of caring, too much pain. "All I can say in my defense is I did it for the right reasons."

Sarah took the folder, skimming the autopsy report of Johanna Nelson.

"Dear God, Jim, why didn't you tell me?"

"You know how this town is, Sarah."

Sarah nodded. The gossip, the scrutiny, the blame. It wasn't just this town, it was all towns. They lived in a very unforgiving world.

Sarah stood at the doorway for just a second, wishing she had time or words to relieve his pain and guilt.

"I have to go, Doc. We'll discuss this later."

Sarah waited for an answer, some acknowledgement that he'd heard her. When none came, she quietly closed the door behind her.

Sarah parked in front of the sheriff's office and turned off the engine, wishing she could turn off her thoughts as easily. The image of Doc Hawthorne standing head bowed, liver spotted hands clutching the desk chair as if he no longer had the strength to stand, haunted her. If she reported him, he'd lose his license. Grabbing the manila folder, Sarah pushed open the door of the Explorer and forced her thoughts away from Doc. There was no time for empathy; Doc would have to deal with his own pain.

Entering the office, Sarah stood for a moment basking in the warmth of her second home. She glanced around the room, surprised to find that Ella Mae and Joshua were still on duty. Not one to look a gift horse in the mouth, she barked out orders.

"Ella Mae, I want the file on Johanna Nelson's accident. Joshua, my office, now."

Sarah saw the questioning look that passed between the two, as Ella Mae jumped to obey, handing the file to Joshua who followed Sarah meekly down the hall.

"Close the door."

Sarah stopped, her eyes drawn to the vase of red roses in the center of her desk.

"Where did these come from?"

Joshua grinned. "Good Reverend delivered them himself. Didn't read the card though."

Sarah removed the small card from the vase. *Sheriff, I hope you'll accept my apology for my wife's rudeness. I assure you, it won't happen again.*

She fingered the card for several seconds. There was something there, something not quite right. Picking up the phone, she placed a call.

"Edgewood Police Department."

"Arthur Daniels, please. Sheriff Sarah Burns calling."

"Hold on."

Sarah fingered the card as she waited for Arthur to pick up.

"Hey, Sarah, what's going on?"

"Need a favor, Arthur."

"Sure. What you got?"

"Run a background check, and see if you can get me a picture of the Reverend Jacob and Sheila Cooper. Came here from Van Cleve about two months ago."

"Take a couple of days, but I'll see what I can get."

"Thanks, Arthur." Sarah hung up the phone, tossed the card into the trashcan, and sat down at her desk. She didn't have time to worry about the Reverend or his marital problems, but she was glad the roses had reminded her to run that background check. Taking the file, she studied the report she'd written and frowned. Nothing seemed unusual.

Joshua fidgeted impatiently. "Sarah, are you ever going to tell me what the hell is going on?"

"I don't think Johanna Nelson's death was an accident. I think she was murdered," Sarah stated, glancing up to emphasize her words.

"Your eyes are blue."

Sarah felt the blood drain from her face. She'd forgotten to put the contact lenses in. And how long had they been out? Joshua's face registered shock, along with the million questions Sarah knew must be running through his mind. There was just not enough time. Recovering quickly, she plunged on.

"I'll explain that later, Joshua. Right now, you're just going to have to trust me that there's a good reason for that. We've got bigger problems. What do you know about David Nix and Johanna Nelson?"

Joshua glanced at the door, uncomfortable under Sarah's scrutiny. Dammit, he'd known she was going to ask eventually. He should have told her. "I know he was seeing her. Hell, Sarah, everyone knew he was seeing her."

Everyone except me, Sarah thought.

"Why didn't you tell me?"

"I didn't think it was important. He didn't kill her. I mean, it had to be an accident. Nix is an ass, but he isn't capable of murder."

"Did you know she was pregnant?"

"Shit." Joshua sank into the old armchair, the word summing it up for both of them. People did a lot of things to cover up mistakes. And if David Nix had gotten Johanna pregnant, that was definitely a mistake. Nix had plans to run for governor next year. Nothing like an affair and an illegitimate child to kill a political career. Then there was Claire. She wanted that governor's mansion. Claire Nix could be ugly when she didn't get what she wanted. Real ugly.

Sarah reread the report, looking for anything that might give her a lead. The car had been towed to George Riley's Body Shop.

"Joshua, I want you to get Tommy over to George Riley's. I want that car checked from top to bottom, brake lines, tires, steering, everything." Sarah slammed the file shut and stood up. "I'll call you after I'm finished with David Nix."

"I'm going with you."

Sarah hesitated, knowing the decisions she made in the next hour could have a drastic effect on her future. "All right, but get Tommy started first."

Sarah didn't wait for Joshua, but left the office, striding determinedly. It was all coming clear now. Ever since Johanna's death something had been niggling at her. She knew now who had been in the car with her. What she didn't know was what had happened after the crash. Sarah thought back over the past few weeks. David had been upset, different. He seemed to have lost some of his obnoxious confidence. When Gavin had told her about the visit from Claire Nix, it had all come together in her mind.

Secrets. Gavin was right, the whole world was full of secrets. She just hoped this one hadn't caused the death of a young woman and her child.

Starting the engine, she waited for Joshua to climb in and fasten his seat belt. "Ready?" Sarah questioned, giving him one more chance to back out.

"Uh, you might want to put your contacts in, Sarah. Save a lot of explanations."

"Oh, God." Sarah reached into the glove box for the green contacts. "Thanks, Joshua."

"No problem." He grinned at her, but Sarah could see the confusion and strain of the past few days reflected in the tautness of his face. She was asking a lot of him.

Darkness descended quickly in the mountains, and the mayor's house was lit up. Sarah hesitated again. If she were wrong, she might be destroying her own career as well as Joshua's.

"Maybe you should stay here. Wait for me."

"No way, Sarah. Comes with the territory, remember? My job."

Sarah felt her eyes mist over, knowing he knew what was about to happen could destroy his future. Yet he would still go in there, stand beside her. Loyalty. It was the one thing she'd seen in his face the day she hired him. Joshua was fiercely loyal to those he cared about.

"Okay. Let's go."

Sarah's stride spoke of confidence, a sureness she didn't feel inside as she rang the doorbell.

"Why, Sheriff Burns, what brings you here?" Claire Nix opened the door herself, eyes watchful, wary.

"This isn't a social visit, Claire. I need to speak with David in private, please."

"Well!" Claire's gaze turned hostile. Sarah stood her ground. She felt no satisfaction in knowing she won, as Claire turned abruptly and hissed, "Follow me." She left them at the library door. "He's in there."

Sarah was suddenly glad for Joshua's presence. The slight pressure of his hand on her shoulder. She knocked, "David, it's Sheriff Burns."

The door opened immediately, and Sarah had the distinct feeling he'd been standing on the other side, listening, waiting.

"Come in. Why, Sheriff, what are you doing here? Why aren't you out there trying to find out who killed that poor girl? Or those other people?"

Good old David, attack before being attacked. It wasn't going to work this time. Her voice cold, authoritative, she addressed him. "Sit down, David."

To Sarah's surprise he obeyed. As he sank into the desk chair his lips quivered, double chins bobbing, as he sobbed, "I'm so sorry."

"What happened to Johanna Nelson?" Sarah felt the anger rising inside her.

"Accident. I swear to God it was an accident. She was driving too fast, couldn't make the curve. I wanted to help her, but I was so scared. Claire...Claire told me I had to end it. I didn't know. She didn't drink. I didn't know."

Sarah gritted her teeth against the rising rage. "You were with her? You left her there to die?"

"No, I swear to God, she was already dead. I didn't know what to do. I called Claire. Claire always knows what to do."

Sarah paced back and forth. She wanted to choke the filthy bastard.

"And the liquor?"

"I was drinking. Claire said we had to do it."

Sarah continued her angry pacing. She could arrest him for leaving the scene of the accident.

"Please don't tell anyone."

Sarah's control snapped. Reaching across the desk she grabbed the front of his shirt, hauling him up face to face. "Don't tell anyone? You spineless piece of trash. She's dead because of you."

"Back off, Sarah." Joshua grabbed her by the shoulders. "He ain't worth it."

Sarah let go of the shirt and stuffed her hands into her pockets. It was too tempting to choke the son-of-a-bitch. Joshua pulled her away from the desk, his voice barely a whisper. "It would only hurt Johanna's parents. They've been hurt enough." He inclined his head toward the door. They both needed a breath of fresh air.

Sarah shook her head. Not yet. The bastard showed no remorse for the death of Johanna and her child. All he was worried about was what it was going to do to his image.

"Did you know she was pregnant?"

Nix's face paled even more, the fat jaws trembling beneath her wrath.

"No, I swear to God..."

"Leave God out of this," Sarah screamed at him. "Where were you this morning? Did you shoot Gavin McAllister?"

"McAllister shot? No, dear God, no. I wouldn't do anything like that."

As much as Sarah hated to admit it, even to herself, she believed him. Still, she wanted a reason, any reason to throw his fat ass in jail. The door slammed open behind them, and Sarah jerked around, hand automatically going for her pistol. Claire Nix stood there, her face contorted, a grotesque mask of hatred.

"I shot McAllister."

CHAPTER TWENTY-FIVE

Carl squirmed in the plush armchair under the chief's penetrating glare, wishing he could light a cigarette. Didn't have to smoke the damn thing, just light it. "It was all my idea, sir. Rob ain't got nothing to do with this."

"That's bullshit, Chief. If anybody is at fault here, it's me."

Chief Walsh sat back, tapping his fingers lightly on the desk. "Why?"

Carl swallowed, his hands fluttering nervously from knees to jacket pocket. Goddamn no smoking rules. "We figured you'd take us off the case when we made the connection between the two cases."

"You figured?" Chief Walsh sat forward and roared, eyes blazing. "You knew goddamn well I'd take you off the case! You're just lucky McAllister wasn't killed!"

"Yes, sir," Carl said, eyes on his feet.

"Two hours. I want a report on my desk in two hours."

Rob cleared his throat as he pulled the sheets of paper from inside his jacket. "Already done, sir." He avoided looking at Carl as he continued. "I was going to give it to you today, along with my resignation."

"Shit." Carl stood up and walked to the window taking the cigarettes from his jacket pocket. Screw the fucking rules. Ignoring the chief's warning look, he shook out a cigarette and placed it between his lips, hands shaking slightly as the lighter clicked loudly in the silent room.

A smiled tugged at the corners of Chief Walsh's lips as he opened the top drawer of his desk and placed an ashtray on the corner of the desk. "Don't get ashes on my floor."

Chief Walsh read the report, nodding occasionally. When he reached the last page, he tore it in half and tossed it into the trashcan. "You don't get off that easy. Take what you've got down to Jefferson and get a profile report."

"Yes, sir." Rob breathed a sigh of relief.

"Well, what the hell are you waiting for? I thought you two were on vacation."

Stubbing out the cigarette, Carl grinned, heading for the door before the chief changed his mind.

"Jackson."

"Yes, sir," Carl turned, holding his breath.

"There's another problem in Glade Springs." Taking a note pad from his desk, Chief Walsh quickly jotted down the name and address, handing it to Carl. *Millie Crawford, 145 Second Street, Glade Springs, West Virginia.*

Carl met the chief's somber gaze and nodded. "I'll see it gets taken care of, sir."

Sarah longed for the comfort of her bed, the warmth of her child. The news of Claire Nix's arrest spread like wildfire through the town. The phone was ringing incessantly. People wanted answers. Answers she couldn't give them.

"Damn, that woman is cold," Joshua stated as he entered the office and tossed the keys on Sarah's desk.

Sarah nodded, absently rubbing her temples. "Did she tell you why she did it?"

"Said she told him to leave. He didn't."

Sarah laughed. As absurd as it sounded, that would have been reason enough for Claire.

Joshua flopped in the old armchair. "She wants to see you."

"Did she say why?"

Shaking his head, Joshua placed a toothpick between his teeth. "Probably wants to explain."

Sarah raised one eyebrow, ignoring the steady hazel gaze. "Explain what?"

"Don't think she meant to shoot him. Probably just wanted to scare him. Her aim just wasn't too good." Joshua laughed softly, imagining the shocked look on Claire's face when the bullet actually struck Gavin.

Sarah failed to see the humor in the situation. "Well, she did shoot at him, and she did hit him. Intended or not." Taking the keys, Sarah headed for the door. The sooner she got this over with the sooner she could try to get some rest.

"Go home, Sarah," Joshua said quietly. "You're gonna crash if you don't get some rest. Claire can wait until tomorrow."

Sarah shook her head, too tired to argue. It was her job to deal with these things.

"You're no good to anyone if you crash. Besides, how long has it been since you really saw Nikki? She needs you, Sarah. And you've got McAllister to deal with. I'll stay here tonight." Joshua had her attention and pushed it home. "We can get by one night without you, you know."

Sarah knew what he was saying made sense. Juanita and José had been practically living at her home, taking care of Nikki. Now she had Gavin McAllister there to be taken care of. Besides, she was so tired she wasn't really functioning. Running on caffeine and fear. Joshua was right, she had to crash eventually.

Tossing the keys on the desk she consented. "Okay, but you call me immediately if anything comes up."

"Don't I always?" Joshua grinned as he watched her leave. Placing the toothpick between his teeth, he moved to the sheriff's chair. He liked it here. Waiting until he was sure Sarah was safely on her way home, he dialed the mayor's number. He could at least listen to what the man had to say.

"Hello."

"Mayor, Joshua Cross. The sheriff's gone."

"I'll be there in fifteen minutes."

Hanging up the phone, Joshua glanced around the bare office. A little redecorating and it would be just fine. Chuckling, he sat back in the chair and propped his feet on the old desk. Yep, he liked it here a lot.

"With all the data we've compiled, I don't believe Williams is your killer."

Rob and Carl exchanged glances before looking at Timothy Jefferson, the Bureau's head profiler.

Jefferson continued in the same droning voice. "The profile of the killer would include some type of abuse when he was a child. Probably sexual. Father, stepfather, maybe even the mother. From what we know of Williams, he came from a stable family, no record of abuse. Both he and his brother had some petty problems with the police as juveniles, but nothing significant. Sorry guys, he just doesn't fit."

Jefferson closed the file and stood up, signaling the meeting was over. "It's getting late. I'll deliver a copy of my report to Chief Walsh in the morning."

Carl smiled at Jefferson. "We'll do that for you. Got a meeting in a few minutes. No need to take up your time."

Jefferson nodded, handing over the file. "That would be great. Thanks."

Carl smiled again, signaling Rob to follow him. Exiting the building, he found the nearest trashcan and dumped the report inside.

"Hey, what the hell are you doing? I thought you said we had a meeting with the chief?" Rob stood open-mouthed as he glanced from the trashcan to his partner stomping back and forth on the sidewalk. Breaking the rules was one thing, but throwing that report away was bound to cost them their jobs.

"Not with that cock-a-mamy bullshit," Carl growled, lighting a cigarette and taking a long drag. "College educated idiots. I was catching killers when he was wearing diapers. And I didn't need no goddamn fucking computer printout to tell me who to look for." Taking another long drag, he blew smoke in Rob's direction. "You want to tell me Williams don't fit the profile?"

Rob shook his head. The profilers always missed one thing. Some people were just born evil. No family abuse, no messed up childhood. Just evil, plain and simple. "He killed Cory. I know it. Knew it the moment I looked into his eyes."

Carl nodded. "Don't need no fucking profile to know evil when you see it. Let's go."

"Where to, partner?" Rob slapped him on the back. They were together in this. Win, lose, or draw, the two of them would go down together.

"Glade Springs," Carl said, tossing the cigarette into the

ditch and reaching for another one. A man had to die from something.

CHAPTER TWENTY-SIX

Nikki lay in the darkness listening to the sound of her mother's deep breathing. Something had awakened her. Sitting up carefully, she waited until her eyes grew accustomed to the darkness. She smiled when she saw the pretty lady standing by the door, one finger pressed to her lips. Nikki nodded, glancing at her mother. She knew how to be quiet.

Cory motioned for her to follow and disappeared through the doorway.

Slipping quietly from the bed, Nikki followed her down the hallway to the closed door of her own room. Mr. McAllister was sleeping there. She could hear the moans coming from inside the room.

"Is he sick?" Nikki looked up at Cory.

He's having a bad dream.

Nikki understood bad dreams. She had them sometimes. Opening the door, she slipped into the room and stood by the bed, watching his face as he clenched and unclenched his hands. Mommy had bad dreams, too. Smiling at Cory, she walked around the bed and climbed on top of the covers. She knew what to do. Lying down next to him, Nikki placed her small hand in his and waited until the moans stopped, and his breathing slowed to a steady rhythm. Yawning, she glanced at Cory, who was still standing beside his bed.

Thank you.

Nikki placed a finger against her lips and smiled as she slipped from the bed. Mommy would be angry if she found her there. She glanced at the bed from the doorway. "He'll be okay now," she whispered, but Cory had already disappeared. Nikki went back down the hall, slipping into bed beside her mother. She liked Mr. McAllister. She placed her hand in her mother's and closed her eyes. Mommy liked him, too.

Sarah woke to the smell of fresh coffee and frying bacon. She lay still for a moment, enjoying the peaceful feeling. Her peace was shattered by the sounds of angry Spanish, giggles, and a deep male voice coming from the kitchen. *What the hell was he doing out of bed? What was it Doc had said...constitution of a mule? A stubborn one at that.*

Sarah glanced at the bedside clock, throwing off the covers. Nine o'clock. She really had crashed. She needed to get to the office, but first she had to deal with what was going on downstairs.

The scene in the kitchen caused a deep ache inside her. Nikki was sitting comfortably on Gavin's lap, head resting against his good shoulder as the two of them watched Juanita fuss around the kitchen. It was apparent Juanita was having the time of her life. Sarah felt left out. How long had it been since she'd simply enjoyed a morning? Too long.

"Mommy." Nikki hopped off Gavin's lap as they all turned to look at her. A look of shock crossed Gavin's face, and Sarah cursed herself silently. She'd forgotten her contact lenses again. Dammit, ever since he'd arrived she'd been making mistakes.

Nikki was tugging at her robe, demanding attention. "Can I go fishing with Juanita? Please Mommy? I'll be good. I promise."

Sarah tousled the strawberry curls. "Run upstairs and get dressed."

"And you." Sarah turned to Gavin. "What are you doing up?"

"I told him. Men!" Juanita summed it up with one word.

"I feel fine. I can go home this morning."

Sarah felt a slight twinge in her heart. Home? Did that mean he was leaving? "I'll be the judge of that. We still haven't had that talk."

He grinned that sexy, beguiling grin that made her want to reach out and touch him.

"Right after breakfast. Juanita has already told me if I don't eat everything on my plate, she's going to hit me with that iron skillet she keeps waving around." His tone was light, but the deep brown eyes were serious. "And you're right, we need to talk."

"Be a good girl." Sarah hugged her daughter.

She stood at the door, watching the car until it disappeared from sight. She hadn't wanted to let her go. Too much was happening. Everything changing.

"She'll be fine, Sarah."

Gavin had come up silently behind her, making her conscious that she was still dressed in the old cotton robe and gown. She must look a mess.

He scanned her face, his gaze coming to rest on the

puffy eyes. Crystalline blue, surrounded by long, dark lashes. Her hair was still mussed from sleep, framing her face. Gone were the strong sheriff features. This morning she was soft, delicate, and a very desirable woman. Her eyes darkened as he came nearer. He'd seen the same look in a doe's eyes once when Rob had finally talked him into tagging along. He'd bumped his brother's arm, just as he took a shot. The doe bounded off into the forest, and Rob had cursed him for weeks about his clumsiness. "Sarah, let me help you. I swear I didn't come here to hurt you."

Sarah smiled tremulously, reaching out to touch his face. "I know. I thought it was you, but it isn't."

Gavin groaned at her touch. He'd planned on being so noble. Strong. One touch and his control shattered. Reaching for her, he pulled her roughly against him, finding her lips in a bruising kiss. His hands roamed her body, coming to rest in the silky hair, pulling her closer. Dear God, he'd never get enough of touching her, tasting her, smelling her. Desire seared his body, making him feel as if he were boiling alive from the inside out.

He came to his senses just enough to realize she wasn't fighting him. Her hands were feverishly sliding over his back, her tongue seeking, soft whimpers escaping her lips.

The ringing of the phone jerked them apart. Sarah stood for a moment, breathing ragged gasps, her body trembling.

"Answer it." Gavin's voice was strained, his own breathing shallow, nostrils flared.

Sarah walked toward the kitchen, unsure if she wanted to thank the caller or kill him.

"Hello."

"Sarah?"

"What's wrong, Joshua?"

The silence grated on Sarah's already tender nerves.

"Joshua?"

"You were right, Sarah. Somebody cut Johanna's brake line."

"I'll be there in an hour."

Sarah hung up the phone and gazed out the kitchen window. She felt Gavin's presence, even before his arms closed around her. "Sarah, I'm sorry. I never meant..."

She cut him off and pulled away. "Don't say it. You didn't do anything I didn't want you to. We both knew this was going to happen. We both wanted it."

"Not like this."

Sarah laughed, "Oh, I think this is exactly what we wanted. Except for the phone ringing."

Gavin felt the sharp drop in the room temperature. She'd pulled away from him, and not just physically. Her words felt like ice water washing over his soul.

"I'm going to get dressed. Then we're going to have that talk."

Gavin sat at the table watching Sarah, her eyes fixated on something he couldn't see. She turned and he gripped the coffee mug to overcome the urge to go to her, take her in his arms. He knew from the look in her eyes that wasn't an option. Her voice quivered slightly as she began.

"My name isn't Sarah Burns. It's Sarah McKnight." She laughed hollowly. "And as you already know, my eyes aren't green, they're blue."

She stopped, sipped her coffee, her attention still focused on something far away. "Six years ago I caught my partner–my lover," she spat out the word, "raping a young girl. I arrested him. To make a long story short, the girl disappeared. He went free. I'd just found out I was pregnant. I ran, and I've been running ever since. I thought we were safe here. Until you came."

She looked at him then, her eyes full of questions, pain, and loneliness.

"I didn't come here to hurt you, Sarah. I came here looking for a killer." Gavin pulled the faded photograph from his wallet and handed it to her.

"Cory was my twin sister. Our parents were killed in an auto accident when we were just fifteen months old. We didn't have any other family, so the state placed us in an orphanage. The Larsons adopted Cory one day before the Walkers adopted me. I didn't even know she existed until three years ago."

The resemblance between the two of them was apparent. Sarah wondered why she hadn't noticed it before.

"Cory came here for a story. Maybe it was you, I don't know. All I know is she sent me here to protect Nikki."

Sarah sank down in the nearest chair, her legs suddenly too weak to hold her.

"Protect Nikki?"

Gavin nodded, placing his hand over Sarah's, the memory of his dream the night before creating a tenderness inside him. He'd been having a nightmare, and then suddenly Nikki was there, placing her small hand in his. Somehow she'd chased the demons away. "As long as there's breath in my body, Sarah, nothing's going to happen to Nikki. I promise you that."

Sarah felt the strength in his grip, the sincerity of his words. "So, where do we go from here?"

"I think it's time Jacody Ives got busy. He really is a

damn good detective."

They rode to town in silence, each lost in their own thoughts. Sarah knew she had a lot of explaining to do. Hopefully, Joshua would understand why she'd lied to him. Why she'd had to lie. Gavin squeezed her hand.

"He'll understand."

Sarah glanced at him out of the corner of her eyes. "How did you know what I was thinking?"

"I don't know. It was like I heard it inside my head. Like I used to do with Cory."

Parking in front of the office, Sarah turned to him. Before they went any further, she needed to tell him about Cory.

"Gavin there's something I need to tell you. About Cory. All my life I've had these dreams. My grandmother said it was a gift." Sarah laughed shakily. "I always thought it was a curse. I knew people were going to die, but I couldn't do anything about it. That's why I went into law enforcement. I hoped maybe I could use it, help someone."

Gavin squeezed her hand, as Sarah continued.

"The night Cory died, she came to me. She warned me someone was coming and that he wanted to destroy me. She's been coming back ever since. She talks to Nikki."

Gavin nodded, not at all surprised. "Cory found something. Something that linked you and Nikki with this sick bastard my brother has been chasing for five years. Every Mother's Day he kills a young girl. The only clue he's ever left is a small pink card. We know it's some kind of message. We just haven't been able to figure it out."

A nagging fear started in Sarah's stomach. "We found one of those cards. It was in the room when Marisa was killed." The fear escalated to terror. "How long?" she whispered.

"How long?" Gavin shook his head, not understanding her question.

"How long has he been leaving the cards?"

"Five years."

The words echoed in Sarah's mind: *You know*. "Oh, my God. It's me. The cards were for me. He knows about Nikki." Sarah turned to Gavin, seeking support, comfort, strength.

"He's Nikki's father."

CHAPTER TWENTY-SEVEN

Rob sniffed, glancing around the motel room. The place smelled stale. The once cream-colored wallpaper was now a dingy, dirty gray. Moving an oval picture, he peered at the circle underneath before letting it drop back into place. Stiff, gaudy flowered spreads covered the beds. Pulling the spread away from the mattress Rob peered at the spread, mattress and sheets. He lifted the pillows and turned them over.

"What the hell are you doing?" Carl gawked at him, flopping on the other bed.

"Looking for bed bugs."

"Shit." Carl sprang from the bed, walked across the room, and opened the drapes. He lit a cigarette, resisting the urge to scratch.

"So, what's the plan?" Rob finished his inspection of the bed and stretched out, hands behind his head.

"As soon as it gets dark, I'll slip into town and scope out the place. Find out how Gavin's doing. See where he's staying."

"What am I supposed to do, twiddle my thumbs?"

"Watch a movie. You're on vacation."

Frustrated, Rob sat up on the side of the bed. "Dammit, Carl, I'm not gonna just sit in this damn room. I'm going with you."

"Not tonight you ain't. Got some business to take care of for the chief." Carl felt the heat from the cigarette singe his fingers, his thoughts in the past. Twenty years in the past.

Sarah pulled away from Gavin, breathing deeply, centering herself. There was no doubt in her mind that Todd Williams was behind this. If not him, then someone he sent, someone as evil as he was. She should have gone to that prison a long time ago, seen for herself. Made sure.

"Okay?" Gavin tucked a stray curl behind her ear.

"Um-hmm."

"You ready to kick some ass?"

Sarah nodded, reaching for the door.

"Uh, Sarah, your contacts?"

"No more contacts, Gavin. Sarah McKnight was a good police officer. And she's going to be a damned good sheriff. No more lies, no more secrets."

Sarah raised her chin, striding into the office, once again a formidable figure with Gavin beside her. There would be questions, but she was ready for them. What was important now was stopping the madness.

"Thank God, you're here," Tommy muttered, nervously eyeing the switchboard lights. "The phone's been ringing off the wall."

"Where's Joshua?"

"Uh…"

"I know, Tommy, my eyes are blue. Now where's Joshua?"

"He's in your office."

A smile tugged at the corners of Sarah's lips. She'd forgotten how good it felt to be herself. The smile widened as Joshua scrambled to get his feet off the desk.

"Stay where you are, Joshua." She closed the door and motioned Gavin to sit down.

"Fill me in, Joshua. What's going on?"

"Not much. Everything's quiet. Mayor came by for a few minutes."

"Any trouble there?"

"None as I know of. Seems to have recovered some of his bluster now that Claire's taking the blame and she's out of the picture. Guess he feels free to carry on as usual."

"We'll see about that."

"Thought we might."

Sarah stopped pacing, her mind churning, turning over facts and theories.

"Sarah, your eyes?" Joshua glanced from Sarah to Gavin.

"I think we all need some coffee," Gavin said. "And you two need to talk."

Sarah waited until the door closed. "My name isn't Sarah Burns, Joshua. It's Sarah McKnight. Six years ago I was a D.C. police officer." She stopped, hating to go into the sordid story again.

"Sarah, you don't have to do this. I trust you."

"Yes, Joshua, I do." Taking the chair Gavin had vacated, Sarah laced her fingers together in her lap. "I fell in love with my partner. We had an affair. I got pregnant. We arrested a young prostitute. I wasn't feeling well, so Todd said he'd take her in. I don't know what it was, some premonition, a hunch. Anyway, I followed him. He took the girl to his apartment. I caught him in the act of rape, arrested him. The girl disappeared. Todd made it look like a love affair gone wrong. Said I'd threatened to ruin him if he broke it off. Things got ugly, I disappeared. With a little help from a friend, I came here and started a new life."

Sarah lowered her eyes; the worst was yet to come.

"I think Todd Williams is here. I think he killed Corrine Larson, Johanna Nelson, and Marisa Hutchins. I think all of this is my fault."

Joshua patted his shirt pocket, looking for a toothpick, stalling for time. A lot depended on what he said in the next few minutes. Glancing at Sarah's bowed head, he rose and walked to the door, opening it. "McAllister, where the hell is that coffee? We got work to do in here."

Sarah raised her eyes, searching his face.

"You're in my seat, Sheriff."

The words were spoken softly, but Sarah understood their meaning. Joshua was ready and willing to stand beside her, no matter what.

Gavin entered, balancing three cups of coffee and kicked the door closed. He looked from one to the other as Sarah rose and took the seat behind the desk.

"Let's start at the beginning, look at what we've got." Sarah took the cup of coffee, sniffing it. "And where the hell is Ella Mae?"

She watched as Joshua's lips tightened, his eyes thunderous as he glanced away from her. "Fell again last night."

Sarah grimaced. She was going to have to deal with that. If she didn't, Joshua would.

Gavin took a seat on the edge of her desk. "Fill me in."

Taking a note pad from the desk, Sarah made notes as she talked. "The best we can figure, Corrine Larson must have arrived here on the night Johanna Nelson was killed. We know now that wasn't an accident. Larson was found murdered the following day." Sarah continued to write, ignoring the tension and pain she felt emanating from Gavin and glancing at Joshua. "Anything on the other bodies?"

Joshua shook his head. "Autopsy confirmed what Doc had already told us. No missing couples reported in this area. Time of death uncertain, but at least two months or more."

"Gavin, you told me that Marisa told you she didn't think Johanna's death was an accident. Maybe that has something to do with her death. She said the wrong thing to the wrong person."

Gavin shook his head. "I don't think Marisa's death had anything to do with that. I think he was sending a message. Letting you know he was here."

Sarah nodded. "Yeah, I think you're right. And I don't think he killed the couple. I think we've got two people here."

"So, who's been here two months?" Gavin asked, Jacody Ives kicking in, searching for secrets.

Sarah exchanged glances with Joshua. "Reverend Cooper and his wife have been here about two months."

Sarah's gaze fell on the roses sitting on the corner of her desk. "Millie says he has black eyes," she whispered. "Williams has black eyes."

Jasmine Little whimpered as she glanced around the old mill. The place was damp and dusty and had a musty odor. Life on the streets had been hard, but this was ridiculous. She couldn't stay here. She wasn't going to stay here.

"We have to go," she whined.

Jeremiah Campbell stopped pacing the floor to look at her. His nerves were already on edge. He'd recognized the

Bureau agents. The stupid bastards must have followed him. Too close. He was too close to let them stop him now. Nobody was going to stop him. Besides they didn't know anything. They couldn't. He'd been too careful.

"You killed them, didn't you? Those bodies they found. You didn't say nothing about killing nobody."

The whiney voice grated on his nerves. He glared at her, black eyes blazing with hatred. Fucking whore. Questioning him.

"Shut up," he spat out.

"What are we going to do?" She continued to whine, ignoring the heated glare as she watched a rat scurry across the dusty floor.

"We're going to do what we came here to do."

She whimpered again. "But you can't. They know. That's why they're here, isn't it? They know."

Her voice had risen to a shriek. Whiney, shrieking whore. Jeremiah hit her, fist bunched, enjoying the sound of bones breaking, the smell of fresh blood.

Tears filled Jasmine's eyes. She spat blood on the floor. "You're crazy," she whispered.

"Fucking whore," he roared, placing his hands around her neck, watching her eyes go large from fear. "Parading around like you was a real minister's wife. Taking on airs. Acting like you was something besides a whore. Pissing off the sheriff."

"Please," Jasmine whispered, spreading her legs and reaching for his groin. He liked it when she touched him there. Men always liked that.

Kill her.

Campbell loosened his grip, straining to hear the voice inside his head. He wasn't crazy.

She deserves to die like a whore, the voice whispered.

Taking his hands from her throat he unzipped his pants and reached for the frizzy blonde hair, pulling her face to his groin. "Suck it."

"You hurt my mouth," Jasmine whined. The thought of putting him inside her mouth gagged her.

"Suck it or die, whore."

Fear made her hands tremble as she finished undoing his pants and pulled out his cock, an angry pulsating red eye. Ugly. She shivered as her lips closed around it, gently sucking.

Jeremiah felt the rage of five years flow through him. Placing his hands around her neck he pulled her closer, shoving deep inside her throat. He felt her gag, hands beating at him. He squeezed harder. "Suck it like the whore you really are."

Her lips closed around him again, and he laughed as she sucked as if her life depended on it. Crazy. That's what they'd said when they'd locked him away. He squeezed harder, semen rushing out, filling her mouth. She gagged and pushed at him, as he shoved deeper into her mouth, his hands clenched tightly around her throat. He heard the slight crack, felt the head loll to one side. The noises stopped, her limp body held up only by the hands clutched tightly around her neck.

Crazy? Tossing the body on the floor, he spat on it as he zipped up his pants. Sounds of laughter echoed inside his head. He'd show them. He'd show them all.

Sarah turned off the lights on the Explorer as they approached the parsonage. Reaching into the glove compartment, she pulled out her extra gun and handed it to

Gavin. "Just in case. If it's Williams in there, he won't go down without a fight."

Gavin nodded, glancing at Joshua who was loading the shotgun in the back seat. They weren't going to take any chances.

The house was fully lit. Sarah motioned Joshua to take the back. She and Gavin would approach from the front. Motioning Gavin to the right of the door, Sarah pounded on it, quickly side-stepping to the left as she called out, "Sheriff! Open up!"

No sound came from inside. Glancing at Gavin, she tried the door and found it unlocked. Gun ready, Sarah shoved the door open and went in at a flying roll, quickly moving to her right. Gavin followed her, surveying the room, looking for places a shooter might hide. Joshua called out as he burst through the back door seconds later.

The house was totally silent. They moved quickly from room to room.

"They're gone." Joshua stated the obvious, noting the open drawers, empty closets.

Sarah cursed silently. She felt Gavin's arm go around her waist and leaned into his strength. If only she'd run that background check sooner.

"Guess I better call Edgewood," Joshua stated, sticking a toothpick between his teeth as he lowered the shotgun.

Sarah nodded. "Tell them they're looking for a missing minister and his wife. Reverend Jacob and Shelia Cooper."

CHAPTER TWENTY-EIGHT

Carl left the motel and headed for Glade Springs at nine-thirty. It was a two-hour drive and he wanted to get there just before midnight. The town was quiet as he pulled onto Main Street and parked in front of the bookstore. He knew where he was going. Millie's house was just down the block, around the corner.

Scouting the street in front of him, he relaxed, pulling out the Sig and screwing on the silencer. He hoped he wouldn't need it. Closing the car door gently, he slipped into the alley beside the store, making his way back and over, toward the house, eyes alert for any signs of movement. Easy as pie, he grinned. Opening the gate, he slipped around the side of the house, and headed for the back door.

Clarence watched the figure moving stealthily around the house, gun in hand. He'd called Millie as soon as he'd noticed the strange car sitting in front of her bookstore. Knew she was waiting on the other side of the door, iron skillet in hand. He'd told her to get the gun, dammit. Stubborn old woman. He clutched the piece of wood he'd grabbed before leaving the flower shop, fear making his heart beat so loud he was afraid the intruder would hear it. Removing his shoes, he slipped through the gate, picking up his pace. Had to stop him before he got to Millie.

Rounding the corner, Clarence stopped. The figure was only a few feet away, one foot on the bottom step, eyes focused on the back door. Rushing forward he swung the club with every ounce of his strength. He heard the loud pop as the wood connected with the side of the man's head. He drew back again, but stopped as the figure slowly fell, gun clattering on the back porch.

"Millie, you okay?" Clarence whispered, his voice strained, as the back door opened slowly.

"Humph, could'a took him out myself." Millie smiled fondly at Clarence. "You old fool, running around in the middle of the night barefoot. You didn't kill him, did you?"

Clarence shook his head, bending over the prone body. "Nope, just knocked him out. Gonna have one hell of a headache, though."

"Turn him over. I want to see his face."

Kicking the gun out of reach, Clarence turned the body over, glancing up at Millie's sharp intake of breath and muttered, "Oh, shit."

"Do you know him? Who is he?" Clarence glanced from Millie to the deathly still black man.

"Carl Jackson, FBI," Millie muttered, bending down to stroke the old man's face gently. "Best damn partner I ever had."

"FBI?" Clarence dropped the club he still clutched in his right hand. "Oh, shit."

"Don't you worry. Always was hard headed. Probably didn't hurt him none. Help me get him inside." Picking up Carl's arms, Millie nodded for Clarence to take his legs. Tugging and pulling, they managed to get him inside and on the couch.

"Make some coffee and fetch me the smelling salts.

He's gonna be madder than a wet hornet when he wakes up."

Ella Mae shied away from her husband. Trembling, she looked into the eyes she'd once thought beautiful. "I didn't tell them anything. I just said I fell."

"That damn deputy comes here again and I'm going to kill him. You understand that, Ella Mae?"

She nodded, her eyes never leaving his face. Waiting for the blink. He always blinked before he hit her. She knew he wouldn't hesitate to kill Joshua.

"You get yourself cleaned up. You're going to work tomorrow."

Ella Mae nodded again, heading quickly for the bathroom. She knew Joshua suspected the truth. She'd have to tell them something. Her breath caught as she touched the darkening bruise just over her ribs. He'd gotten smart after the last time. At least he wouldn't hit her in the face again.

He's going to kill you.

Ella Mae shrugged, pulling off her clothes and stepping into the shower. She didn't need the voice to tell her that. Turning the water on cold, she let it run over her burning body. She must already be dead. This had to be hell.

Millie ran the smelling salts beneath Carl's nose, stepping away from the huge black fist that struck out at her as Carl woke, sputtering oaths before grabbing his head and groaning.

"What the hell hit me?"

"What'd you expect, you old coot. Sneaking around an old woman's house at night."

Carl struggled to sit up, moaning louder as the effort

sent a fresh wave of pain through his head.

"Didn't expect an old biddy like you to hit a man so hard." He groaned, opening his eyes and glaring at Millie.

Clarence stepped next to Millie, placing an arm protectively around her shoulders. "I'm afraid I hit you, Mr. Jackson. Saw you skulking around and followed you."

Carl turned his fierce gaze on Clarence, but held his tongue. The old fart looked pretty tough, even barefoot. Besides, he wasn't in any shape to take on the two of them.

Millie glanced fondly from one to the other. "Why don't you two get to know each other while I get some coffee."

Clarence sat down, eyes alert, watching Carl suspiciously.

"You can relax. I didn't come here to hurt her." Carl patted his pocket for his cigarettes.

"Why the gun then?"

Carl managed a shaky grin, pulling the pack from his pocket. "In case I ran into some son-of-a-bitch with a big stick."

Clarence laughed, relaxing as Millie came in with three mugs of steaming coffee and an ice pack.

"Glad to see you two made up. No hard feelings?" She handed Carl the mug and watched as he sniffed it, sighed, and placed the ice pack on the lump that had begun to swell.

"No hard feelings." Carl sipped the coffee laced with brandy and watched Millie take a seat on the arm of the chair next to Clarence. Loneliness washed over him. He'd missed Millie. Missed Sharon. It was hard getting old. He was glad Millie had somebody.

Carl finished the cup of coffee and held it out for a refill. "Bring the bottle."

Millie refilled the mugs and handed Carl the bottle of brandy. "Want to tell me what you're doing here, sneaking around in the middle of the night?"

Carl took a long swig of brandy, chasing it with hot coffee. He glanced at Clarence, his meaning clear.

"Ain't no secrets here, Carl Jackson. Anything you got to say, you can say it in front of Clarence."

"We gotta move you, Millie. Right away."

"Ain't going nowhere." Millie stood up, pacing the room. "This is my home. Been my home twenty years." Her gray eyes flashed fire.

"Ain't got no choice. Things are about to break wide open here. Can't take a chance on you being seen on the media. Chief says we gotta move you."

"Ain't going." Millie's chin quivered, but her voice was strong and clear.

Carl muttered to himself, lighting another cigarette. "Fool headed, stubborn old woman. Knew you'd be this way. You're going, if I have to knock you over the head and carry you out of here."

"We'll see about that." Millie walked to the phone, dialing the number from memory.

He answered on the second ring. "Walsh."

"You got an agent here with a knot on his head. Says I gotta leave. I ain't going. You hear me, Junior?"

"Millie?" Walsh rubbed his eyes, glancing at the bedside clock. Two a.m.

"I told you, I ain't going." Millie glared across the room at Carl.

"Put Jackson on the phone."

Millie handed the phone to Carl and sat down next to Clarence with a resounding "humph."

"Chief?"

"What the hell's going on there, Jackson?"

"Well, first some old codger clobbered me, and now the old biddy says she ain't going nowhere." He smiled at Millie, seeing the sparks in her eyes at his reference to Clarence.

"Should have known. All right. All right. Fill her in. Make sure she stays out of the spotlight."

"Yeah." Clarence hung up the phone wondering just how he was supposed to do that.

"Chief says you can stay." Carl snarled, noting the satisfied grin. "Give me some more of that coffee. And don't look so damn smug."

Millie grinned, but stifled the giggle. She sure had missed the old coot.

Sarah filled the coffee pot with water, peering into the darkness surrounding the house. She'd been awakened by the dreams again. She shivered. Two men were going to die, and she couldn't do anything to stop it. She didn't even know who they were or where to start looking for them. Dammit, it wasn't fair. What kind of gift was it if she couldn't stop what she saw?

"Sarah?"

Gavin stood just inside the kitchen doorway, his face a pale ghostly mask. "You saw it too?" she whispered.

Gavin nodded, unable to find his voice and put into words the horror the dream had instilled in him.

"Gavin, do you know who they are?" Sarah approached him, reaching out to him. He moved into her arms, body trembling.

"Rob Walker and Carl Jackson. My brother and his

partner."

CHAPTER TWENTY-NINE

The sound of the key turning in the lock woke Rob from a light sleep. He'd stayed up as long as he could, prowling the room, cursing, worrying like a father waiting for his child to come home. He met Carl at the door.

"Where the hell have you been?"

"Taking care of business." Carl tried to grin, but the spinning of the room made it come out lopsided. His head still hurt, and the brandy was fermenting in his stomach. He belched loudly.

"Shit, you're drunk." Rob grabbed him, placing one arm around his shoulder and half lifted, half dragged him to the bed.

Carl tried to grin again. "Jus' a little bit. Hep' the headache." He closed his eyes to shut out the spinning room and immediately fell asleep.

Rob stood, mouth gaped open, listening to the sound of Carl's snores. "Well, I'll be damned." He grinned as he pulled off Carl's shoes and gently covered him with a blanket. The grin stiffened on his face as his eyes took in the knot and slight oozing of blood. He shook Carl gently.

"Go 'way," Carl slurred, turning over and continuing his snoring.

Rob examined the knot. What if he had a concussion? He shook him again.

"Carl, what happened out there?"

Carl pushed at Rob's hands feebly, muttering, "Said she ain't going." He giggled. "Called him Junior."

Rob sat down, watching his partner snore. Carl was too hard-headed to have a concussion. Pulling the blanket up over him, Rob patted his shoulder. "It must have been some night, buddy."

Sarah refilled their coffee cups and sat down at the table, waiting for Gavin to hang up the phone.

"Chief says they're here somewhere. He doesn't know where, but he'll keep trying to reach them." Gavin raked his hands through his thick wavy hair, a look of desperation on his face.

Sarah wanted to say something, but stopped as José came down the stairs carrying Nikki. Juanita followed closely behind, carrying the small suitcase she'd packed.

José nodded to them, carrying Nikki out to his car. Sarah felt the tears behind her eyelids as Gavin's arms slipped around her. He whispered, "Go with her. This isn't your fight."

Sarah shook her head, enjoying the comfort of his arms before she pulled away. "It is my fight, Gavin. I should have faced him six years ago. I should have killed him then."

Joshua pulled into the driveway of the old Sampson place, cutting the engine. There were no lights on, and only one car sat in the driveway. Maybe the bastard had left. His hands were white from gripping the steering wheel. He'd promised Sarah he wouldn't do this. He was here. The least he could do was check on Ella Mae. The radio squawked as his hand touched the door handle.

"Deputy Cross," he answered, never taking his eyes off the silent house.

"Joshua, I need you to meet me at the office right away."

"What's up, Sarah?"

"Not on the radio. Just get here as fast as you can." Sarah clicked off.

"Shit." Replacing the microphone, Joshua sat for a second, hand poised over the door handle. He started the Jeep, spun around, and headed toward town. "I'll be back," he whispered to the silent house.

Ella Mae whimpered, shying away from the icy metal pressed against her back.

"You fucking that deputy?" he spat out, hand raised to hit her again.

"No. He's just a friend."

"Friend!" He raised the bottle of whiskey to his lips, the word leaving a sour taste in his mouth. "Get out," he snarled.

Ella Mae whimpered again, raising her hands in front of her. "Please…"

He jumped at her, laughing as she scurried up the basement stairs. "Fix my breakfast. I got things to do today."

Gavin hung up the phone, shaking his head at Sarah's questioning look. "Still no word from them. Rest of the department is out on some terrorist threat."

Joshua paced the floor. "So, we're on our own?"

Gavin nodded. "Looks like it."

"How much time do you think we have?" Sarah asked.

Gavin shook his head again. "I don't know. The dreams have never been like that before. It's always been during or afterwards, not before."

"Dreams don't always mean something, though. Maybe it was just a fluke." Sarah touched his hand, wishing she could ease the pain she knew he was feeling.

Joshua glanced back and forth between them. "You two sure need an education."

Sarah frowned at him.

"Dreams have forecast the future since the beginning of time." Joshua sat down, warming up to his subject, surveying his audience. "Ever read Cayce?"

They both shook their heads.

Joshua shifted in the chair. "Edgar Cayce, born March 18, 1877, in Hopkinsville, Kentucky. From the age of 24 he gave over 14,000 readings."

"What's a reading?" Gavin took a seat on the edge of Sarah's desk.

"Sort of a prediction. Something like your dreams."

"But that's different than the dreams we're having," Sarah stated flatly. "Cayce was physic, we're not."

Joshua shrugged. "Everybody's psychic, Sarah. Some know it, some don't. Comes in all forms, too. You got your dreamers, your meditators, people like Cayce that go into trances, and empaths that feel what other people feel. Then you've got those with the voices in their heads. Most people are scared to death of it."

Joshua knew he had their attention, but they were still skeptical. "Pharaoh's dream, remember? The seven cows that were fat and the seven cows that were lean. The lean cows ate up the fat cows. Then he dreamed about seven ears of corn on one stalk. Good corn. Then seven thin ears, which devoured the good ears. Joseph interpreted the dream for him. Seven years of plenty, followed by seven years of famine."

Sarah laughed. "Coincidence, Joshua."

Joshua shook his head. "No such thing. What about President Lincoln? He dreamed his own assassination. And surely you've heard of Jeanne Dixon?"

Gavin picked up the story, familiar with Dixon. "She dreamed about the White House with the numerals 1-9-6-0 formed above the roof. A dark cloud appeared covering the numbers and rippled onto the White House. She saw a young man, tall, blue-eyed, crowned with a shock of thick brown hair, quietly standing in front of the main door. She heard a voice that told her the young man was a Democrat to be seated as President in 1960. He would be assassinated while in office."

Sarah drew in a shaky breath. "John F. Kennedy."

Joshua nodded and grinned. Thank God. Slow but not impossible. He grabbed a notebook from Sarah's desk and sat down. "Doctor Cross, open for business. Tell me about your dreams."

Sarah couldn't believe her ears, and yet it made perfect sense. She'd suspected for some time that Joshua had a gift similar to hers. His instincts were good. A little too good. Sarah glanced at Gavin, her eyes alight with excitement as she realized what Joshua was trying to do.

"It's dark. I can see the two men sitting in a car. Someone's approaching." She glanced at Gavin, who nodded and picked up from there.

"It's dark, but I think it may be early morning. There seems to be a grayness in the air. Just before dusk or just before dawn."

Joshua nodded, writing down early morning. "Okay, someone's approaching. Male or female?"

Sarah shook her head, glancing at Gavin for confirmation. "I don't know. It's too fuzzy."

"Okay. What happens next?"

"There's a streak of light or a blaze of some kind. And I can see blood. Lots of blood." Sarah stopped talking, her eyes on Gavin's pale face, closed eyes.

Joshua glanced at Gavin, but continued. "What happens then?"

Sarah frowned, closing her own eyes as she tried to remember what she'd seen next. She knew it was important.

"I'm in Sarah's living room. Holding my brother. Trying to stop the blood gushing from his chest."

"I'm on the porch, checking his partner. He's dead."

Joshua stood up. "Okay. Now we know who, and we know where. All we have to do is be ready for it, sit back and wait."

Sarah took a deep breath and squeezed Gavin's hand. Maybe this time they could stop it. She glanced at Joshua. "You believe in psychics?"

He nodded, sitting down and sticking the toothpick between his teeth. Grinning, he placed his feet on her desk.

"Why haven't you ever said anything?"

"Remember Joan of Arc?"

Sarah nodded.

"Joan heard voices in her head. Those voices prompted her to lead the French army against the English at Orleans. They burnt her at the stake as a heretic." Joshua stood up and reached for the door. "Some things are better left unknown."

Ella Mae looked up from the files she'd been sorting as Joshua came down the hall whistling. She hadn't mentioned seeing him outside the house that morning. "I just made some fresh coffee," she said, smiling hesitantly.

Joshua stopped whistling, noticing the way she favored one side, the look of pain that occasionally crossed her face.

"Ella Mae, does your husband hit you?"

Ella Mae lowered her eyes, placing the files into the drawer. "It was an accident. He likes to play games. Sometimes they get a little rough."

Making his way to the coffee pot, Joshua poured a cup to go and headed for the front door. Anger seethed inside him. "He gets rough again, he's going to have to deal with me," Joshua stated, slamming the door behind him.

Ella Mae trembled, wringing her hands.

He'll kill him.

"No," she whispered. She wouldn't let him kill Joshua. She'd kill him first.

Rob closed the door and glanced at the empty bed. He could hear the sound of the shower running and breathed a sigh of relief. At least he hadn't gone off without him again. Hearing the water cut off, he sat down on the bed and waited.

"Boo!"

Dropping the towel draped loosely around him, Carl lunged at the sound of the voice. Rob quickly rolled to the other side of the bed, roaring as he watched Carl bounce off the bed, landing hard on the floor, buck-naked.

"You fucking son-of-a-bitch," Carl yelled, holding his head. "What the hell do you think you're doing?"

Rob tried to answer, but laughter overcame him. The sight of Carl sitting naked on the floor, holding his head from last night's hangover was too priceless.

"Payback's hell," he finally managed.

Carl's look was thunderous. "First I get cold-cocked by some old codger old enough to be my grandfather, and then pushed around by an old woman, and now you."

Rob tried to stifle the laugh, but failed miserably.

"That's pretty old, partner."

"You gonna help me up or not?"

Rob reached over, offering a hand, pulling it away as he noted the gleam in Carl's charcoal eyes. "Almost had me there." He picked up the towel, tossed it to Carl, and grinned.

"Just remember, payback's hell," Carl snarled as he stood up wrapping the towel around him.

Rob held out the cup of coffee he'd brought back from the restaurant. "Truce?"

Carl uttered a curse, but took the coffee.

Rob's tone turned serious. "What happened last night?"

Carl sat down on the bed, fingering the small lump on the side of his head. "Chief sent me to get a witness out of Glade Springs before we got started. Afraid the media might pick up on her. Damned old fool got herself a boyfriend." He fingered the lump tenderly.

Rob couldn't help the snicker that escaped his lips, bringing another murderous look from Carl.

"Ain't funny. Old witch got the chief out of bed." He chortled. "Called him Junior."

"You're kidding?" Rob stated. "She called Walsh 'Junior'?"

Carl started to nod, but stopped as the movement hurt

his head. He snickered again. "I'd give a month's pay to have seen his face when she said that."

Rob grinned, shaking his head. She must be something else.

"Millie was the best," Clarence continued, voice serious. "She had my back for almost twenty years. I can't let nothing happen to her, Rob. We gotta get in and find this bastard quick."

Rob nodded. The stakes were growing daily. "We'll get started as soon as it gets dark."

CHAPTER THIRTY

"What do you think?" Rob glanced over at Carl from his position in the tree.

"Hell if I know. Deputies strung out all over the place. They must be expecting somebody." Carl held up the field glasses. "Gavin and Sarah are still in the kitchen talking. Ain't seen the kid."

Rob couldn't shake the feeling of impending doom. They were in the wrong place. "I think it's the kid he's after. Let's get back to the car."

Gavin paced the kitchen, his nerves on edge. He wanted to be out there in the darkness stalking whoever was stalking them.

"Call Nikki, Sarah. Make sure she's okay."

Sarah glanced out the window. The shadows seemed deeper, darker, more menacing. She knew Joshua and Thomas were out there, along with her reserve deputies, Jed Burdock and Matt Carter. Still she could feel the evil coming closer. Smell the distinct odor of death. Death was stalking them. Where the hell were Rob and Carl?

Gavin placed a hand on her shoulder. "Call her, Sarah. You need to get some sleep."

Sarah nodded, picked up the phone, and dialed José's number.

"Hello."

"Hey, José it's me. I was just checking on Nikki." She listened for a second. "No, don't wake her up. I'll see you in the morning."

Turning to Gavin she hung up the phone. "She's asleep. A little angel, according to José."

Taking her in his arms, Gavin rested his head on hers. "Why don't you go upstairs and get some sleep? I'll keep watch down here."

Sarah smiled shyly, turning off the lamp and taking his hand. "Sleep isn't what I need right now."

Gavin knew at that moment what Rob had felt for Cory. He couldn't imagine living the rest of his life without Sarah. He wanted her. She wanted him. Tonight might be their last night. Pulling her into his arms, he whispered her name. He wanted her, but not like this. Not with the fear of death surrounding them. Not with thoughts of Rob and Carl out there somewhere bleeding, maybe already dead. When they came together, it would be out of love, not fear.

Sarah pulled away, sensing his feelings, gazing into the deep brown eyes. "Lie down with me then. Let's see if we can get some rest."

Gavin checked the windows and doors again, making sure everything was locked up tight before following her up the stairs.

Moonlight filtered through the window, illuminating her still form lying on the bed. Gavin stretched out beside her, taking her hand in his. He didn't want to sleep, but exhaustion had taken its toll, and within minutes he found himself drifting off in darkness.

Sarah lay awake, listening to the sounds of his even breathing. Tears coursed down her face. She loved this man, and when he left, a part of her would die.

Turning, she snuggled against him as emotional exhaustion overcame her, and she drifted into sleep.

Sarah woke with a start, lying with Gavin's arms tightly wound around her. She glanced at the bedside clock. Five-thirty a.m. She snuggled deeper into his embrace. They'd made it through the night and nothing had happened.

Closing her eyes, Sarah waited for sleep to come. Something was wrong. Tension filled the air around them. She'd missed something. She thought back over the dream, seeing it, reliving it. When they'd opened the door, Rob had fallen into Gavin's arms. She'd rushed out to check Carl. Squirming out of Gavin's arms, Sarah sat up, concentrating hard on the fleeting images. She saw herself re-enter the room, glance at Gavin, and shake her head. Carl was dead. Gavin had looked at her then, his eyes reflecting the horror he felt, as blood flowed through the fingers he'd pressed against Rob's chest. Terror hit her in the pit of her stomach as she heard the words echo, *Sarah, check on Nikki.*

Oh, God. Nikki had been here. They'd changed it. Changed the course of the dream.

"Gavin, wake up. We have to hurry." Sarah dashed from the bed, feeling for her shoes.

"Sarah?" Gavin opened his eyes, sleepy, reaching out to draw her back to bed.

She strapped on her revolver and tossed him his shoes. "We changed the dream, Gavin. Nikki was here when Rob and Carl were shot."

Understanding wiped the last remnants of sleep from his eyes as he pulled on his shoes and followed her down the stairs.

He stopped mid-stride as laughter flowed around him.

Too late, McAllister. You're too late.

Millie crawled out of bed, groaning as she headed for the kitchen. Damned old bones hurt, keeping her awake all hours of the night. After filling a pot with water, she sat down at the table. She should be out there. Helping Carl. Damned old fool would probably get himself killed without her.

A smile tugged at her lips. It sure had been good to see him again. She thought about Clarence. A gentle flush crept up her neck spreading across her wrinkled face. Wanted to get married, sell flowers and books. He knew what he was asking for.

Reaching under the counter, she pulled out a bottle of Kentucky bourbon, pouring a healthy dose into the mug before filling it with steaming hot coffee. Placing it on the table to cool, she paced around the kitchen, pondering what she should do. Couldn't just sit here. Things were happening. Bad things. She sat down, allowing her thoughts to drift back over the past few months. New people moving into Glade Springs. She thought about the young girl who'd stopped by the bookstore looking for work. What was her name? Ella something another. Mousy little thing. Always looking at the ground. Millie chastised herself and took another sip of coffee. Should have checked on her. Poor thing probably didn't have a friend in the world. Besides, Millie wanted to see her husband anyway. See what kind of man made a woman look like that.

Humming softly, Millie set down the coffee and pulled out her mixing bowl. Chocolate cake. Why, the girl could be quite pretty if she'd put on a little weight. And a good neighbor would take a chocolate cake, wouldn't she?

Everybody loved chocolate cake.

"What do you think?" Rob glanced at Carl, handing him the binoculars.

"I think Gavin is gonna kick our ass when he finds out we tapped his girlfriend's phone." Carl grinned.

Rob laughed softly. "They did look kind of cozy there."

"No sign of anybody." Carl handed the binoculars back to Rob. "You ready?"

Rob nodded. "Back yard or forest?"

"I'm taking the forest. At least there I can hide out and smoke."

"Be careful."

Grabbing her cell phone, Sarah rushed from the house, Gavin right on her heels. She dialed José's number as she swung open the door of the Explorer, ignoring Joshua's frantic yells.

Climbing in quickly, Gavin called out "Follow us," just as Sarah put the car into gear and spun out of the driveway.

"There's no answer," Sarah whispered, closing the phone and handing it to Gavin as she pressed down harder on the gas pedal.

"Maybe they're asleep, Sarah." Gavin placed his hand gently on her knee, offering comfort, as his own chest tightened in fear.

The drive to José's took only minutes, but to Sarah it felt like an eternity. She should never have let Nikki out of her sight. She shouldn't have left. Her hand tightened on the wheel. No, she should have killed Todd Williams six years ago. She wouldn't make that mistake again. She'd find him, and this time she'd kill him.

The small frame house was dark as they pulled into the driveway and parked. Sarah could hear the sound of other vehicles approaching quickly. A shadow moved near the rear of the house. Pulling her revolver, she opened the door quietly, motioning for Gavin to stay in the truck. Sarah moved silently toward the house.

Her gut instinct told her something was wrong. The sound of approaching vehicles should have caused the intruder to flee. She waited for Joshua to join her as the others fanned out, surrounding the house. After climbing the steps, Sarah peered cautiously through the living room window. Her face paled at the sight of José lying motionless on the floor.

Motioning to Joshua, Sarah slipped around the side of the house, headed for the spot where she'd seen the shadow move.

Sarah heard the sound of a high-powered rifle, saw the blaze of flame, just before someone rushed toward her, pushing her aside. The sound of bullet striking flesh thudded loudly. She heard the grunt, saw Joshua reach out to grab the young man before he fell. Answering gunshots went off in the woods. Someone yelled. Seconds. Everything had happened in seconds.

Joshua lowered the body to the ground, placing his hands over the chest wound trying to stem the flow of blood. Sarah gasped. She knew the face. She'd seen it in her dreams. Rob.

"Oh, God," Gavin whispered. Kneeling beside Rob, he took Joshua's place, applying pressure to the wound, cursing silently as blood gushed over his fingers. Not too late. Dammit, not this time.

"Gavin?" Sarah placed her hand on his shoulder.

"Find Nikki." Gavin didn't look up. He couldn't meet her eyes. Couldn't bear the sympathy and pain.

"Call Edgewood, Joshua. Get us some help over here."

Gavin could hear Joshua on the cell phone, heard Sarah's pounding footsteps as she raced toward the trees.

"Gavin…" The whisper pulled his attention from the blood seeping through his fingers. He looked into Rob's eyes.

"Don't talk. The doctor's on the way."

"Couldn't let her die. Not like Cory. Knew the son-of-a-bitch was gonna shoot." Rob coughed, a trickle of blood spilling from the corner of his lips. "Carl?"

Gavin thought about lying, telling him Carl was okay. The pale blue eyes pinned him with a steady gaze and he shook his head. "I don't know."

A smile tugged at Rob's lips as he gazed at something behind Gavin. "Can you see her?"

Gavin turned, looking in the direction of Rob's gaze. Cory stood there. "Yeah, I see her."

"I gotta go, bro."

"No." Gavin spoke through clenched teeth, hot tears spilling down his face.

With great effort, Rob moved his hand, covering Gavin's. "That Sarah, she's pretty special."

Gavin nodded, clutching Rob's hand.

"And the little girl?"

Gavin smiled through his tears. "Very special."

Rob coughed again, and Gavin could hear the death rattle.

"Do me a favor?" Rob whispered.

"Anything."

"Marry her." Rob squeezed his hand. "And tell Carl I

said payback's hell."

Gavin felt the hand grow limp. He stared into the sightless blue eyes through blinding tears. Bowing his head he let the tears flow freely. Too late. He was always too damn late.

CHAPTER THIRTY-ONE

Ignoring the branches that slapped at her face, Sarah raced through the trees, lungs on fire. Somewhere ahead of her a madman had her little girl. She cried out in frustration, as the pain became unbearable. Holding her side, she hunched over trying to catch her breath. How far had she run? A mile? Two? The roaring in her ears drowned out all other sound, as sweat burned her eyes, blinding her. She had to stop. She leaned against a tree for support as she wiped the sweat from her face, slowing her ragged breathing. Dawn was breaking, and she scanned the forest in front of her. She'd broken her own rules, rushing in blindly. She didn't even know where her own men were. What if she'd shot one of them? What if she'd shot Carl?

The roaring subsided and she stood listening, straining her ears to catch the slightest whisper or breaking branch. The forest was silent except for her ragged breathing, pounding heart. Where the hell were they? Grief threatened to overcome her. She didn't know if Juanita and José were dead or alive. The body count was way too high. Five little girls had lost their lives because she'd run away. Closing her eyes, she struggled for control; the image of Gavin kneeling beside his brother flashed before her eyes. She heard his anguished voice, "Find Nikki." That was all that was important now. She swore softly as she straightened her spine. "No more, Williams. You're not taking one more person from me."

"Sheriff!"

"Over here, Matt."

"We've got somebody here."

Sarah turned toward the sound, moving swiftly, but cautiously this time, her eyes scanning the trees around her. Matt and Jed approached her, carrying a huge black man, cursing and yelling. Blood flowed from the bullet wound in his left leg.

"Put him down." Holstering her gun, Sarah knelt beside Carl, gently probing the wound. "Looks like the bullet went straight through. I need your belt, Matt."

Sarah took the belt, fashioned a makeshift tourniquet, and stood up. "Take him to the house. I'm going after Williams."

"Wasn't Williams. And you're too late." Carl struggled to sit up, grimacing as the movement started a fresh wave of pain.

"What do you mean it wasn't Williams?"

"Campbell. Bastard had a car parked other side of the woods. Heard him drive off right after he shot me." Carl fumbled in his pocket for his cigarettes.

Sarah knelt again, her eyes level with Carl's. "Tell me everything you know about the man who's got my daughter."

Gavin watched quietly as Rob's body was loaded into the hearse. Doc had made the call official at six-thirty a.m. The forest loomed in front of him. Sarah was in there, maybe lying somewhere bleeding, dying. He ached to go after her. Do something, anything besides stand here helpless. He knew Joshua was right, though. Too many people in the woods made it more dangerous. At least they hadn't heard any additional shots. He had to believe she was okay. Otherwise, he'd go insane.

"At least Juanita and José are going to be okay." Joshua had come up behind him.

"Yeah, at least," Gavin stated flatly, turning toward the house.

"McAllister," Joshua called after him. "We need to talk."

"What about?" Gavin couldn't seem to take his eyes off the blood covering Joshua's hands. Rob's blood.

"Claire Nix."

Rage flared in Gavin's eyes. He'd just lost his brother. Nikki was missing and Sarah might already be dead. Right now he didn't give a damn about Claire Nix.

Joshua approached him, ignoring the rage. "Just listen to me. Hear me out, okay? Sarah's already got her hands full. So have you. From the looks of things, we're all going to have our hands full. I worked out a deal with the mayor. You agree not to press charges; he agrees they'll get out of Glade Springs. Hell, out of West Virginia. All I'm trying to do is eliminate one more problem for Sarah. What do you say?"

Gavin unclenched his hands, allowing the rage to flow out of him. What difference did it make? And it would eliminate a problem. One he'd totally forgotten about. Meeting the steady green gaze he nodded. "Get it in writing."

"I'll get the damn thing notarized."

Gavin noted the change in Joshua's posture, the slight glazing of the eyes, head tilted to one side. He was listening to something, or someone.

Down by the Old Mill Stream... The melody played loud and clear inside Joshua's head.

Joshua turned abruptly and headed for his Jeep. "Tell Sarah I had to go. Something I had to do."

Gavin grabbed his arm, turning him around. "Not so fast. What'd they tell you?"

Joshua hesitated. "It's not really words. Usually it's a song, a melody. Sometimes it's not really clear. Sometimes it's crystal clear."

"This time?"

"I'm going to the old mill out on Elliott Pike."

Gavin let go of his arm. "I'm going with you."

He paced the floor, glancing out the window. He needed a drink. No...no drinking. He had to be clear, ready. Everything was going just as planned.

You left the note.

"Fuck." He kicked the wall. That fucking whore was shacked up with McAllister. He'd seen them together. The ache was becoming a constant pain. He needed to hear her scream. Ease the pain. Needed to ease the pain.

Reaching for the whiskey, he poured a shot, downing it. The bitch was too old.

But she screams.

He laughed viciously. She screamed.

An hour later he felt exhilarated. The pain gone. He laughed with joy, the sound of her coarse screams still echoing through the room. Why hadn't he thought of this before?

Because it's perverted. Sick.

He laughed again, his eyes on the blood stains on her

buttocks, the sound of her whimpers exciting him. Just like a virgin. Nothing that felt that good could be sick. It was the killing that was wrong. And that was her fault.

The image on the bed shimmered, changed, the dull brown hair becoming flaming locks of red. He closed his eyes, remembering how he'd felt the night he stood over her, watching her sleep. It would have been so easy to slit her throat. Too easy. He wanted her to know he was here, feel his presence around her until she could think of nothing else. Then he would take her. Pleasure coursed through his body. He wouldn't kill her. Sarah was strong. A fighter. Whistling, he jogged up the steps. If he was careful, she might even last a week.

"There was always something about that man that made my skin crawl." Millie poured another cup of coffee, glancing fondly at Clarence as she cut him a piece of applesauce cake.

"What about the wife?"

"Never met her. Don't think she got out much."

"Nobody found that a little strange for a minister's wife? I mean, shouldn't she be out in the community, ministering to the sick or whatever?"

"Humph," Millie snorted. "You men, always categorizing. Have us all still barefoot and pregnant if it was up to you."

Clarence grinned sheepishly. "Now, Millicent, you know I don't think that way. Didn't you think it a little odd that she never left the house? They were here more than two months."

Millie pondered what Clarence had said. "Didn't really think about it. Don't make no never mind, though.

Disappeared just like they came."

"Could be they're still here somewhere." Clarence took another bite of cake and washed it down with Millie's special coffee. "Makes sense they were here for a reason. Seems like they'd stick around until they got whatever it was they came for."

Millie frowned, considering Clarence's statements. The Reverend had taken an awful lot of interest in Nikki. Almost seemed obsessed with her. For the second time that morning Millie felt the spine-tingling chill. She reached for the phone, dialing the sheriff's office. The chill deepened, sinking into her bones as the rings went on and on. She hung up and dialed Sarah's number.

"Damn," she whispered as she hung up the phone. There was no answer at Sarah's either. She hesitated only seconds before dialing Joshua's home number.

"Hello."

"Mary?"

"Hey, Millie. I wondered when you were going to call. Grandpa's got that liniment ready for you."

"Why bless you, child. But that's not the reason I called. Need Joshua's cell phone number."

"Is everything okay?"

Millie heard the panic in Mary's voice. Dammit, she didn't want to upset the girl.

"Everything's fine. Got a cat stuck up in my tree."

Mary laughed, relief in her voice. "It's 449-3456."

"Thank you, honey. I'll be by real soon."

"Bye, Millie."

Millie dialed the number, impatiently tapping her fingers as she listened to the rings.

"Cross."

"Joshua, it's Millie. Why ain't nobody answering at the sheriff's office? Ain't nobody answering at Sarah's either."

Joshua hesitated, knowing he'd never get away from Millie unless he told her the truth. "Cooper's got Nikki."

"Oh, God." Millie sat down, reaching up to clutch the hand Clarence laid gently on her shoulder.

"What can we do?"

"We'll get him, Millie." A nagging worry had begun in the back of Joshua's mind. Millie said there was no answer at the sheriff's office. Ella Mae should have been there by now.

"Millie, there is one thing you can do for me. Run out to the old Sampson place and check on Ella Mae. Got one of those bad feelings."

Millie nodded as she hung up. She grabbed her purse and the chocolate cake. "Come on Clarence, we gotta go."

Clarence had only heard a small portion of the conversation, but it was enough to know that Millie was rushing into danger. He followed her to the car and reached into the glove compartment pulling out the .38. He checked to make sure it was loaded, and clicked off the safety. Patting Millie's hand, he put the car in gear. "Prepare for the worst, hope for the best."

CHAPTER THIRTY-TWO

Nikki shivered as she glanced around the small dusty room. Her chin quivered, tears coursing down her cheeks. She didn't like it here. She wanted to go home.

Be brave, Nikki.

"Where's my mommy?" Nikki whispered. She was glad the pretty lady was here. She wanted to be brave, but she was scared.

Cory patted her hand as they listened to the sound of approaching footsteps. *He won't hurt you.*

Jeremiah Campbell looked at the little girl sitting hunched on the bench. So much like his little Isabella. Betty would see it. Know that God had sent her to them. A gift. That's what she was. A gift from God. The three of them would go away somewhere and live happily ever after.

"I brought you some breakfast." Jeremiah placed the plate on the bench along with a glass of milk and sat down a few feet away. He loved to just look at her.

Nikki glanced at the plate filled with bacon, eggs, and fruit. The pretty lady had said he wouldn't hurt her. And she was hungry. Picking up the plate she nibbled at the fruit. It tasted old. The bacon and eggs were salty and cold. Putting the plate on the bench she drank the glass of milk.

Jeremiah watched her face as she tasted each item. He'd done something wrong. She didn't like the food. At least she'd drunk the milk. He smiled at her, reaching out to push the hair back behind her ear.

"I'm sorry, Issie. I'm not a very good cook. Soon we'll be home and Mommy can fix you a real meal."

"My name's Nikki."

Jeremiah blinked, the smile disappearing from his face. "Of course it is."

Taking the plate and glass he left, closing and locking the door behind him.

Carl met the steely blue gaze. Gorgeous and dangerous. Gavin sure had landed himself one hell of a package. No wonder he'd been bowled over. *Why, hell, if I was thirty years younger...*

Sarah repeated her demand. "I said, tell me everything you know about the man who's got my daughter."

"Name's Jeremiah Campbell. He and his wife Betty live in New York. Their little girl, Isabella, was the first one killed. Campbell went off his rocker. Crazy as a loon. Thought the bastard was institutionalized, but I guess they let him out." Carl grimaced as pain shot through his leg again. "Dammit, woman, can't we do this at the house? Or are you gonna let me sit here and bleed to death?"

"What's he want with Nikki?" Sarah ignored the grimace, and the questions.

"Damned if I know. Didn't know he was after the girl until tonight."

"What else do you know?"

Carl lit a cigarette and puffed on it, blowing the smoke in Sarah's face. "I know if you don't get off your ass and get me out of here, you're gonna have a dead FBI agent on your hands. It's a wonder Rob ain't already got here and shot the lot of you. Damn fools."

Sarah couldn't ignore the grief that washed over her at the mention of Rob's name. Carl didn't know his partner had been shot. Or that he might already be dead. José and Juanita might be dead. So many losses. All of them her fault.

Sarah closed her eyes, taking a deep breath as a single tear slid down her face. "I'm sorry, Mr. Jackson. Matt, Jed, let's get him back to the house."

Sarah ignored the urge to run, setting a steady pace, stopping occasionally to check the tourniquet. Her efforts were met with stony glares and bursts of profanity. Relief surged through her at the sight of the three Edgewood police officers headed their way.

"Thank God," she whispered, hugging Arthur Daniels.

"We got here as quick as we could." Turning to Matt and Jed struggling under the weight of Carl's huge frame, he grinned. "Looks like you guys have got your hands full."

"Everybody's a fucking comedian," Carl grumbled.

Ignoring the comment, Daniels turned to Sarah. "What can we do to help?"

Sarah motioned him to walk a short distance away with her. Keeping her voice low she filled him in on what she knew and what had happened so far.

"What happened at the house?" Sarah asked, her heart clenching as she held her breath.

"José and Juanita are fine. Knocked out, but Doc doesn't think there's any concussion or anything." His gaze slid to Carl, and then quickly away. "The other agent died about half an hour ago."

Closing her eyes Sarah let relief and guilt wash over her. Thank God, José and Juanita were okay. She'd

221

expected the news about Rob, but somehow it hurt so much worse to have someone put it into words.

"Does he know?" Daniels nodded toward Carl.

"I didn't tell him. Thought it might be better to get him back to the doctor first. I understand they were really close."

Daniels nodded. "I'll have Bill and Sam take over for Matt and Jed. They look really bushed."

"Let Matt and Jed help. He's lost a lot of blood. Would you mind if I went on ahead?"

"Get on out of here. I can handle this."

"Thanks, Art. You might want to check the tourniquet before you leave." As an afterthought Sarah added, "Mr. Jackson's bark is a lot worse than his bite."

Daniels smiled. "I think I can handle him."

Sarah waved, taking off at a steady jog. Arthur Daniels was six foot five inches of solid muscle. There weren't many people he couldn't handle.

Millie felt the slight tremble in her legs as she approached the door. She was suddenly thankful that Clarence had the gun. And she knew without asking he knew how to use it. The door opened, just as she raised her hand to knock.

"Can I help you?"

"Why, Mr. Thomas, you shocked me. I was just getting ready to knock. I'm Millie Crawford, from the bookstore." Millie knew she was rambling, but the black eyes had shocked her. She watched as he scanned the driveway, eyes narrowing as they fell on Clarence sitting in the car.

"Can I come in?"

"Perhaps another time, Mrs. Crawford. My wife isn't

feeling well. Perhaps you," he glanced at Clarence, "and your husband, could come back tomorrow."

Millie shivered, chills running down her spine. She smiled, hoping her face didn't reveal the terror she felt inside. It had been a long time since she'd played these games.

"Husband? Oh, no, he's not my husband. I'm a widow. That's Mr. Archibald from the flower shop. He's such a dear. I hate driving, and he was kind enough to offer to drive me over."

The black eyes narrowed again.

Sticking out the cake, Millie rambled on. "I'm so sorry about Mrs. Thomas. Why, if I'd known I'd have made some homemade soup. Is there anything I can do?"

"No."

Millie smiled again. "Well then, perhaps you're right. Tomorrow would be better."

Millie shoved the plate into his hands and struggled to walk slowly to the car, feeling the dark eyes boring into her back. Every nerve in her body screamed run. Reverend Cooper had made her skin crawl, but Philip Thomas gave her the willies. Slamming the door she fastened her seatbelt. "Get us out of here, Clarence."

Starting the car, Clarence glanced at her pale face. "Where to?"

"José Minguela's. And step on it."

"There's an extra gun in the glove compartment." Joshua glanced over at Gavin McAllister.

Hitting the latch to open the glove compartment, Gavin pulled out the .38 and checked it to make sure it was fully loaded.

"Have we got a plan, or are we just going to play it by ear?"

"Thought we'd park over on Crenshaw. We'll hike in behind the mill. After that, well I guess we're playing it by ear."

Gavin nodded. He'd suspected as much. "Tell me about the mill."

Joshua shrugged. "Imagine an old barn with windows and a tobacco stripping shed attached, add a big wheel, and you've pretty much got an image of the old mill. Haven't been out there in years."

"How about inside? Is it rooms, open?"

Joshua frowned, drawing on his childhood memory. "Pretty much open on the bottom floor. Might be a small room or two. Seems I remember some rooms on the second floor, but I'd say the floors are rotted through by now."

Pulling to the side of the road, Joshua parked and turned to Gavin. "Before we go, I just want to say I'm really sorry about your brother."

Gavin nodded, trying to swallow the lump stuck in his throat. "Yeah, me too."

Joshua cleared his throat. "You know dreams as predictions sometimes take a twist or turn. They're not always exact. And then, you know, sometimes things just have to be the way they are."

"Rob said something like that. Something about he had to go. I think it was what he wanted."

Joshua clasped him on the shoulder. They were in this together. "He also wanted to protect Nikki. Let's go get her."

"Let's go."

The trail to the old mill was overgrown and Gavin

found himself fighting not only bugs, but briars that cut into his skin and clothing. He followed Joshua's lead, and stopped when he held up his hand. From their spot among the trees they could see the back of the old Mill. Joshua's recitation had been perfect. To Gavin it looked just like a dilapidated old barn that might fall in on their heads if they were stupid enough to venture inside.

Movement caught Gavin's eye and he patted Joshua on the shoulder, pointing in the direction of the man just coming around the side of the mill.

"That's Cooper," Joshua whispered, crouching lower and signaling Gavin to do the same. They watched as he dumped something on the ground and proceeded to dig. Gavin glanced at Joshua, fear taking his breath, clutching at his heart. They couldn't be too late. Not this time. Joshua shook his head and motioned for Gavin to follow him into the forest.

Joshua waited until he was sure they were out of hearing distance. He'd read the fear reflected in Gavin's eyes. "Too large to be Nikki."

"Who then?"

"Well, since that's the good Reverend Cooper, I'd say maybe Mrs. Cooper."

Gavin was horrified at the thought. "You think he killed his wife?"

Joshua shrugged. "Maybe she wasn't his wife."

"You know, you're beginning to freak me out just a little," Gavin stated. "My psychiatrist would have a field day analyzing you."

Joshua grinned, placing a toothpick between his teeth. "That's why they burned Joan of Arc. Just didn't understand. Let's go."

Gavin followed Joshua through the trees in a different direction until they reached the front of the mill.

"I figure it's gonna take him a couple of hours to dig that grave. Give me about ten minutes and then you head in. Find Nikki and get out of there. We'll deal with Cooper after we get her away from here."

Gavin nodded and glanced at his watch.

"Gavin?"

Gavin caught the keys Joshua tossed his way. "Just in case anything goes wrong. You hear shots, get Nikki, and get the hell out of here."

Gavin nodded again. "No hero shit, okay?"

Grinning, Joshua stuck the toothpick between his teeth and disappeared quietly into the trees.

CHAPTER THIRTY-THREE

"How are you doing, buddy?" Daniels reaffixed the tourniquet.

"I've been a hell of a lot better." Carl growled, fumbling for his cigarettes. "Shit," he mumbled, pulling out the empty pack.

"Bill, give the man a smoke."

"Yes, sir." Bill pulled out a pack and handed it to Carl.

"Thanks."

Daniels grinned as Carl shook out a cigarette and pocketed the remaining pack, huge charcoal eyes daring the young officer to complain. The old man was a fighter.

"You gonna tell me about my partner?" Carl struggled to raise his shaking hands to light the cigarette.

Daniels reached out and steadied his hands, waiting until the cigarette caught and Carl took a deep drag. He'd known the question was coming.

"He didn't make it."

Carl nodded, eyes misting over. "Thought so. Seen it in the sheriff's eyes."

Daniels knew there was nothing else he could say. Nothing he could do to ease the pain. Jackson was getting weaker from loss of blood, and they needed to move. Reaching out, he patted him on the shoulder. "Ready?"

Carl nodded.

"Okay, guys let's move." Daniels watched as the officers carefully lifted Carl, placing one arm over each of their shoulders. Satisfied the tourniquet was holding, he took the lead, his thoughts turning to the loss of his own partner ten years ago. Jackson would never quite be the same. Losing a partner was like losing a part of yourself. You never quite got over it.

Gavin waited the full ten minutes before he pulled off his shoes and sprinted toward the front of the old mill. Stepping inside, he let his eyes adjust to the dim light change and studied the floor. The patterns in the dust told a gruesome story. He could see where the body had fallen and then been dragged across the floor. Easing around the wall, he approached the small room in the far left corner. Small bare feet had stood there. A key hung on the wall just to the right of the door. *Not too smart, Cooper.*

Taking the key, Gavin unlocked the door and pulled it open cautiously. Nikki sat hunched against the wall with her legs pulled up underneath her. Her face was pale, but a small smile creased it when she saw him. Placing one finger to his lips, Gavin smiled, motioning her to join him at the door. Nikki nodded, crept across the creaking floor slowly until she reached Gavin, and placed her small hand in his. Gavin could feel the tremors in the small body and cursed Cooper silently. Squeezing her hand, he motioned for her to walk behind him as he slowly made his way back to the open door. He glanced right and left, making sure the area was clear. Reaching down, he picked Nikki up, allowing her to wrap her arms around his neck and bury her head in his shoulder. Taking a deep breath, he sprinted back to the trees.

"Are you okay?"

Nikki nodded, reluctant to let go of his neck. Gavin held her tight for another minute, enjoying the feelings of tenderness that filled his body. He untangled her arms, set her down, and slowly checked her to make sure she was really okay.

"The pretty lady said you'd come," Nikki whispered.

Gavin smiled at her, retying his shoes. "She always was a pretty smart lady. Her name's Cory." Gavin glanced at the mill. Still no sign of Cooper. Taking off his shirt he wrapped it around Nikki and over her head before picking her up again. "Keep your face down, honey, there's a lot of briars in here." Holding her tightly pressed against him, Gavin started in the direction Joshua had gone.

"What are you doing here?" Joshua whispered. "I told you to take her and get out of here."

"We go together," Gavin stated emphatically. "No heroes."

Joshua glanced back to where Cooper was still digging. "I'll stay and keep an eye on him. You can send reinforcements after you get Nikki out of here."

Nikki struggled in Gavin's arms and he set her down. She immediately went to Joshua, holding up her arms.

Joshua knelt down beside her. Her tiny face was grimy and smudged, the tracks of tears clearly visible. He hated Cooper. "You're going with Gavin, sweetie. Mommy's waiting for you." Joshua's voice cracked, emotion choking him.

Shaking her head, Nikki wound her arms around his neck, refusing to let go.

Joshua held her, glancing over her head. "You put her up to this?"

Gavin smiled at him and shrugged his shoulders. "Nope."

"Let's get out of here then."

Gavin grinned again as Nikki winked at him over Joshua's shoulder. Five years old and already she knew how to control men. She was going to be a real heartbreaker when she got older.

Millie gasped as Clarence pulled slowly into the driveway. She reached for Clarence's hand and gripped it, seeking comfort.

"We going in?" Clarence asked.

Millie hesitated. With this many police cars around, some type of news media would only be a short distance behind them. The sound of Juanita wailing in Spanish made up her mind for her. She was needed here.

"Yep."

Exiting the car, Millie clumped up the sidewalk, her keen eyes taking in the scene, digesting it, and not liking the conclusions she came up with.

"Sorry, ma'am, you can't go in there." Officer Pete Anderson stood guard at the door, stopping the couple on the porch steps.

"Humph," Millie snorted, eyes flashing. "That's my friends in there, sonny. And unless you're planning on arresting me, I'd suggest you step aside."

Juanita set off in another burst of Spanish, and not waiting for an answer, Millie pushed by the young officer. "Come on, Clarence."

Shrugging, Clarence grinned at the officer and followed Millie inside.

Doc Hawthorne glanced up from his patient as the door

opened. "Thank God," he muttered as Millie and Clarence closed the door behind them. Leaving Juanita wailing over José, he filled Millie in on what he knew.

"Is José okay?" Millie asked.

"Would be if I could get that damn woman to stop her blubbering long enough for me to finish stitching up his head," Doc growled.

Millie nodded and crossed the room. "Juanita, you stop all that moaning and groaning right now. We got things to do."

Juanita stopped her wailing but continued to wring her hands.

"You got coffee?"

Juanita nodded.

"Good. You come in the kitchen and help me. Got lots of people out there that could use some good coffee, and probably a good breakfast." Nodding to Doc, Millie guided Juanita toward the kitchen.

Sarah stopped at the edge of the yard to catch her breath, motioning Officer Anderson to join her.

"We need to set up roadblocks. Jackson said he took off in a car." Sarah gasped out the words.

"I'll get on it right away."

"Wait. How are they?"

"Doc says they'll be fine."

"Where's Joshua?"

"He and the other guy took off right after we got here."

Sarah frowned. "Did they say where they were going?"

"Nope, just took off."

"Set up the roadblocks. I'll see if I can raise Joshua on the radio."

Anderson nodded. "Oh, there's an old man and woman inside. Wouldn't take no for an answer."

"They're okay." Sarah almost smiled. Nobody said no to Millie.

"Damn." She cursed as she slammed the microphone in place. Tears of frustration filled her eyes. Where the hell were they?

Be strong, Sarah.

"What?" Sarah turned toward the sound, feeling the hair rise on the back of her neck. A sudden chill in the wind. Rob stood only a few feet away, his image shimmering.

Be strong.

Sarah shuddered as she watched the image dissipate. She must be losing her mind. Or was she? Did it really matter? Whatever she'd seen, heard, real or hallucination, was right. She had to be strong now for Nikki.

The front door opened and Millie came out, balancing a tray of mugs. "Lord be, child," she exclaimed, shoving the tray at Officer Anderson. "Drink that." Millie hurried over to Sarah.

Millie fought the urge to take Sarah in her arms. One look told her the young woman was hanging by a thread that might break at any moment. She opened her mouth to speak just as the radio squawked.

"Sarah, are you there?"

Jerking open the door, Sarah grabbed the microphone. "Joshua, where the hell are you? And where's Gavin?"

"We love you, too." Joshua chuckled before turning serious. "Got somebody here you might want to talk to. Say hi to your mommy, honey."

"Hi, Mommy."

Sarah's knees buckled and she sat down on the front seat, clutching the microphone. "Nikki." Her voice quivered and broke, tears coursing down her face.

"Don't cry, Mommy. I'm okay. Gavin came and got me, just like Cory said he would."

Taking the microphone, Joshua lowered his voice. "Listen, Sarah, get everybody you can out to the old mill on Elliott Pike. I'm sending Gavin back with Nikki. I'll stay here and watch Cooper until backup arrives." Joshua clicked off, his eyes meeting Gavin's over Nikki's head. "That's the way it's gonna be, partner."

Gavin nodded. He knew somebody had to stay. "No heroes?"

Joshua grinned, popping a fresh toothpick between his teeth. "I ain't the hero type."

CHAPTER THIRTY-FOUR

Sarah dropped the microphone, burying her face in her hands as sobs shook her body. Relief had finally broken the thread holding her together.

"There, there, honey. It's gonna be all right now. We got our baby back." Millie wrapped her arms around Sarah, patting her gently on the back. Her hand stilled at the sight of the five shirtless officers struggling to carry the makeshift stretcher. "Carl?" Her voice was barely a whisper, her heart racing at the sight of Carl's haggard face. Disentangling herself from Sarah, she shook her. "Pull it together, Sarah. We got work to do."

Sarah struggled, breathing deeply, pulling her sobs under control as her eyes followed the direction of Millie's stare.

Millie strode across the yard issuing orders to the officers.

"Hurry up and get him inside. You boys need to get out to the old mill and collar Cooper."

Arthur Daniels stopped mid-stride, a startled look on his face as he took in all five foot two inches of gray fury standing in front of him. He had a feeling he'd just met his match.

"Now you boys be careful," Millie urged as she led them up the front stairs and opened the door. "Don't hurt him."

Doc looked up from washing his hands, taking in the gravity of the situation in one glance. "Put him over here."

Millie stood vigilant as they transferred Carl to the cot. She rubbed Carl's face tenderly. "It's gonna be all right, Carl. Knew you'd get your damn self shot," she grumbled affectionately.

"Millie, quit blubbering all over my patient and get out of the way," Doc ordered. "Get these men some coffee."

"Me, too," Carl mumbled weakly. "And put some of that goddamn brandy in it."

"No brandy." Doc ordered, cutting away the cloth around Carl's wound.

"Shit," Carl mumbled just before passing out.

Arthur Daniels glanced from the doctor to Millie. An even match if he'd ever seen one. "Don't have time for coffee, Doc. What was that you were saying about the old mill and Cooper, Ms. Crawford?"

Sarah spoke up from the doorway. "Joshua is there keeping an eye on him. We need to get everyone out there as soon as we can."

"What about Nikki?" Daniels shrugged into his shirt.

"She's safe. Gavin's bringing her here. We can't wait."

Daniels nodded. "I'll ride with you. Let's get going."

Joshua continued to watch Cooper from his spot among the trees. The grave was almost finished. Cooper's attitude fascinated him. The man was humming and smiling as he dug. "You'd think the son-of-a-bitch was planting flowers instead of a body," Joshua muttered to himself.

Finished, Jeremiah stood, admiring his handiwork, as he wiped the sweat from his face. He glanced at the bag, a small stirring of guilt. He shouldn't have killed her. Shaking his head, he quelled the thoughts. Why should he feel guilty? He wasn't crazy. Issie was waiting for him, and soon they'd be going home. She was just a whore he'd picked up off the streets. Probably would have been dead in a few months anyway. This was just a nightmare. The doctors had said he'd have nightmares. All he had to do was get home. Then everything would be okay. Issie was alive. He'd told them she wasn't dead.

He dragged the body to the open hole and pushed it in. A song. That's what was needed. Smiling, Jeremiah gripped the shovel and started refilling the grave. "Amazing grace, how sweet the sound, that saved a wretch like me. I once was lost, but now am found, was blind but now I see."

Joshua shuddered as the strong clear voice carried through the forest. Nuts. The guy was totally nuts. Shifting for a comfortable position, he glanced behind him. They should have been here by now. The forest became deathly quiet as the singing stopped.

"Oh, hell," Joshua muttered as he watched Cooper drop the shovel and head around the side of the mill. He couldn't wait any longer. Slashing and darting through the trees, he made his way around to the front of the mill just as Cooper entered the open door. Wiping the sweat from his eyes, he crouched waiting as the seconds ticked by.

I'm going there to meet my mother, I'm going there no more to roam, I'm only going over Jordan...

The song played softly inside Joshua's head as he watched the doorway.

I'm only going over home.

"Oh, crap," Joshua muttered as he realized what the song meant. He rushed for the open doorway.

* * *

"How is he?" Millie bent over the motionless form lying on the old cot.

"Lost a lot of blood." Doc met Millie's concerned gaze, his own eyes frank, honest. Never was much for lying to people. "We got to get him to a hospital quick."

Millie nodded, eyes misting again as she walked to the front door. Clarence joined her there, placing one arm around her shoulders. "He should have been here by now," Millie whispered, leaning into the comfort of Clarence's shoulder. Her body tensed at the sound of the approaching helicopter. "It's about time." She muttered. "Come on, Clarence."

They stood on the front porch, hands locked tightly together, as they watched the helicopter slowly descend in the front yard.

"Took your damn time," Millie yelled over the sound of the whirring blades as the huge figure climbed down from the passenger seat.

Chief Walsh stopped, his face breaking into a wide grin. "Millie, you sure are a sight for sore eyes." Striding quickly up the steps he captured her in a bear hug before sticking a hand out to Clarence. "Robert Walsh."

"Junior." Millie sniffled, wiping away a tear. "We gotta get Clarence to a hospital."

Walsh nodded, his face lined with worry. "How is he?"

"Doc says he's lost too much blood," Millie answered, leading the way inside.

Robert Walsh, Jr., forgot he was the Chief of the FBI as he looked down at the old man who had started it all for him. He'd take a bullet for any of his guys, but this one, this one was really dear to his heart. Kneeling beside the cot, he lowered his head in silent prayer.

"Sooner we move him the better," Doc stated flatly. Prayer was good, but he wanted to get his patient on the way to the hospital.

"Let's get him to the helicopter. We'll fly him to Richmond."

"Edgewood's closer. We'll go there," Doc stated, reloading his medical bag.

Walsh didn't bother arguing. Something in the doctor's eyes told him he'd lose.

Sarah shivered as the anguished scream seemed to come from all directions.

"Shit," Daniels muttered, pushing through the briars. "Move it guys!"

The single gunshot stirred fear in their hearts. Ignoring the branches and briars, they raced the remaining distance to the mill.

Sarah stopped them at the edge of the forest, surveying the clearing around the mill. "Fan out. Move in slow."

Sarah was once again seized by gut-wrenching guilt as looked the freshly disturbed ground. Another grave. Another death she was responsible for.

"I'm going in." She stood up, and before Arthur could stop her, darted across the open space behind the mill.

"Dammit. Work your way around, but hold your position." Daniels issued orders, as he stood up and sprinted after Sarah.

Catching up with Sarah, he stopped her, motioning for her to take one side and he'd take the other. They arrived at the open doorway together.

Taking a deep breath, Sarah glanced at Daniels and

nodded. The two entered the dim interior, guns extended, glancing around the huge room for places to hide.

"Joshua," Sarah called out, eyes watchful for signs of any threat.

"In here, Sarah."

Joshua sat on the far bench, gazing at the remains of Jeremiah Campbell.

"I tried to stop him. Said he couldn't take it any more. Couldn't stand to see her body again. He thought Nikki was his little girl."

Holstering his gun, Daniels nodded to Sarah. "I'll go get the guys, start searching, and call it in."

Sarah sat down next to Joshua, placing her hand over his as she tried to summon up the hate she'd felt for Cooper. All she felt was immense relief. She was glad he was dead. "It's over, Joshua."

Joshua squeezed her hand, his grip tightening as the laughter flowed around him. *Too late, Joshua. You're too late.*

"Now, Millie, are you ready to go?" The chief was pacing back and forth. He'd insisted on coming to her house with her when she left José's.

"Wondered why you didn't go with Carl." Millie huffed around the kitchen, clearing cups and dishes.

"The capture of Campbell is going to be big news, Millie. My people will be here in about four hours. The media will be here long before that. I'm going back, and you're going with me."

Millie turned, wringing the dishrag in her hands. "Ain't going without Clarence."

Walsh looked the older man over. He'd stayed in the

background, but never too far, close enough to protect Millie if the need arose.

"All right."

Millie glanced at Clarence, who nodded approval.

"Gotta pack some clothes. Say some goodbyes." Millie sniffed, then blew her nose loudly.

Walsh stood up and extended his hand to Clarence. "Give you an hour to pack. No goodbyes."

Clarence returned the strong grip and placed his arm around Millie as they watched the chief drive away. He understood perfectly what Walsh was saying. When they left Glade Springs, Millie Crawford and Clarence Archibald would cease to exist. It didn't matter to Clarence. He'd be home wherever Millie was.

"Come on, honey. We'll take the Millicent."

Millie pulled away from him. "You making fun of me?"

Clarence laughed. "Just wait 'til you see her. A real beauty."

Clarence ushered her out of the house and down to the garage attached to the flower shop. He opened the door and stepped aside, his face beaming as Millie gasped.

"Why, Clarence, it's a 1947 Cadillac."

"Told you she was a beauty!"

Millie ran her hand over the creamy white exterior, gold trim. Clarence was right; it was a thing of rare beauty.

"But, Clarence, these things weigh 18 tons. We could walk to Richmond faster."

Clarence chuckled. "Can't judge a book by its cover, Millie. Got a 396 high performance engine with a 400 turbo transmission in this baby. Give her an open road and she'll fly."

Millie smiled, still running her hand over the smooth surface. "She's a real classic."

"Yep." Clarence moved in, putting his arm around her. "Classics are hard to find today. When I find one, I tend to hold onto it."

Millie flushed, reaching up to kiss him. "We better get started packing. Junior only gave us an hour."

"Junior will have to wait. We're going to Edgewood. Got another old classic there we need to check on."

Millie clapped her hands in pure joy. "Clarence Archibald will you marry me?"

Clarence flushed, his eyes glowing like stars, "I thought you'd never ask."

CHAPTER THIRTY-FIVE

Sarah dangled her feet, wrapping her arms tighter around Nikki as Chief Walsh finished talking. Gavin sat quietly beside her in the swing.

"I promised Millie I'd tell you she was okay. Said you'd understand."

Sarah nodded, her eyes misting. She was going to miss Millie and Clarence. She was going to miss Glade Springs and the life she'd built here. She hated uprooting Nikki, but the media had done a thorough job of exposing both of them. If Williams got out of prison, he'd know right where to find them. She couldn't take that chance.

Gavin cleared his throat. "It's still hard to believe that Campbell killed his own child and then killed the others to cover it."

"Yeah, he had us fooled, too. We found the box of pink cards in the trunk of his car, along with several items that belonged to the children, as well as Jacob and Sheila Cooper's belongings."

Standing up, Walsh held his hand out to Sarah. "Sheriff, I wish we'd met under better circumstances."

Shifting Nikki to her hip, Sarah stood and shook his hand. "Me, too."

"Gavin, I'll see you tomorrow?"

Gavin stood up, shaking the chief's hand. "I'll be there.

I've got a message for Carl."

Walsh smiled. "He's probably cursing the nurses about now. If I don't get back, he'll probably take off, find Millie, and the two of them will cook up some scheme to get back here."

Gavin and Sarah stood silently watching the chief drive away. There were too many unspoken words between them. And yet Sarah couldn't bring herself to ask the question haunting her, breaking her heart. Was he coming back?

Gavin took Nikki from Sarah's arms and sat her down. "Why don't you go pick Mommy some flowers?"

"You won't tell her?"

"I promised." Gavin tousled the strawberry curls.

Sarah frowned, watching the interplay between the two before Nikki bounded off the steps in search of flowers.

"Tell me what?"

"I promised." Gavin smiled at her. "Even crossed my heart." He gazed into the blue eyes, violet in the early morning light.

"Gavin, I'm so sorry about Rob."

His smile surprised her. "He's where he wants to be, Sarah. He's where he belongs."

Sarah thought about the pretty young brunette who had saved her life as well as Nikki's.

"Listen," Gavin was talking again, his tone serious, "one of the agents told me about a small town in Wyoming that's looking for a sheriff. I stopped there once. Quiet peaceful town, good people. Perfect for raising children."

Sarah nodded, looking away from him to hide the pain, the tears threatening to fall. She swallowed hard.

"It has an extra bonus, too."

"Bonus?"

"You'll have a couple of friends there."

Millie. She'd have Millie.

Gavin touched her then. His hand gently caressed her face, turning it toward him, eyes searching. "You'll need a name change. I thought maybe you'd consider McAllister."

The ice around her heart melted, flowing like warm butter, smoothing away the years of pain and loneliness. Gavin pulled her into his arms, lips gently capturing hers for a kiss, a promise, the future.

"You told!"

Gavin felt the slight tug on his pants leg, and looked down at the tiny figure scowling up at him. She would definitely keep him in line.

"I didn't."

"Tell me what, sweetheart?"

The scowl turned to a mischievous grin, as Nikki reached up to take Gavin's hand.

"We're going to write stories about a beautiful ballerina who travels all over the world solving crimes."

Sarah raised an eyebrow.

"Children's books. No more secrets." Gavin looked at her, seeking her approval. "Cross my heart."

Sarah took a deep breath, unable to believe what she was hearing.

"You haven't answered my question." Gavin held his breath, searching her face.

"Say yes, Mommy. I'm hungry." Nikki tugged on their hands.

Sarah laughed, reaching down to hug her daughter. "Yes."

"It's about fucking time somebody got here." Carl

raised himself up in the bed.

"You watch your language, old man, or I'll have Clarence put another knot on your head." Millie smiled fondly at him as she set the vase of flowers on the bedside table.

"Don't need no damn flowers. Where the hell are my cigarettes?"

"Now, Carl, you know you can't smoke in the hospital. You just settle down and we'll have a nice long chat." Millie plumped his pillows, fussed around, straightening the covers on the bed. Curiosity and weakness got the better of him.

"All right. Quit your damn fussing and tell me what happened. Won't nobody tell me nothing in here. Chief was supposed to be here last night. Called to say he'd run into some kind of problem."

Millie grinned and sat down on the edge of the bed, motioning Clarence to take the seat. She knew exactly what problem Walsh was talking about. Still, she knew enough of the story to calm Clarence down.

"Well, after you were shot, Gavin and Joshua tracked Cooper–I mean Campbell–to the old mill and rescued Nikki. Didn't surprise me at all he turned out to be a killer. Never did trust that man."

"Yeah, go on."

"Campbell killed himself. End of story."

"What about Williams?" Carl sat up straighter.

"Who?" Millie asked, a perplexed look on her face.

"Todd Williams, the Mother's Day killer. Sarah's old partner. What happened to him?"

"Oh, he's still in prison. Wasn't him. They found the pink cards in the trunk of Campbell's car."

"Shit," Carl cursed, swinging his legs over the side of

the bed amidst Millie's protests. "Where's my clothes?"

"Carl Jackson, you lay down. You ain't in no shape to go nowhere."

Carl glanced at Clarence, his eyes pleading for understanding, as he jerked the I.V. out of his arm. "Williams ain't in prison. He's in Glade Springs. And if somebody don't get me my goddamn clothes, I'm gonna walk out of here bare assed."

"Millie, go outside, find a wheelchair." Clarence headed for the closet and pulled out Carl's clothes.

"What?" Millie gasped.

"We need a wheelchair, Millie." Clarence's voice was quiet, but his tone commanded action.

"Humph," she muttered, heading for the door. "Damned old fools."

"We better make this quick," Clarence stated, pulling underwear and socks from the drawer.

Carl nodded, pulling on his shorts and socks, beads of sweat popping out on his forehead from the effort. "Help me stand up." Hands shaking, Carl took Clarence's hand, pulling himself up, face set against the pain he knew was about to come.

Clarence helped Carl to his feet and pulled up his slacks before lowering him down to the bed, and reaching for his shirt.

"How come you didn't ask?" Carl gasped, pain shooting through his leg.

"Served my country for thirty years. Judge a man by what I see, not what he says," Clarence stated, pulling the shirt up over Carl's shoulders and buttoning it. It wasn't the total truth, but it was enough to satisfy Carl.

"You want the jacket?"

Carl shook his head.

Nodding, Clarence knelt down and slipped the shoes on Carl's feet. "You won't be able to walk very far on that leg. All we've got for pain is aspirin."

"Don't matter," Carl grunted. "I been in pain before."

Clarence nodded. He'd seen the scars as he dressed him. Opening the door slowly, he saw Millie hurrying down the hallway pushing a wheelchair. Taking the chair, he kissed her fondly on the cheek, and wheeled the chair over to the bed. "Give me a hand, Millie."

Millie reached out to place one of Carl's arms around her shoulder as Clarence took the other. "Be careful with him," she whispered as they shifted him from the bed to the chair.

"Millie, you bring him downstairs through the emergency exit. I'll get the car. If anybody stops you, tell them you're taking him outside for a smoke." Clarence reached into his pocket and tossed Carl a pack of cigarettes. "Got a whole carton in the car."

Carl grinned, placing the pack in his shirt pocket. "You heard the man, Millie. What are you waiting for?"

Sarah watched as Gavin slammed the lid of the trunk and then walked towards her. She wished she were going with him. There was just so little time.

"I'll be back in three days. Can you finish up here by then?"

Wrapping her arms around his neck, she kissed him, passion igniting between them. "I'll be ready," she whispered, her mind checking off all that had to be done. The wedding, packing, saying good-bye to their friends. Making Joshua sheriff.

"He'll make a good sheriff, Sarah."

Sarah laughed, her blue eyes glowing with love. "He's been sitting in my chair for a long time anyway. Might as well make it official."

"I've got to go."

"I know. Take my cell phone. That way, if you have any trouble, you can call." Sarah kissed him again, unashamed of her passion, expressing her love. Stepping back, she smiled, "Or if you miss me, you can call."

Gavin took the phone, his brown eyes dark with desire. "I'll be calling."

CHAPTER THIRTY-SIX

Sarah pinned the sheriff's badge on Joshua, grinning up at him. "You knew it all along, didn't you?"

Joshua grinned, sticking the toothpick between his teeth, a sign he wasn't nearly as comfortable as he was pretending. "Had a feeling. Mary's the one been biting at the bit to get in here and start decorating." He placed his arm lovingly around his wife, pulling her close.

"Are you sure about this, Sarah?"

Sarah nodded. "I've never been more sure of anything in my whole life." She hugged Mary and stuck out her hand. "Sheriff?"

"Dammit." Joshua reached out and pulled her in for a hug, his eyes misting. "I'm gonna miss you. What about tonight? You and Nikki want to join us for dinner?"

"No, I think we'll just spend the evening alone. Say good-bye to the house."

"We are getting an invite to the wedding, right?" Mary wiped the tears from her eyes.

"I'll have it served on you."

"Come on you two, before we all start blubbering. We'll walk you to the car."

"No, stay here. Talk about redecorating. I want to say good-bye to Ella Mae before I leave."

Joshua nodded. He knew good-bye wasn't exactly what

Sarah was going to say.

Closing the door, Sarah stood for a moment, eyes closed. This place was as much a home as any place she'd been in her life. Leaving it was like leaving a loved parent for the first time. She thought of Gavin, the way he looked at her, the way he loved Nikki as if she were his own child. She'd been lucky. She wasn't going to waste another minute on regret.

"Ella Mae?" Sarah reached out her hand to steady the young woman who jumped at the sound of her voice. "Are you okay?"

"Yes, ma'am," Ella Mae answered turning back to the table she'd been vigorously scrubbing.

Taking her by the shoulders, Sarah gently turned her around. "There's something you need to hear. Look at me." Sarah waited patiently as Ella Mae wrung the cleaning cloth between her hands, finally lifting the huge doe eyes to look at her.

"You are a lovely person."

"No, I'm not," Ella Mae whispered, looking down at the floor. "I'm ugly."

Sarah lifted her head gently. "I was once you Ella Mae. Scared of everyone and everything. I thought I was ugly, too. We're all beautiful. And you deserve to be treated that way."

Ella Mae shifted beneath Sarah's steady gaze.

"Do you understand what I'm saying?"

Nodding, Ella Mae continued to wring the cloth, eyes fixated on the tips of her shoes.

"He hurts you, doesn't he?"

Ella Mae nodded, eyes filling with tears.

"The next time he hurts you, I want you to promise me

you'll tell Joshua. Okay?"

He'll kill him.

Ella Mae nodded, knowing she'd never do it.

Sarah reached out and hugged her, surprised at the strength in the arms that clung to her. "He can only hurt you if you let him. Don't let him do it any more."

Wiping her nose on the back of her hand, Ella Mae sniffled. "Thank you."

"You take care of yourself." Sarah placed her keys to the office on the desk and stepped out into the evening breeze. She breathed deeply. Everything smelled fresh. New. Just like the life she was beginning. Smiling, she hurried to the Explorer. She could hardly wait to begin.

Gavin groaned as consciousness slowly returned. Struggling, he opened his eyes, groaning again as pain sliced through his head. He tried to remember, but could get no further than the tree in the road. He'd stopped to remove the tree, then everything went black. Opening his eyes again, slower this time, he glanced around and assessed his situation. He was in some kind of basement. He'd been strapped into a chair, hands tied tightly behind his back. Twisting, he struggled against the ropes, only to be overcome with dizziness and nausea. Slumping forward, he breathed slowly, controlling the urge to vomit by sheer will. He wasn't gagged, meaning there was no one to hear him even if he had the energy to cry out. *Assessment–you're in deep shit, McAllister.*

Gavin could hear the sound of footsteps overhead, pacing back and forth. His situation was grave, but he had a feeling it was all downhill from here. Light filtered down the steps, the footsteps descended. Closing his eyes against the light, Gavin bowed his head again. He needed to buy time, think.

Pain sliced through his head, a groan escaping, his hair pulling free from the scalp, as his head was jerked up roughly.

"Don't play games with me, McAllister. I know you're awake."

Breathing deeply, Gavin waited for the dizzy spell to subside. "Well, you've got the advantage on me, then," Gavin spat out. If he was going to die, then he was going quick. "Who the hell are you?"

The laugh chilled the air; a cold, wet chill that sank into Gavin's bones. He knew that laugh.

"What say we give Sarah a call, see just how much she loves you?"

The rage that had simmered beneath the surface boiled over. Gavin fought the ropes, his eyes fierce, piercing, filled with hate. "You touch her and I'll kill you."

Laughter filled the basement, echoing off the walls. "Too late, McAllister. You're too late."

Gavin shouted at the silhouette retreating up the steps. "I'll kill you! You hear me?"

Clarence glanced in the rearview mirror, checking on Carl. Millie would never forgive him if anything happened to Carl. Thirty years of military service had given him a sixth sense. Something about the situation with Campbell/Cooper had smelled fishy. Something not quite right. Walsh was going to have his head for taking off with Millie. Might even make it impossible for him to go with her. He knew little about the witness protection system, only that people disappeared never to be heard from again.

Glancing at Millie out of the corner of his eye, he knew he'd never accept that. Life was too short and beauty too rare. He'd fight the whole damn Bureau if he had to.

Carl lit another cigarette, smiling as Millie "humphed," giving him a mutinous glare. He wasn't really concerned that she was pissed at him. But poor old Clarence looked miserable. The man was sharp for his age. Would have made a hell of an agent. Clarence fingered the small bump.

Carried one hell of a wallop too. Carl knew they were all worried about Gavin and Sarah. But dammit, he liked the old codger, and a couple of minutes couldn't hurt nothing. Desperate situations called for desperate measures. They'd been driving for over an hour, the only sound in the car the occasional flicking of his lighter. Tossing the cigarette out the window, Carl groaned loudly and slumped over in the seat.

"Clarence, honey, stop the car. Something's wrong with Carl."

Carl coughed to cover the snicker. He continued to groan loudly as Clarence pulled the car to the side of the road and parked. In seconds the two had jerked open the back doors and were hunched over him.

"Carl, honey, what's wrong?" Millie touched his face gently, her voice quivering.

Grabbing an arm of each he pulled himself up in the seat, the strength in his hands belying the act of frailty. "It's time the two of you kissed and made up, that's what's wrong. Tired of sitting in this goddamn car, with nothing to do but watch you sulk."

Millie's face flushed, and she struggled to pull her arm free.

"We'll just sit right here until I bleed to death and that

sick pervert kills Sarah and Nikki."

Concern flashed in Millie's eyes as she glanced at Carl's wounded leg. Blood was seeping through.

"Damned old fool. I told you."

"Yeah, yeah, you told me. Now kiss him so we can get out of here. Ain't got time for this foolishness."

Reaching across Carl, Millie planted a sound kiss on Clarence's lips. "Can we go now?"

"Just waiting for you to lovebirds to quit smooching." Carl winked at Clarence as the two climbed back in the car.

Clarence glanced in the rearview mirror. The groaning wasn't all an act. Clarence was growing weaker. They needed to get him back to the hospital and the sooner the better. The silence broken, Clarence voiced the questions that had been bugging him since they'd left the hospital.

"Chief Walsh said Williams was still in prison. What makes you think he's in Glade Springs?"

Carl flushed, lowering his gaze. "Didn't put it in the report. Rob and I visited Williams in prison. Son-of-a-bitch had his brother take his place. Even had his fingerprints grafted on the brother's fingers. Somehow the bastard found Corrine Larson, followed her here and found Sarah and Nikki. Not sure how Campbell got in the picture. Might have gone to Cory, when he felt the police weren't doing enough. Got her to looking. Followed her out here, too. Went crazy as a fucking loon after his daughter was killed. Must have seen Nikki and thought she was Isabella."

Millie nodded. It made more sense that way.

"But where could Williams be? I mean other than the Coopers, everybody else has been in Glade Springs for years."

"What about the Thomases?" Clarence reminded her.

Millie's face paled. "Oh, God, that poor girl. I'll bet he killed her."

"Can't this bag of bolts go any faster?"

Millie chuckled. "You ain't seen nothing, Carl. Hit it Clarence."

Clarence grinned, pressing the gas pedal to the floor. Yep, he'd found himself a real classic this time.

Sarah shut the lid on the box and then peeked in at Nikki. It had been a long day, but she'd accomplished at least a third of what needed to be done. Joshua was sworn in as sheriff, and most of the packing was done. Now she could concentrate on the wedding. She raced the last few steps down the stairs as the phone rang. Glancing at the caller I.D., she smiled. Gavin.

"Miss me already?" She laughed into the receiver.

"Hello, Sarah."

Sarah felt her hands begin to tremble, her body shake. It couldn't be.

"Miss me?"

"What have you done to Gavin?"

He laughed that cruel, sick laugh she remembered. "You always were a whore."

"What do you want, Todd?"

"Why, I want you Sarah. That's what I've always wanted. I want my family."

"We're not your family," Sarah spat out vehemently.

"Don't fuck with me! You want to see McAllister alive, you'll meet me at the Sampson place. And, Sarah, bring the brat."

"Nooo!" The sound of the dial tone echoed in the room as she stood trembling, the phone pressed against her lips.

CHAPTER THIRTY-SEVEN

Sarah hung up the phone, leaning her head against the cool surface of the kitchen wall. Flashes of lightning illuminated the shadows. Thunder rolled across the sky. An angry God.

Fitting, Sarah thought. The heavy leaden sky had to choose this moment to open up. If she went outside, would God's tears mix with her own? Would the rain wash her clean? "Damn you, Todd Williams."

"Mommy, we have to go."

Nikki stood at the foot of the stairs, her favorite teddy bear clutched to her chest. Her powder blue eyes huge in the tiny face.

"I know." Sarah turned away, gazing into the night. Rain slashed at the window. "Get dressed, sweetheart. Find your raincoat and galoshes." Simple things. Normal things.

"No, Mommy. We have to go get Gavin."

"We can't." Sarah's voice caught on a sob. Dear God, what could she do? If they went, they all died. If she didn't, could she live with herself? Could she ever look into Nikki's eyes again?

"Please, Mommy!"

Sarah reached for her daughter, holding her close. How could she make her understand?

"Sweetheart, Gavin wouldn't want us to do that. He'd

want us to go away, somewhere safe."

Nikki struggled against her, tiny arms flailing. "No, no, no! We have to go get Gavin, Mommy. We have to. We have to." Sobs shook the tiny body. Hands clutched into fists she pounded at Sarah's chest. "We have to."

Pulling her closer, Sarah stroked the strawberry curls, her mind in torment as she fought back the tears, swallowed her own sobs. Gavin would want her to leave. Protect Nikki. What was it Millie had said? The past always catches up with you, and if you're going to lose either way, then you might as well stay and face the music. If she left here now, like this, Nikki would never be the same. She would never be the same. What difference did it make if they were alive? They'd both be dead inside.

"All right, sweetheart," Sarah whispered, "go get dressed, and we'll go get Gavin."

Sarah waited until she was sure Nikki was safely upstairs. Picking up the phone, she dialed the number for the cell phone, waiting for the tale-tale click that would tell her he'd pressed the talk button. She could see him, standing there, a smug smile plastered to his face, listening to the rings.

Click.

"We're on our way."

"I'll see you tomorrow, Thomas." Joshua called out as he left the Sheriff's office. Ella Mae was just backing out and he waved, calling a quick "Good night."

Shops were closing along Main Street, and Joshua pulled up in front of the flower shop, looking across at Millie's bookstore. The town seemed lonely. Joshua found himself torn between happiness for Sarah and Nikki and sadness at the loss of his friends. He glanced down at the sheriff's badge pinned to his chest. He'd thought this was what he wanted. What he really wanted was his town back the way it was before Campbell came here and tore everything apart.

Dizziness hit him in waves as he started to turn the key.

Many a tear has to fall, but it's all in the game...in the game...in the game...

Time stood still as Joshua found himself back inside the mill, gun extended, eyes fixed on Campbell hunched against the wall, holding the gun to his head.

Cooper, don't! Joshua screamed, stepping into the small room. *Put down the gun. Let's talk.*

Campbell shook his head. *Name's not Cooper. It's Campbell. Jeremiah Campbell. He killed her again. Killed my little girl.*

She isn't dead. Nikki's okay.

Joshua felt the hair at the nape of his neck stand on edge as he looked into Campbell's sightless eyes. He wasn't seeing Joshua standing before him. His eyes were seeing something else. Some terror only he could see.

I killed them, you know. The Coopers. Good people. He's in my head. Makes me do things. Makes me kill people.

Don't do it, Campbell. Put the gun down. We can talk about this. Just you and me.

Joshua would never forget the smile that crossed Campbell's face. Relief, understanding, conviction.

He says I have to kill you.

Don't do it. Don't listen to him.

He's in my fucking head.

Memory of the anguished scream still sent shivers

down Joshua's spine. The sound of the gun going off in the small room. The splattering of blood, flying through the air in slow motion.

Joshua shook his head, clearing the vision. What was it Gavin had said?

I don't know if I'm connecting with the killer or the victim. It's like the son-of-a-bitch is inside my head, playing games.

Ella Mae. *He likes to play games. Sometimes he gets rough.*

"Oh, God." Joshua slammed his fist against the steering wheel and grabbed for the cell phone, dialing Sarah's number. "Answer the phone, Sarah. Please, answer the goddamn phone."

Laughter echoed in the cab. *Too late, Joshua. You're too late.*

Sarah parked the car and cut the engine. A curtain fluttered back into place. The bastard was watching them. There were no vehicles in the drive, and Sarah wondered where Ella Mae was. Surely she couldn't be part of this.

"Mommy?"

Sarah smiled bravely at Nikki. "It's okay, sweetheart. I need you to listen to me carefully, though, okay?"

Nikki nodded, her face pale, eyes huge.

"If you get a chance to run, you take it. Don't look back and don't worry. I'll find you. I promise."

Nikki nodded again, her bottom lip quivering.

Taking a deep breath, Sarah opened the door and stepped out. The door to the house slowly creaked open. "Let's go, sweetheart." Sarah picked Nikki up, needing to hold her close. There was no turning back now. She had reached the eleventh hour.

Sarah stopped on the first step, the sound of an approaching car creating a sense of hope. She turned as Ella Mae parked and stepped from her car, smiling nervously.

"Why, Sheriff, I mean...what are you doing here?"

"You'll have to ask your husband," Sarah answered, noting the paling of Ella Mae's features. The way her eyes darkened, as she glanced toward the house, then back to Sarah and Nikki.

Closing her eyes, Sarah prayed silently and climbed the steps. She could see nothing inside the house. Darkness. Where had the rain gone? The lightning? If she'd ever needed God, she needed him now.

Sarah found herself propelled forward, Nikki jerked from her arms.

"Mommy!"

Sarah righted herself, her eyes meeting the cold black gaze of Todd Williams. "Leave her alone," she begged, arms reaching for Nikki.

He laughed. "Oh, I will. At least until I'm finished with you." Glancing out the door he yelled, "Ella Mae, get you ass in here!"

Never taking her eyes off Williams, Sarah listened to the sound of Ella Mae's scurrying footsteps.

"Philip, what's going on? What's the sheriff doing here?"

The slap was quick, vicious. "What have I told you about questioning me? Now shut up and take the kid upstairs. Lock her in the bedroom and join us in the basement." He thrust Nikki into Ella Mae's arms.

Seeing her opportunity, Sarah took it. She rushed Williams, her only hope to catch him off guard. She'd forgotten. Forgotten those damn eyes in the back of his head. How quick he could move. The fist caught her on the left temple, spinning her around.

"Mommy!" Nikki squirmed in Ella Mae's arms.

Williams grabbed Sarah by the arm, his smile cruel, fingers digging in. "See, Sarah, you're upsetting the kid." He looked at Ella Mae, his eyes fierce, deadly. "I told you to take her upstairs."

Ella Mae scurried up the stairs, shushing Nikki.

Sarah could taste blood, her head still spinning. Fear gripped her, but she wasn't going to show it. Meeting his gaze, she spit in his face.

Williams laughed, wiping the spittle from his face. "Still the same old Sarah."

Grasping her hair, he pulled her up and pushed her toward the stairs. "Let's go see your lover."

Sarah walked in front of him, down the stairs into the dimly lit basement. She glanced around the room, her mind racing. The room was bare except for a cot along one wall and two chairs in the center. Her eyes filled with tears as she spotted Gavin. He sat slumped in the chair, face swollen, bloody.

Williams pushed her, laughing as she fell down the last three steps, landing hard, scraping her hands on the concrete floor.

"Crawl to him, Sarah. I want to see you crawl."

Sarah crawled the remaining distance between her and Gavin. She tried to smile, convey her love. At least if they were going to die, they would die together.

Sarah felt Williams' hands in her hair again. Biting her lip against the pain, she stifled a scream, as he jerked her up pushing her into the second chair.

"What should I do first, Sarah? Rape you? Or should I tie you up and let you watch while I rape the kid?"

Rage boiled inside Sarah. She wanted to claw his eyes out. Beat him until there was nothing left but bloody pulp. Torture him like he'd tortured her for the past six years.

"Do whatever you want," she spat at him.

He turned away from her as Ella Mae descended the stairs. "Good." Tossing the rope he'd been holding to Ella Mae, he laughed again. "Tie her up."

"Philip, what are you going to do?" Ella Mae whimpered.

He slapped her hard, the sound echoing in the room. "See what you've reduced me to, Sarah? A mousy little piece of shit for a wife."

He drew back his hand to hit her again, but Ella Mae shied away from him, taking the rope and approaching Sarah.

"Tie her tight," he ordered, taking a long thin blade from the scabbard on his waist.

Grabbing Gavin by the hair, he pulled his head back, exposing the neck. His black eyes focused on Sarah's face, as he laid the blade against Gavin's throat. "You're gonna scream for me, aren't you, sweetheart?"

CHAPTER THIRTY-EIGHT

Nikki.

Nikki glanced away from the door she'd been tugging and kicking on. Cory stood in the shadows, motioning to the window.

"The bad man?" Nikki whispered, her voice quivering.

Cory nodded. *It's time to hide.*

Nikki didn't want to hide. She wanted to find her Mommy and Gavin. Mommy's radio was in the truck. She could call for help. Pushing aside the curtains, she pushed upward on the window. It wouldn't budge.

"I can't do it!" she cried.

Yes, you can. Push harder.

Nikki's face screwed up in concentration as she studied the window. Mommy always locked their windows. Reaching up as far as she could on tiptoes, she felt along the top of the window, finding the clasp and turning it. *"Shew,"* she breathed out hard and pushed again. She felt the window move. She pushed again and again until the window was wide open. She glanced down at the ground. It was a long way off.

You'll have to jump to the tree and climb down.

Nikki glanced at the tree growing a few feet away, to the right of the window.

"I wish I was a ghost like you; then I could just go

through the walls."

Cory smiled, her eyes sad as she shook her head. *It's not your time.*

"It wasn't your time either," Nikki cried. "He did it, didn't he? Just like he's going to kill Mommy and Gavin." Her tiny face screwed up, tears flowing from her eyes.

It's time to go. Time to hide.

Nikki wiped the tears from her face. She climbed up on the windowsill, steadying herself. She could do this. She had to. Taking a deep breath, she jumped for the huge branch a few feet away. Her fingers clutched and held. Moving slowly, she swung herself up onto the branch and quickly climbed down. Cory was waiting for her at the bottom of the tree.

Come on. Cory motioned for Nikki to follow and headed toward the woods.

Nikki shook her head. "I have to help Mommy and Gavin." Not waiting for an answer, Nikki raced around the house, headed for the car. She darted quick looks toward the house as she opened the car door slowly, quietly closing it behind her. Mommy had never let her use the radio before, but she'd watched her. Taking the microphone, she hit the button on the left panel and whispered, "Help! Mommy needs help."

Joshua heard the crackle of the radio, the quivering whisper, and grabbed the microphone.

"Nikki, honey, is that you?"

"Mommy and Gavin need help."

Joshua tried to steady his voice, calm the fear that gripped him. "It's gonna be okay, honey. Tell me where you are."

"Ella Mae's."

"Nikki, honey, listen to me. I want you to hide. I'm on my way, sweetheart."

"The bad man's here."

The fear turned to terror. "I know, sweetie. But I'm the sheriff, remember. The sheriff always puts the bad men away."

Nikki dropped the microphone and crawled behind the seats, hunching down on the floorboard. She shivered at the night sounds, the darkness. What if Joshua was too late? Her fingers touched a holster, and Nikki pulled out the small .22 pistol her mother kept hidden for emergencies. Mommy had told her she could never touch the guns. That was a grown up thing, and guns were only used when lives were in danger. The bad man had killed Cory. He probably killed Marisa, too. Now he was going to kill Mommy and Gavin. She'd be all alone. Nikki didn't want to be all alone. Taking the gun, she climbed out of the car and started toward the house.

"Thomas, get everybody you can out to the old Sampson place. Sarah's in trouble." Joshua closed the cell phone, maneuvering another sharp curve. He cursed himself for missing the signs. It had been there right in front of him all the time.

"Damn." Joshua swerved to miss the 1947 Cadillac headed straight at him. The Jeep careened off the road, plowing into a tree.

"Oh, God, Clarence, that's Joshua," Millie screamed as Clarence slammed on the brakes, the car skidding into a spin. Clarence fought the wheel, letting off the brake and allowing the car to right itself. He tapped the brakes lightly as the car turned 180 degrees, before coming to a stop.

Clarence pushed open the car door and ran to the steaming truck. He jerked its door open, Millie right at his heels.

"Joshua, are you all right?"

Joshua stared at them blankly, blood oozing from the knot swelling on his forehead. "What the hell are you doing here?"

"No time," Clarence stated, pulling him out of the truck.

"Sarah's in trouble," Millie added, grabbing one arm and helping Clarence load him in the back seat next to Carl.

Clarence climbed into the driver's seat and started the engine. He whipped the car around.

"You're going the wrong way," Joshua yelled.

Slamming on the brakes, Clarence stopped the car.

"He's already got them. Old Sampson place."

Clarence nodded, not bothering to ask questions. He spun the car around again, and floored it.

Joshua glanced at Carl. "You don't look so good, partner."

"Shit," Carl groaned, "look in a fucking mirror. Ain't no sleeping beauty yourself."

"He's just mad because I told him he couldn't smoke in the car," Millie yelled over the screeching wheels, as Clarence took another curve.

Carl lit a cigarette and blew smoke into the front seat. "Hell, way Clarence's driving, I figure he's gonna kill us all anyway. Dying man gets one last request."

Standing at the top of the porch steps, Nikki held tightly to the pistol, holding it out in front of her with both hands, the way she'd seen her mother do. She studied the pistol, trying to remember what it was Mommy always did.

Something about safety. Turning the pistol over, she found the small lever and pushed it. Slipping off her shoes, she crept silently into the house and over to the basement door. She stood for a moment, listening to the sound of the evil man's voice.

Don't do it, Nikki. Come with me.

Cory stood in the shadows near the front door. Nikki shook her head, biting her lip to control the trembling. She wiped the tears from her face and steadied the gun. Mommy needed her.

Sarah's eyes widened in fear at the sight of Nikki descending the stairs. She shook her head no, straining against the ropes.

"Get away from my mommy!" Nikki's voice rang out in the room, loud, clear.

Williams stepped away from Sarah, edging toward Nikki.

"Nikki, run," Sarah screamed.

"Get the gun, Ella Mae."

Ella Mae reached for the gun, grabbing it from the child's shaking hands.

"She's got spirit, Sarah. Just like you. I like that. Yeah, I like that," he growled, reaching out and grabbing the strawberry curls, jerking Nikki toward him. "I'll bet you scream real good, don't you, sweetie?" He flung her across the room towards Sarah.

Gavin strained against the ropes as Nikki buried her face in Sarah's lap, her sobs echoing off the basement walls.

"I'm going to kill you, Williams," Gavin stated in a voice harder than steel.

"Oh, I don't think so." Williams smiled sardonically.

The sound of a vehicle approaching fast, bouncing over

the rocky driveway, wiped the smile from his face.

He glared at Ella Mae, his eyes filled with disgust.

"I'll bet it's that goddamn deputy of yours. Give me the gun."

He'll kill him.

Ella Mae trembled, her foot on the bottom step. Poised for flight. She couldn't let him kill Joshua. She struggled to hold the pistol in her shaking hands, bringing it upright, pointed at William's chest.

"Stay away from me," she whispered.

He'll kill him.

He held up both hands, laughing. "You gonna shoot me, Ella Mae? An unarmed man? That's murder. You'll go to jail." He walked towards her, covering the distance slowly. "You don't want to go to jail, do you, Ella Mae? They beat you there, you know. Every day. Beat you and shove things up inside you."

"Stay away from me," she screamed, her finger tightening on the trigger.

His face twisted as he snarled contemptuously, "You ugly whore. Do you know how ugly you are? How much touching you made me want to puke? You disgust me."

It isn't murder. Some people deserve to die.

Ella Mae heard the voice inside her head. He drew closer, almost within reaching distance. It wouldn't be murder. Some people deserved to die.

Steadying her hands on the gun, she looked straight into the black eyes.

"I'm not ugly," she whispered. She pulled the trigger again and again, watching as his shirt turned red and the black eyes dimmed. He stumbled once, hands outstretched, clutching the air. Ella Mae continued to pull the trigger, the hammer clicking on empty chambers uselessly.

"Give me your gun." Clarence turned to Joshua as the shots rang out inside the house.

"I'm going in," Joshua stated, hand on the doorknob.

Carl reached over and grabbed Joshua's arm. "Give him your gun, son. You ain't in no shape, and neither am I." Carl met Clarence's gaze over the back seat. "Besides, I have a feeling he knows how to use it."

Clarence nodded, taking the revolver and checking it quickly. He glanced at Millie. "I ain't got time to argue. You're staying here."

Millie opened her mouth, but shut it as Clarence slammed the door and raced up the steps, slipping quietly into the now silent house.

Joshua glanced at Carl. "Can't do it. Can't just sit here."

"Me neither." Carl muttered. "Help me out of this damned death trap."

Joshua opened the door, standing up slowly, letting the dizzy spell subside.

"Damned fools," Millie muttered, getting out of the car. "Come on, Joshua, let's get him out. Probably get his fool self shot again."

"Lord, God," Millie whispered, her eyes growing huge as Clarence came out the front door with Sarah, the two of them supporting Gavin between them. Ella Mae followed behind them, Nikki cradled in her arms.

Joshua helped Carl from the backseat, motioning for Millie to help. "Come on, pard. Looks like we missed all the fun."

Sirens blared in the distance, headlights bumping and

jolting as the cars sped over the rocky road.

"Yeah, and here comes the Calvary," Carl grumbled. "Late, as usual."

Clarence helped Sarah lower Gavin to the porch and waited for the trio. Joshua and Millie lowered Carl slowly to the porch, seated next to Gavin.

"Williams?" Joshua placed his hand on Sarah's shoulder.

"In the basement." Her voice was thick, one arm wound tightly around Nikki, the other around Gavin.

Tommy, Matt, and Jed raced up to the porch, guns drawn, glancing from Joshua to the group seated on the old porch steps to the silent dark house.

"In the basement," Joshua stated, sinking down on the step beside Sarah, placing an arm around her. Delegation. Sarah had told him he'd have to learn to delegate. Now seemed as good a time as any to start.

Sarah glanced up just in time to see Ella Mae walk away from the others. A lonely silhouette with head bowed. Moonlight created dancing shadows from her trembling hands. Placing Nikki in Gavin's lap, she kissed him. "I'll be right back."

"Ella Mae?"

She jumped, startled, but raised her head. "It was murder. I guess you'll have to tell Joshua. Put me in jail."

Sarah shook her head, holding out her arms. "No one's arresting anybody. You saved our lives."

Ella Mae stepped into the arms, sobs shaking her thin frame, arms grasping Sarah.

"It's okay," Sarah whispered, stroking the stringy hair, much as she'd stroked Nikki's earlier. "It wasn't murder, Ella Mae. Some people deserve to die."

* * *

Sarah glanced in the mirror, her face glowing with anticipation. The church was full to capacity with Glade Springs residents. Gavin had insisted they get married immediately. He wasn't letting her out of his sight again.

"Ain't you ready yet?" Carl jerked on the tie that threatened to choke him. "Damn monkey suit is killing me."

"Shush, Carl," Millie chastised him, reaching up to loosen the tie. "Won't hurt you none to look civilized for once in your life."

"Humph," Carl grumbled.

"I'll be ready in just a minute."

Sarah turned around, smiling at them before turning back to the mirror and smoothing her hair into place. She stared into her own blue eyes, shining with excitement. She'd never have to wear contacts again. And with Williams gone, she didn't have to leave Glade Springs. David and Claire Nix were gone. She could stay here. Millie and Clarence were staying. She smiled, remembering the look on Joshua's face when she'd told him she wanted him to stay on as sheriff. She was trading in her badge for an apron. She knew the dreams would continue. But Jacody Ives could deal with those. She'd convinced Gavin not to give him up. After all, he was a part of what she'd fallen in love with. True love didn't force people to change. It only enhanced what they really were.

Her thoughts turned to Ella Mae. She was talking about attending night classes, maybe becoming a deputy. Millie had taken her under her wing. It wouldn't be easy, but with the love of Joshua and Mary, Millie and Sarah, maybe Ella Mae could finally find herself.

The last week had been a nightmare. Carl and Gavin

had been right about the cards left with the bodies of the young girls. Williams had hoped the cards would hit the paper. Hoped that Sarah would see them. Know it was him. Show herself. Campbell had speeded up the process by looking for his daughter's killer. Somehow he'd uncovered Sarah's story, gone to Corrine Larson, put two and two together. They still weren't sure how he'd found and killed the Coopers, taking the Reverend's place. Finding a starving prostitute to play his wife. They didn't know why he'd killed Jasmine Little. There would always be questions. He'd come here, seen Nikki, and confused her with his own daughter. His tortured mind had seen what it wanted to see.

They still didn't know for sure who had cut the line on Johanna Nelson's brakes, but they were pretty sure Williams was responsible for Marisa's death. Gavin had called it a Gordian puzzle.

Sarah shook her head. Today wasn't for questions. Today was meant for happiness, love, and laughter. Today was the first day of a new life. A real life, without secrets and lies.

Smiling again, she turned from the mirror and picked up Carl's cane. She handed it to him and took his arm. "Let's go get married."

"About damn time," Carl grumbled, the glow of pride on his face belying his ire, as he pushed Millie out of the room ahead of him. "Get on down that aisle, woman. We ain't got all day."

"Humph," Millie snorted, signaling the organist to start playing.

Sarah could see Gavin standing at the altar, his eyes sparkling with promise. Nikki walked slowly in front of her, tossing rose petals.

"Look, Mommy, rainbows," Nikki whispered, just loud enough to be heard. Laughter rang out in the church.

The sun was shining through the stained glass windows, creating rainbows on the rose petals. The only thing missing was Joshua and Mary. The baby had chosen a perfect day to enter the world. They were all going to the hospital as soon as the ceremony was over.

Reaching the altar, Carl placed Sarah's hand in Gavin's, squeezing them both before he took his seat on the family row next to Millie.

"Do you, Gavin McAllister, take Sarah McKnight to be your lawfully wedded wife, to love, honor, cherish and obey until death do you part?"

Gavin smiled at her, his eyes full of love.

"I do."

"Do you, Sarah McKnight, take Gavin Colin McAllister to be your lawfully wedded husband, to love, honor, cherish and obey until death do you part?"

Nikki was pulling frantically on her dress.

"Look, Mommy!"

Sarah glanced at Gavin before they both looked in the direction Nikki was pointing. Standing in the back of the church, shimmering like the rainbows, stood Rob and Cory, hand in hand. Tears filled Sarah's eyes as she turned to Gavin. Smiling tremulously, she squeezed his hand, and in a clear, loud voice said, "I do."

EPILOGUE

"It's almost time, Mrs. McAllister. Would you like me to turn on the television?"

"Please."

Sarah smiled up at the nurse before turning her attention to the small child snuggled in her arms. "Daddy and Nikki are going to be on TV. What do you think of that?"

"Humph," Millie grumbled from the side of the bed. "You gonna hog him all day, Carl?"

"Hush up, woman. You wake him and he'll start that caterwauling again." Carl sat in awe of the tiny figure snuggled inside the blue blanket, sleeping peacefully in his arms. His old face beamed as the boy wiggled.

Sarah smiled fondly at both of them. "Here, Millie, you can hold Cory. I don't think Carl is ready to give up Rob yet."

Millie grumbled as she beamed down at the little girl. "You just wait until Clarence gets here."

Sarah turned her attention to the television screen. Pride filled her as she watched the unveiling of the new series of children's books, *The Ballerina Tales* by Gavin and Nikki McAllister.

They stood side by side, hand in hand, both grinning from ear to ear. Picking up Nikki, Gavin took the microphone.

"It's an honor to be here today. Writing *Ballerina Tales* with my daughter was one of the greatest experiences of my life. However, there's something else that's even more wonderful. Nikki, you want to tell them?" Gavin grinned as he handed the microphone to Nikki.

"I have a new baby brother and sister." Nikki beamed at the camera.

"Isn't there something else?" Gavin urged her on.

"We taped the show, Mommy."

The door opened at that moment. Love filled the room, surrounding Sarah with its warmth, as Nikki bounded from behind Gavin, a dozen red roses clutched in her tiny hands. Nikki stopped in mid-stride, her eyes widening, as she gazed in wonder at the two babies.

Leaning over the bed, Gavin kissed Sarah and whispered, "We came to take you home."

Jacody Ives: The Gifts

Meet the Author:

Hi. My name is Linda S. Prather. I was born in Kentucky in 1955, the youngest of six siblings. I live in Lexington, Kentucky with my fiancé, Coby W. Fuson. I have two wonderful sons, Charles and Steven.

I have always loved reading and writing. And although perhaps not one of the greatest literary works, my earliest memory of a book that inspired me was *Old Yeller*. The characters in that book were so real to me. I laughed and cried with every page. When I started writing, it was my greatest desire to write characters, which were real, and stories that opened the hearts and minds of the readers.

Knowledge was another love. I wanted to learn everything about everything. In the late 1980's I started my studies in metaphysics, delving into touch healing, dream analysis, meditation, psychic phenomena, and hypnosis. I received my degree in metaphysics in 1992 and continued from there to become a Certified Clinical Hypnotherapist. I spent the new two years studying the effects of hypnosis on cancer and pain. I taught meditation and self-hypnosis, as well as dream analysis through Eastern Kentucky University's Special Programs for four years. The power of the mind has always fascinated me, and continues to fascinate me.

The Gifs is actually the fourth novel I've written, although it is my first attempt at publishing one of my works. I am currently working on a new novel, and find myself in the jungles of Africa, enthralled by its culture and beauty. Hopefully, I will share that with you in the near future.

My greatest accomplishments–my children. My sons have been the light in my life. Their love and encouragement has sustained me through the bad times and enhanced my joy during the good times.

My favorite pastimes–good friends, good food and good conversation.

My favorite quote: *"Be known for unwavering commitment to the people and ideals you choose to live by."*

Echelon Press Publishing

Echelon Press Publishing

Celebrating Five Years of

Unique Stories

For

Exceptional Readers

2001 -2006

WWW.ECHELONPRESS.COM

Also available from Echelon Press Publishing

Situation Sabotage (*Global Adventure*) Graeme Johns

*Contamination...sabotage...*terms feared by food industry executives around the world. They prefer to announce the problem as a potential...*situation*. Now, Investigator Barton has been called in to solve the case before word leaks out. A frantic dash across the Pacific uncovers three murders before he discovers the mastermind behind the sabotage.

$12.99   ISBN 1-59080-477-5

Invasion of Justice (*Women's Adventure*) Regan Black

In 2096 an empath with a penchant for all things retro, Petra Neiman is making a good name for herself reading crime scenes for the judicial system. That is until a serial killer drags her into his crimes and pins a gruesome murder on her brother! Now she must sort through myriad feelings and memories to unravel a plot that began before her birth.

$12.99   ISBN 1-59080-443-0

Dangerous Affairs (*Romantic Suspense*) Kelle Z. Riley

A man fighting his past. A woman fleeing hers. When fate throws them together they form an unlikely—and temporary— alliance. Soon real passion infuses their fake marriage and they begin to dream of more. But someone has other plans. Someone who would rather see them dead than happy.

$12.99   ISBN 1-59080-468-6

Fractured Souls (*Suspense*) T.A. Ridgell

*People aren't always what they seem...*Terrifying accidents have Dr. Benita Kyser on edge. Teaming up with private investigator, Sean Turner, they work against time to identify the threat. *Cracked Minds Lead to Fractured Souls...*One man wants more from Beni. She's the reason for his success--or failure. He will have her as his own. And if he can't--then no one will...

$12.99   ISBN 1-59080-471-6